The Rendezvous and other stories

Daphne du Maurier was born in London and was educated at home and in Paris. Her first novel, *The Loving Spirit*, was published in 1931, since when she has written many highly successful novels, including *Rebecca*, *Frenchman's Creek* and *Jamaica Inn*. Disliking town life, she lives in Cornwall.

Daphne du Maurier

The Rendezvous

and other stories

Pan Books London and Sydney

First published 1980 by Victor Gollancz Ltd
This edition published 1981 by Pan Books Ltd,
Cavaye Place, London SW10 9PG
© Daphne du Maurier 1980
ISBN 0 330 26554 7
Made and printed in Great Britain by
Hunt Barnard Printing Ltd., Aylesbury, Bucks.

Contents

Preface

The last chapter in my book of memoirs, *Growing Pains,* is entitled "Apprenticeship"; the sub-title of the book itself, *The Shaping of a Writer.* In brief, the chapter "Apprenticeship" explains how I began to write short stories before embarking on my first novel, and some of these stories are included here. One or two were published in *The Bystander,* thanks to the interest and kindness of my maternal uncle, William Comyns Beaumont, who was editor at the time; and two or three of the others also found space in magazines. The rest, to the best of my recollection, were written later, between the ages of thirty and forty, when I had become known as a professional writer.

The stories are set in various locations—in France, in London, in Cornwall, in Switzerland—for it so happened that I had spent much of my time in these places. The early stories especially show something of my development as a writer. I would let my imagination have full play as I sat in a café in Paris, or listened to the conversation of my dear French friend Fernande Yvon, while she chatted to her fellow-countrymen, and something observed, something said, would sink into the hidden places of my mind, and later a story would form.

The same thing held good for London, and for my home in Hampstead: conversations overheard in my father Gerald's dressing-room, or at lunch at Cannon Hall on Sundays. Nothing definite, nothing solid or factual, but an impression, an association of persons, places and ideas, so that weeks, possibly months, later the germ of a short story suddenly became quite clear in my mind, and I knew that I must write it down and rid my system of it. Whether it would be published or not did not bother me; the writing down was all.

"So?" asks the reader, disenchanted. "Nobody in any of the stories is real? They are all made up?"

Made up . . . My father Gerald made up his face to become

another man upon the stage. Whereas I sit in front of a seedy hotel in the Boulevard Montparnasse and imagine what happens inside it, or I wander into a small empty church in Brittany. I see two men and a woman greeting one another at Victoria station. Or a young couple hurries past me on a London pavement, averting their eyes from a cripple selling matches. I am in the foyer of a theatre. I am in a dressing-room. I watch a queue of people hoping for my father's autograph. A distinguished clergyman comes to a Hampstead garden-party. A middle-aged man and a young woman are dining together in a Geneva restaurant; I wonder what they are discussing. Back home in England a laundry-van races down a steep hill, narrowly missing me. Staring across Fowey harbour I think of all those who go down to the sea in ships, from the crew of a tramp steamer in wartime, sailing in convoy because of the threat of enemy submarines, to the lone yachtsman in peacetime, seeking adventure and seclusion. And so on and so on . . .

The people and the places and the events are real to the writer, and that is all that matters. Read for yourself and see!

No Motive

Mary Farren went into the gun room one morning about half-past eleven, took her husband's revolver and loaded it, then shot herself. The butler heard the sound of the gun from the pantry. He knew Sir John was out and would not be back until lunchtime, and no one had any business to be in the gun room at that hour of the day.

He went to investigate, and there he saw Lady Farren lying on the floor, in a pool of her own blood. She was dead. Aghast, he called the housekeeper, and after consultation they agreed he must first telephone the doctor, then the police, and lastly Sir John himself, who was at a board meeting. The butler told the doctor and the police, who arrived within a few minutes, what had happened; his message on the telephone had been the same to each. "Her ladyship has had an accident. She is lying in the gun room with a gunshot wound in her head. I fear she is dead." The message summoning Sir John was worded differently. It just said, would Sir John please return home at once, as her ladyship had met with an accident. The doctor, therefore, had to break the news to the husband when he came.

It was a painful, wretched business. He had known John Farren for years; both he and Mary Farren were patients of his—a happier married couple did not exist—and they were both look-ing forward to the baby that was to be born to them in the spring. No difficulties were expected; Mary Farren was normal, healthy, and delighted at the prospect of being a mother.

The suicide, therefore, did not make sense. Because it was suicide. There was no doubt about it. Mary Farren had scribbled three words on a writing pad, which she had put on the desk in the gun room. The words were, "Forgive me, darling." The gun had been put away unloaded, as always. Mary Farren had quite definitely taken out the gun, loaded it, then shot herself. The police corroborated that the wound had been self-inflicted. Mercifully, she must have died at once.

Sir John Farren was a broken man. In that half-hour, talking to the doctors and the police, he aged about twenty years. "But why did she do it?" he kept asking in agony. "We were so happy. We loved each other; the baby was on its way. There was no motive, I tell you, absolutely no motive."

Neither the police nor the doctor had an answer for him.

The usual formalities were gone through, the official business of an inquest, with the expected verdict, "Suicide, with no evidence to show the state of mind of the deceased."

Sir John Farren talked to the doctor again and again, but neither of them could come to any conclusion.

"Yes, it is possible," said the doctor, "women can become temporarily deranged at such a time, but you would have noticed signs of it, and so would I. You tell me she was perfectly normal the night before, perfectly normal at breakfast. So far as you know, there was nothing on her mind at all?"

"Absolutely nothing," said Sir John. "We breakfasted together, as we always did; we made plans for the afternoon; after I returned from the board meeting I was going to take her for a drive. She was cheerful and completely happy."

Lady Farren's cheerfulness was also corroborated by the servants. The housemaid, who had gone to the bedroom at half-past ten, found her ladyship examining shawls that had come by the parcel post. Lady Farren, delighted with the work, had shown the shawls to her and had said she would keep both pink and blue, for boy or girl.

At eleven a travelling salesman had called from a firm that made garden furniture. Her ladyship had seen the man, chosen two large garden seats from his catalogue. The butler knew this, because Lady Farren had shown him the catalogue after the man had gone, when he had come to enquire if there were any orders for the chauffeur, and her ladyship had said, "No, I shan't be going out until after lunch, when Sir John will be taking me for a drive." The butler had gone from the room, leaving her ladyship drinking a glass of milk. He was the last person to see Lady Farren alive.

"It comes to this," said Sir John. "Between that time, which was approximately twenty minutes past eleven, and eleven-thirty, when she shot herself, Mary went off her head. It doesn't make sense. There *must* have been something wrong. I've got to find out what it was. I shall never rest until I do."

The doctor did his best to dissuade him, but it was no use. He himself was convinced that Mary Farren had succumbed to a sudden brainstorm, owing to her condition, and, not knowing what she was doing, had made an end of herself. Let it stay there. Let it rest. Only time would help John Farren to forget.

John Farren did not try to forget. He went to a private detective agency and interviewed a man called Black, recommended by the firm as trustworthy and discreet. Sir John told him the story. Black was a canny Scot. He didn't talk much, but he listened. It was his private opinion that the doctor's theory was right, and a sudden brainstorm, owing to pregnancy, was the motive for the suicide. However, he was thorough at his job, and he went down to the country and interviewed the household. He asked many questions that the police had not asked, chatted with the doctor, checked up on the mail that had come for Lady Farren during the past few weeks, enquired about telephone calls and encounters with personal friends; and still there was no answer he could give his client.

The one obvious solution that had come to his practised mind —that Lady Farren was expecting a child by a lover—did not work. Check and double-check revealed no possibility of this. Husband and wife were devoted and had not been apart since their marriage three years previously. The servants all spoke of their great attachment for one another. There were no financial worries. Nor could the shrewd Black trace any infidelity on the part of Sir John. Servants, friends, neighbours, all spoke of his high integrity. Therefore, his wife had not shot herself through any fault of his that had come to light.

Temporarily Black was baffled. But not beaten. Once he took on a case, he liked to see it through to the end, and, hardened though he was, he felt sorry to see Sir John's agony of mind.

"You know, sir," he said, "in cases of this sort we often have to go back in a person's life, rather further than the immediate past. I've been through every inch of your wife's desk, with your permission, and searched her papers and all correspondence, and I have found nothing to give the faintest clue to the trouble on her mind—if there was trouble. You have told me that you met Lady Farren—Miss Marsh, as she was then—while on a visit to

Switzerland. She was living with an invalid aunt, Miss Vera Marsh, who had brought her up, her parents being dead."

"That is correct," said Sir John.

"They lived in Sierre and also in Lausanne, and you met both the Misses Marsh at the house of a mutual friend in Sierre. You struck up a friendship with the younger Miss Marsh, and by the end of your holiday you had fallen in love with her and she with you, and you asked her to marry you."

"Yes."

"The elder Miss Marsh made no objection; in fact, she was delighted. It was arranged between you that you should make her an allowance to cover the expenses of a companion to take her niece's place, and within a couple of months or so you were married at Lausanne."

"Correct again."

"There was no question of the aunt coming to live with you in England?"

"No," said Sir John. "Mary wanted her to—she was much attached to her aunt—but the old lady refused. She had lived in Switzerland so long, she couldn't face the English climate or the English food. Incidentally, we have been out twice to see her since we married."

Black asked if Sir John had heard from his wife's aunt since the tragedy. Yes. He had written, of course, at once, and she had seen the news in the papers too. She was horrified. She could give no reason why Mary should have taken her life. A happy letter, written a week before, full of her delight at the prospect of the future baby, had arrived in Sierre only a few days prior to the calamity. Miss Marsh had enclosed the letter for Sir John to read. And Sir John gave it to Black.

"I take it," said Black, "that the two ladies, when you met them first three years ago, were living very quietly?"

"They had this small villa," said Sir John, "and about twice a year they used to go down to Lausanne and take rooms in a pension. The old lady had some sort of trouble with her lungs, but not serious enough for a sanatorium or anything like that. Mary was a most devoted niece. It was one of the first things that drew me to her—her gentleness and sweet temper to the old lady, who, like many elderly people, semi-invalid, was apt to be fractious at times."

"So your wife, the younger Miss Marsh, did not get about much? Not many friends her own age, and that sort of thing?"

"I suppose not. It did not seem to worry her. Hers was such a contented nature."

"And this had been her life since she was quite small?"

"Yes. Miss Marsh was Mary's only relative. She had adopted her when Mary's parents died. Mary was a child at the time."

"And how old was your wife when you married her?"

"Thirty-one."

"No history of a previous engagement or a love affair?"

"Absolutely none. I used to tease Mary about it. She said she had never seen anyone to give her the slightest flutter. And her aunt agreed. I remember Miss Marsh saying to me when we became engaged, 'It's rare to find anyone so unspoilt as Mary. She's got the prettiest face and is quite unaware of it, and the sweetest nature and doesn't realise that either. You're a very lucky man.' And I was."

Sir John sat staring at Black with such abject misery in his eyes that the tough Scot hardly liked to cross-question him further. "So it really was a love match on both sides?" he said. "You are quite certain there was no pull in your title and position? I mean, the aunt might have told her niece that here was a chance she mustn't miss, another man like you might not come along. After all, ladies do think of these things."

Sir John shook his head. "Miss Marsh might have had an eye to the main chance, I don't know," he said, "but certainly Mary had not. Right from the beginning it was I who sought out her, not the other way round. If Mary had been looking about for a husband, she would have shown signs of it when we first met. And you know what cats women can be. The friend at whose chalet I originally met the Marshes would have warned me that here was a girl, past thirty, in search of a husband. She said no such thing. She said, 'I want you to meet a perfect darling of a girl whom we all adore and feel rather sorry for because she leads such a lonely life.' "

"Yet she didn't appear lonely to you?"

"Not at all. She seemed perfectly content."

Black handed back Miss Marsh's letter to Sir John. "You still want me to go on with this enquiry?" he said. "You don't think it would be simpler to decide, once and for all, that your doctor was right about Lady Farren, and she had some sort of a blackout which affected her mind and made her take her life?"

"No," said Sir John. "I tell you, somewhere there is a clue to this tragedy, and I shan't give up until I've found it. Or rather you find it for me. That's why I'm employing you."

Black rose from his chair. "Very well," he said, "if that's the way you feel about it, I'll go right ahead with the case."

"What are you going to do?" asked Sir John.

"I shall fly to Switzerland tomorrow."

Black handed in his card at the Chalet Bon Repos at Sierre and was shown into a small salon that gave on to a balcony with a fine view across the Rhone valley.

A woman, Miss Marsh's companion, he supposed, led him through the salon on to the balcony. Black had time to notice that the room was furnished neatly, with good taste, but nothing out of the way, very much the room of an elderly English spinster living abroad who did not fling her money around. There was a large picture of Lady Farren on the mantelpiece, taken recently, a duplicate of the one he had seen in Sir John's study. And another on a writing bureau of Lady Farren aged about twenty, he judged. A pretty, shy-looking girl, her hair worn rather longer than in the more recent portrait.

Black went on to the balcony and introduced himself to the elderly lady seated there in a wheeled chair as a friend of Sir John Farren. Miss Marsh had white hair, blue eyes, and a firm mouth. From the way she spoke to her companion, who immediately left them together, Black decided she was hard on those who served her. She seemed, however, genuinely pleased to see Black, and at once asked after Sir John with much concern and wanted to know if any light at all had been thrown on the tragedy.

"I'm sorry to say, none," answered Black. "In fact, I am here to ask you what you know about it. You knew Lady Farren better than any of us, even her husband. Sir John thinks you may have some ideas on the subject."

Miss Marsh looked surprised. "But I wrote and told Sir John I was horrified and completely baffled," she said. "I enclosed Mary's last letter. Did he tell you?"

"Yes," said Black, "I saw the letter. And you have others?"

"I kept all her letters," said Miss Marsh. "She wrote to me

regularly, every week, after she married. If Sir John wants me to send him the letters I shall be pleased to do so. There is not one letter that isn't full of her affection for him, and her pride and delight in her new home. It was her one regret that I wouldn't stir myself to go and visit her. But you see, I am such an invalid."

"You look hearty enough," thought Black, "but perhaps you just didn't want to go."

"I gather you and your niece were much attached?" he said.

"I was deeply fond of Mary, and I like to think she was equally fond of me," was the swift reply. "Heaven knows I can be cantankerous at times, but Mary never seemed to mind. She was the sweetest-natured girl."

"You were sorry to lose her?"

"Of course I was sorry. I missed her terribly, and still do. But naturally her happiness came first."

"Sir John told me he made you an allowance to cover the cost of your present companion."

"Yes. It was generous of him. Will it continue, do you know?"

The inflection in her voice was sharp. Black decided that his original idea of Miss Marsh as someone who did not wholly disregard money was probably sound.

"Sir John didn't say. But I feel sure, if it was otherwise, you would have heard from him or from his lawyers," said Black.

Black looked at Miss Marsh's hands. They tapped the sides of the wheeled chair in a little nervous gesture. "There was nothing in your niece's past that would account for her suicide?" he said.

She looked startled. "What on earth do you mean?"

"No previous engagement, or love affair gone wrong?"

"Good heavens, no."

Curious. She seemed relieved at the wording of his question.

"Sir John was Mary's only love. She led rather a solitary life with me, you know. Not many young people in the district. Even in Lausanne she never seemed to seek out people nearer her own age. It was not that she was particularly shy or reserved. Just self-contained."

"What about school friends?"

"I taught her lessons myself when she was small. She had a few terms in Lausanne when she was older, but as a day girl; we lived in a pension close by. I seem to remember one or two girls coming in for tea. But no especial friend."

"Have you any photographs of her at that age?"

"Yes. Several. I've got them all in an album somewhere. Would you care to see them?"

"I think I should. Sir John showed me several photographs, but I don't think he had any that dated from before their marriage."

Miss Marsh pointed to the bureau in the salon behind and told him to open the second drawer and bring back an album. He did so, and putting on spectacles she opened the album and he drew up his seat beside her. They went through the album at random. There were many snapshots, none of any particular interest. Lady Farren alone. Miss Marsh alone. Lady Farren and Miss Marsh in groups with other people. Snaps of the chalet. Snaps of Lausanne. Black turned the pages. No clue here.

"Is that the lot?" he said.

"I'm afraid it is," said Miss Marsh. "She was such a pretty girl, wasn't she? Those warm brown eyes. It is the most dreadful thing . . . Poor Sir John."

"You haven't any snaps of her when she was a child, I notice. These seem to start when she was around fifteen."

There was a pause, and then Miss Marsh replied, "No . . . no, I don't think I had a camera in those days."

Black had a well-trained ear. It was an easy matter for him to detect a falsehood. Miss Marsh was lying about something. About what? "What a pity," he said. "I always think it's interesting to trace the child in the adult face. I'm a married man myself. My wife and I wouldn't be without the first albums of our youngster for the world."

"Yes, it was stupid of me, wasn't it?" said Miss Marsh. She put the album down in front of her on the table.

"I expect you have the ordinary studio portraits?" said Black.

"No," said Miss Marsh, "or if I once had, I must have lost them. In the move, you know. We didn't come here until Mary was fifteen. We were in Lausanne before that."

"And you adopted Mary when she was five, I think Sir John said?"

"Yes. She would have been about five." Again the momentary hesitation, the inflection in her voice.

"Have you any photographs of Lady Farren's parents?"

"No."

"Yet her father was your only brother, I understand?"

"My only brother, yes."

"What decided you to adopt Lady Farren as a child?"

"The mother was dead, and my brother did not know how to take care of her. She was a delicate child. We both of us felt it was the best solution."

"Of course your brother made you an allowance for the child's upkeep and education?"

"Naturally. I couldn't have managed otherwise." Then Miss Marsh made a mistake. But for this one mistake, Black might have let the whole thing go. "You ask the most extraordinarily remote questions, Mr Black," she said with a hard little laugh. "I don't see that the allowance paid to me by Mary's father can be of the slightest interest to you. What you want to know is why poor Mary killed herself, and so does her husband, and so do I."

"Anything even remotely connected with Lady Farren's past life is of interest to me," said Black. "You see, Sir John has employed me for that very purpose. Perhaps it is time that I explained to you I am not a personal friend of his. I am a private detective."

Miss Marsh turned grey. Her composure went. She became suddenly a very frightened old woman. "What have you come to find out?" she said.

"Everything," said Black.

Now it was a favourite theory of the Scots, which he often expounded to the director of the agency for whom he worked, that there are very few people in this world who haven't got something to hide. Time and time again he had seen men and women in the witness box, under cross-examination, and one and all were afraid; not of the questions put to them, which they must answer, and which might shed light on the particular case then under trial; but that in answering the questions they would, by some mishap, by some slip of the tongue, reveal a secret pertaining to themselves which would discredit them. Black was certain that Miss Marsh found herself in this position now. She might know nothing of Mary Farren's suicide or of its cause. But Miss Marsh herself was guilty of something that she had long sought to hide.

"If Sir John has found out about the allowance and thinks I

have been defrauding Mary all these years, he might have had the decency to tell me himself, and not employ a detective," she said.

"Oh, ho, here we go," thought Black. "Give the old lady enough rope and she'll hang herself."

"Sir John did not mention the word fraud," he replied to Miss Marsh. "He merely thought the circumstances were rather strange."

Black was taking a chance, but he felt the result might be worth it.

"Of course they were strange," said Miss Marsh. "I tried to act for the best, and I believed I did. I can swear to you, Mr Black, that I used very little money on myself, and that most of it went for Mary's upkeep, according to the agreement with the child's father. When Mary married, and as it happened married well, I did not think there was any harm in keeping the capital for myself. Sir John was rich, and Mary would not miss it."

"I take it," said Black, "that Lady Farren knew nothing of what was going on?"

"Nothing," said Miss Marsh. "She was never interested in money matters, and she believed herself entirely dependent on me. You don't think Sir John is going to prosecute me, Mr Black? If he won a case against me, which he undoubtedly would, I should be destitute."

Black stroked his chin and pretended to consider. "I don't think Sir John intends anything of the sort, Miss Marsh," he said. "But he would like to know the truth of what happened."

Miss Marsh sank back in her wheeled chair. No longer stiff and upright, she looked a tired old lady. "Now that Mary is dead, it can't hurt her, the truth coming out," she said. "The fact is, Mr Black, she wasn't my niece at all. I was paid a large sum of money to look after her. The money should have gone to her on her majority, but I kept it myself. Mary's father, with whom I signed the agreement, had died in the meantime. Living here in Switzerland, no one knew anything about the matter. It was so simple to keep it secret. I intended no harm."

It was always the way, thought Black. Temptation came to a man or woman, and they succumbed to it. They never "intended" harm.

"I see," he said. "Well, Miss Marsh, I don't want to go into the details of what you did or how you spent the money intended for Lady Farren. What does interest me is this. If she wasn't your niece, who was she?"

"She was the only daughter of a Mr Henry Warner. That is all I ever knew. He never told me his address, or where he lived. All I knew was the address of his bankers, the branch in London; four cheques were paid to me from that address. After I took Mary in my care, Mr Warner went to Canada and died there five years later. The bank informed me of this, and as I never heard from them again I believed myself safe to do—what I did —with her money."

Black noted the name Henry Warner, and Miss Marsh gave him the address of the bank.

"Mr Warner was not a personal friend of yours?" he asked.

"Oh no. I only met him twice. The first time was when I answered his advertisement to a box number for someone to take charge, indefinitely, of a delicate girl. I was very poor at the time and had just lost a post as governess to an English family returning to England. I did not want to take a position in a school, and this advertisement came as a godsend, especially as the sum to be paid for the child's upkeep, which the father intended to accumulate, was so generous. I knew I should be able to live as I had, frankly, never lived before. You can hardly blame me." Something of her former confidence was returning. She looked sharply at Black.

"I am not blaming you," he said. "Tell me more about Henry Warner."

"There is little to tell," she said. "He asked very few questions about myself or my background. The only point he made clear was that he wanted Mary to remain with me for good; he had no intention of having her back with him again, or corresponding with her. He planned to go to Canada, he told me, and cut himself off from all former connections. I was entirely free to bring up his daughter as I thought fit. In other words, he washed his hands of her."

"A callous sort of customer?" suggested Black.

"Not exactly callous," replied Miss Marsh. "He looked anxious and careworn, as though the responsibility of looking after the child had been too much for him. His wife apparently was dead. Then I enquired in what way his daughter was delicate, because I knew little of nursing and did not particularly relish an ailing child. He explained to me that she was not physically delicate, but that she had witnessed a terrible train accident a few months previously, and the shock of this had caused her to lose her memory. She was perfectly normal otherwise, perfectly sane. But she remembered nothing previous to the shock. She did not even know he was her father. This was the reason, he told me, why he wanted her to begin a new life in another country."

Black jotted down some notes. The case at last was beginning to show possibilities. "So you were willing to take the risk of having this child—suffering from mental shock—on your hands for life?" he asked.

He had not intended his question to be cynical, but Miss Marsh saw a sting in it. She flushed. "I am used to teaching and used to children," she said. "Also, independence was dear to me. I accepted Mr Warner's offer, on condition I took to the child and the child took to me. At our second meeting he brought Mary with him. It was impossible not to feel an affection for her at once. That pretty little face, those large eyes, and the soft gentle manner. She seemed quite normal, but young for her age. I chatted with her and asked her if she would like to come and stay with me, and she said she would; she put her hand in mine in the most confiding way. I told Mr Warner 'Yes', and the bargain was struck. He left Mary with me that evening, and we neither of us ever saw him again. It was easy enough to tell the child she was my niece, as she remembered nothing of her past; she accepted anything I cared to tell her about herself as gospel truth. It was all too easy."

"And from that day she did not once recover her memory, Miss Marsh?"

"Never. Life began for her when her father handed her over to me at that hotel in Lausanne, and it really began for me too. I could not have loved her better had she been in truth my niece."

Black glanced through his notes and put them in his pocket. "So beyond the fact that you knew she was the daughter of a Mr Henry Warner, you were completely ignorant as to her background?" he asked.

"Completely," said Miss Marsh.

"She was merely a little girl of five years old who had lost her memory?"

"Fifteen," corrected Miss Marsh.

"How do you mean, fifteen?" said Black.

Miss Marsh flushed again. "I forgot," she said. "I misled you earlier in the afternoon. I always told Mary, and everybody else, that I had adopted my niece when she was five. It made it so much easier for me, and easier for Mary too, because she remembered nothing of her life previous to the time she came to live with me. She was, in point of fact, fifteen. You will realise now why I have no snapshots or photographs of Mary as a child."

"Indeed, yes," said Black. "And I must thank you, Miss Marsh, for being so helpful. I don't think Sir John is likely to raise any questions about the money, and for the present, at any rate, I shall keep the whole story of what you have told me as entirely confidential. What I have now to find out is where Lady Farren —Mary Warner—was living for the first fifteen years of her life, and what that life was. It may have some bearing on the suicide."

Miss Marsh rang for her companion to show Black out. She had not quite recovered her equanimity. "There is only one thing that has always puzzled me," she said. "I feel her father, Henry Warner, did not speak the truth. Mary showed no fear of trains at any time, and though I made several enquiries of many people, I could learn of no severe train accident that had happened in England, or anywhere else for that matter, during the months before Mary came to me."

Black returned to London, but he did not get in touch with Sir John Farren, because he thought it best to wait until he had more definite news to communicate. It seemed to him unnecessary to reveal the truth about Miss Marsh and the adoption. It would only unsettle Sir John further, and it was hardly likely that this fact had suddenly come to light and driven his wife to suicide. The more intriguing possibility was that Lady Farren had received a shock which, in a moment, had pierced the veil that had shrouded her memory for nineteen years. It was Black's business to discover the nature of that shock.

The first thing he did in London was to go to the branch of the bank where Henry Warner had kept an account. He saw the manager and explained his mission. It appeared that Henry Warner had indeed gone to Canada, had married again when he was out there, and had subsequently died. The widow had written, closing the account in England. The manager did not know whether Henry Warner had left a second family in Canada, nor did he know the address of the widow. Henry Warner's first wife had died many years previously. Yes, the manager knew about the daughter of the first marriage. She had been adopted by a Miss Marsh in Switzerland. Cheques had been paid to Miss Marsh, and they ceased when Henry Warner married a second time. The only positive information that the bank manager could give Black which might be helpful was Henry Warner's old address. And the piece of news, which Henry Warner had certainly not told Miss Marsh, that his profession was the Church, and that at the time Miss Marsh had adopted his daughter he was vicar of All Saints, in the parish of Long Common, Hampshire.

Black travelled down to Hampshire with a pleasurable feeling of anticipation. He always began to enjoy himself when the clues started to unravel. It reminded him of boyhood days of hide-and-seek. It was his interest in the unexpected that had called him to be a private detective in the first place, and he had never regretted his call.

He believed in keeping an open mind about his case, but it was difficult not to see the Reverend Henry Warner as the villain of this piece. The sudden handing over of a mentally sick daughter to a perfect stranger abroad, and then cutting himself loose from her and going to Canada, seemed an extraordinarily heartless thing for a clergyman to do. Black smelt scandal, and if the taint still lingered in Long Common after nineteen years, it would not be difficult to ferret out what the scandal had been.

He put up at the local inn, describing himself as a writer on old churches in Hampshire, and with this same excuse he wrote a polite note to the present incumbent, asking if he might call. His wish was granted, and the vicar, a young man, an enthusiast on architecture, showed him every corner of the church from nave to belfry, with a wealth of detail about fifteenth-century carving. Black listened politely, disguising his own ignorance, and finally led the vicar round to talking of his predecessors. Unfortunately the present vicar had been at Long Common for only six years, and he knew little about Warner, who had been succeeded by someone who had moved to Hull, but Warner had definitely held the living for twelve years, and his wife was buried in the churchyard. Black saw the grave and noted the headstone. "Emily Mary, dearly beloved wife of Henry Warner who passed to rest safe in the arms of Jesus." He also noted the date. Their daughter Mary would have been ten years old at the time.

Yes, said the present vicar, he had heard that Warner had given up the living in a great hurry and gone to the Dominions, Canada, he believed. Some of the people in the village would remember him, especially the older ones. Possibly his own gardener would remember most. He had been gardener at the rectory for thirty years. But as far as he, the vicar, knew, Warner had not been a historian or a collector; he had done no research work on the church. If Mr Black would care to come to the rectory, he had many interesting books on Long Common history.

Mr Black excused himself. He had got all he wanted out of the present incumbent. He felt that an evening at the bar of the inn where he was staying would prove more profitable, and it did. He learnt no more about fifteenth-century carving, but a good deal about the Reverend Henry Warner.

The vicar had been respected in the parish, but never deeply liked because of his rigid views and his intolerance. He was not the sort of man to whom his parishioners went when they were in trouble; he was always more likely to condemn than to console. He never entered the bar of the inn, never mixed in friendly fashion with the humble. He was known to have private means, and he was not dependent on his benefice. He liked to be invited to the few large houses in the neighbourhood, because he placed social values high; but he had not been particularly popular there either.

In short, the Reverend Henry Warner had been an intolerant, narrow-minded snob, which were three poor qualities for a vicar to hold. His wife, on the contrary, had been much loved by all, and it had been universally regretted when she died after an operation for cancer. She had been a most sweet-tempered lady, very thoughtful for others, most kind-hearted, and her little girl took after her.

Had the child been much affected by her mother's death? No one remembered. It was thought not. She went away to school and was only home during the holidays. One or two recollected her riding about on her bicycle, a pretty, friendly little thing. The gardener and his wife had acted as married couple for the Reverend Henry Warner, the same gardener that was up at the rectory now. Old Harris. No, he did not come down to the pub of an evening. He was a teetotaller. He lived up in one of the cottages near the church. No, his wife was dead. He lived with a married daughter. He was a great rose fancier and won prizes for his roses every year at the local show.

Black finished his pint and departed. The evening was yet young. He dropped out of his disguise as a writer on old Hampshire churches and slipped into the role of a collector of Hampshire roses. He found old Harris smoking a pipe outside his cottage. There were roses growing up his fence. Black stopped to admire them. The conversation was launched. It took him the better part of an hour to lead Harris from roses to past vicars, from past vicars to Warner, from Warner to Mrs Warner, from Mrs Warner to Mary Warner, but the picture unfolded, and there was nothing remarkable to see in it. The same tale was repeated that he had heard in the village.

The Reverend Warner was a hard man, not given to being friendly-like; very sparing, he was, with his praises. Took no interest in the garden. Stuck-up sort of chap. But down on you like a ton of bricks if anything was wrong. The lady was very different. Proper shame when she died. Miss Mary was a nice child too. His wife had been very fond of Miss Mary. Nothing stuck-up or proud about her.

"I suppose the Reverend Warner gave up the living because he was lonely after Mrs Warner died?" said Black, offering Harris some of his own tobacco.

"No, it wasn't nothing to do with that. It was along of Miss Mary's health, and her having to live abroad after being so ill with the rheumatic fever. They went off to Canada, and we never heard from them no more."

"Rheumatic fever?" said Black. "That's a nasty thing to get."

"It wasn't anything to do with the beds here," said old Harris. "My wife kept the place aired and looked after everything, just as she used to when Mrs Warner was living. It was at school Miss Mary caught it, and I remember saying to my wife that the vicar ought to sue the teachers up there for neglect. The child nearly died of it."

Black fingered the rose Harris had picked for him and placed it neatly in his buttonhole. "Why didn't the vicar sue the school?" he asked.

"He never told us if he did or not," said the gardener. "All we was told was to pack up Miss Mary's things, and send them off to the address in Cornwall he gave us, and then to get his own things packed, and dust covers put over the furniture, and before we knew what was happening a great van came to pack the furniture and take it to store, or to be sold—we heard afterwards it was sold, and then that the vicar had given up the living and they was going off to Canada. My wife was most upset about Miss Mary; she never had a word from her or from the vicar, and we had served them all those years."

Black agreed that it was a poor return for what they had done. "So the school was in Cornwall?" he observed. "I'm not surprised at anyone catching rheumatic fever in Cornwall. A very damp county."

"Oh no, sir," said old Harris. "Miss Mary went down to Cornwall for her convalescence. Place called Carnleath, I believe it was. She was at school at Hythe, in Kent."

"I have a daughter at school near Hythe," lied Black with ease. "I hope it's not the same place. What was the name of Miss Mary's school?"

"Couldn't tell you, sir," said old Harris, shaking his head, "it's too long ago. But I remember Miss Mary saying it was a lovely place, right on the sea, and she was very happy there, fond of the games and that."

"Ah," said Black, "can't be the same then. My daughter's school is inland. It's funny how people get hold of the wrong end of the stick. I heard Mr Warner's name spoken down in the village this evening—queer, if you hear a name once in a day you hear it again—and someone was saying the reason they went to Canada was because the daughter had been badly injured in a train accident."

Old Harris laughed scornfully. "Them fellows at the pub will say anything when they've a drop of beer inside them," he said. "Train accident, indeed. Why, the whole village knew at the time it was rheumatic fever and that the vicar was almost out of his mind with the worry of it, being sent for so sudden up to the school and all. I've never seen a man so demented. To tell you the truth, neither the wife nor myself had ever thought him so fond of Miss Mary until that happened. He used to neglect her, we thought. She was so much her mother's girl. But his face was terrible when he came back from being sent for to the school, and he said to my wife that it was for God to punish the head teacher there for criminal negligence. Those were his words. Criminal negligence."

"Perhaps," said Black, "he had an uneasy conscience and blamed the school for neglect, when at heart he blamed himself."

"Could be," said old Harris, "could be. He'd always look for the fault in the other fellow."

Black considered the time had come to pass from the Warners to the roses once again. He lingered five more minutes, made a note of the blooms recommended for planting by an amateur like himself who wanted quick results, said good evening, and went back to the inn. He slept soundly and caught the first train back to London in the morning. He did not think he would secure any more information at Long Common. In the afternoon he took a train to Hythe. On this expedition he did not bother the local vicar, but addressed himself to the manageress of his hotel.

"I am looking around the coast for a suitable school for my daughter," he said, "and I understand that there are one or two in this part of the world that are very good indeed. I wonder if you happen to know the names of any you could recommend?"

"Oh yes," said the manageress, "there are two very good schools in Hythe. There is Miss Braddock's, up at the top of the hill, and of course there is St Bees, the big co-educational school right on the front. Here at the hotel we mostly get parents with children at St Bees."

"Co-educational?" said Black. "Has it always been so?"

"Since it was first founded, thirty years ago," said the manageress. "Mr and Mrs Johnson are still the principals, though of course they are both elderly now. It's very well run and has an excellent tone. I know there is sometimes prejudice against a co-educational school, because people say it makes the girls masculine and the boys effeminate, but I've never seen a sign of that myself. The children always look very happy and just like other children, and they only take them up to fifteen anyway. Would you care for me to make an appointment for you to see either Mr or Mrs Johnson? I know them well."

Mr Black wondered if she got a commission on pupils to whom

she had recommended the school. "Thank you very much," he said, "I would be pleased if you would." The appointment was made for eleven-thirty the next morning.

Black was surprised at St Bees' being co-educational. He had not thought that the Reverend Henry Warner would have been open-minded on mixed tuition, St Bees it must be, however, from the description given by old Harris, the gardener. St Bees was certainly facing the sea, with a fine surround. The other school, Miss Braddock's, was tucked away behind the hill at the top of the town, with hardly any view at all and no playing fields. Black had made sure of this by going to look at the outside before keeping his appointment at St Bees.

A smell of shining linoleum, scrubbed floors, and varnish greeted him as he stood at the entrance. A parlourmaid answered his bell and showed him into a large study on the right of the hall. An elderly man with a bald head, horn spectacles and an effusive smile rose to his feet and greeted him.

"Glad to meet you, Mr Black," he said. "So you are looking for a school for your daughter? I hope you are going to leave St Bees believing that you have found it."

Mr Black summed him up in a word. "Salesman," he said to himself. Aloud, he proceeded to spin a neat yarn about his daughter Phyllis, who was just reaching the awkward age.

"Awkward?" said Mr Johnson. "Then St Bees is the place for Phyllis. We have no awkward children here. All the odd spots get rubbed off. We pride ourselves on our happy, healthy boys and girls. Come and have a look at them."

He clapped Black upon the back and proceeded to lead him round the school. Black was not interested in schools, co-educational or otherwise; he was only interested in Mary Warner's rheumatic fever of nineteen years ago. But he was a patient man and allowed himself to be shown every classroom, every dormitory—the two wings were separated for the two sexes —the gymnasium, the swimming bath, the lecture hall, the playing fields, and finally the kitchen. He then returned with a triumphant Mr Johnson to the study.

"Well, Mr Black?" said the principal, smiling behind his horn rims. "And are we to be allowed to have Phyllis?"

Black sat back and folded his hands, the picture of a fond father. "Yours is a delightful school," he said, "but I must tell you that we have to be very careful of Phyllis's health. She is not a robust child and gets colds very easily. I am only wondering whether the air might not be too strong for her."

Mr Johnson laughed and, opening a drawer in his desk, took out a book. "My dear Mr Black," he said, "St Bees has one of the best health records of any school in England. A child develops a cold. He or she is isolated at once. That cold does not spread. In the winter months noses and throats are sprayed as a matter of routine. In the summer months the children do exercises for the lungs in front of open windows. We have not had an influenza epidemic for five years. One case of measles two years ago. One case of whooping cough three years ago. I have here a list of illnesses contracted by the boys and girls over the years, and it is a list I am proud to show to every parent."

He handed the book to Mr Black, who took it with every sign of pleasure. It was just the evidence he wanted.

"This is remarkable," he said, turning the pages, "and of course modern methods of hygiene have helped you to have such a good health record. It can't have been the same some years ago."

"It has always been the same," said Mr Johnson, getting up and reaching for another volume on his shelf. "Choose any year you fancy. You won't catch me out."

Without hesitation Black chose the year that Mary Warner had been removed from the school by her father. Mr Johnson ran his hand along the volumes and produced the year in question. Black turned the pages in search of rheumatic fever. There were cold cases, one broken leg, one German measles, one sprained ankle, one mastoid—but not the case he sought.

"Have you ever had a case of rheumatic fever?" he enquired. "My wife is particularly afraid of that for Phyllis."

"Never," said Mr Johnson firmly. "We are too careful. The boys and girls always have a rub-down after games, and the linen and clothing are most scrupulously aired."

Black shut up the book. He decided upon direct tactics. "I like what I have seen of St Bees," he said, "but I feel I must be frank with you. My wife was given a list of schools, with yours amongst it, and she at once struck it off the list because she remembered being very put off it by a friend many years ago. This friend had a friend—you know how it is—but the long and short of it was that the friend was obliged to remove his daughter from St Bees and even talked of suing the school for criminal negligence."

Mr Johnson's smile had gone. His eyes looked small behind the horn-rimmed glasses. "I should be very much obliged if you would give me the name of the friend," he said coldly.

"Certainly," said Black. "The friend afterwards left this country and went to Canada. He was a clergyman. And his name was the Reverend Henry Warner."

The horn-rimmed glasses did not disguise the odd, wary flicker in Mr Johnson's eyes. He ran his tongue over his lips. "The Reverend Henry Warner," he said, "now let me see." He leant back in his chair and seemed to be pondering. Black, trained to evasion, knew that the principal of St Bees was thinking and playing for time.

"Criminal negligence was the word used, Mr Johnson," he said, "and oddly enough I ran across a relative of Warner's only the other day, who happened to bring the matter up. I was told that Mary Warner nearly died."

Mr Johnson took off his horn glasses and slowly polished them. His expression had quite changed. The over-genial schoolmaster had turned into the hardheaded businessman. "You obviously know the story from the relative's point of view only," he said. "Any criminal negligence was on the part of the father, Henry Warner, and not on ours."

Black shrugged his shoulders. "How can a parent be sure?" he murmured.

His words were calculated to draw the principal further.

"How can you be sure?" shouted Mr Johnson, all pretence at geniality gone, and slapping his hand on his desk. "Because I would have you know that Mary Warner's case was one isolated incident that had never happened before and has never happened since. We were careful then. And we are careful now. I told the father that what had occurred must have occurred during the holidays, and most definitely and finally not at school. He would not believe me, and insisted that our boys here were to blame, through lack of supervision. I had every boy over a certain age up here before me, in this very room, and questioned them privately. My boys spoke the truth. They were not to blame. It was useless to try to get any sense out of the girl herself; she did not know what we were talking about or what we were asking her. I need hardly tell you, Mr Black, that the whole thing was the most frightful shock to myself and my wife, and to the whole staff, and the story is one which, thank God, we have lived down and which we had hoped was forgotten."

His face showed fatigue and strain. The story may have been lived down, but it had definitely not been forgotten by the principal.

"What happened?" asked Black. "Did Warner tell you he was going to remove his daughter?"

"Did he tell us?" said Mr Johnson. "No, indeed, we told him. How could we possibly keep Mary Warner here when we found she was five months pregnant?"

The jigsaw puzzle was fitting together rather nicely, thought Black. It was remarkable how the pieces came to hand if you set your mind to the job. Finding out the truth through other people's lies was always stimulating. First Miss Marsh; he had to break through her iron curtain. The Reverend Henry Warner, too, had certainly gone out of his way to build a fictitious barricade. A train accident to one, rheumatic fever to another. Poor devil, what a shock it must have been to him. No wonder he packed his daughter off to Cornwall to hide her secret, and shut up the house and left the neighbourhood. Callous, though, to wash his hands of her when the business was through. The loss of memory must have been genuine enough. But Black wondered what had caused this. Had the world of childhood suddenly become nightmare to a schoolgirl of fourteen or fifteen, and nature taken charge and mercifully blotted out what had happened?

It looked this way to Black. But he was a thorough man; he was being paid well for his time of research, and he was not going to his client with a tale half-told. It must be the whole story. He remembered Carnleath was the place where Mary Warner had gone for her convalescence after the supposed rheumatic fever. Black decided to go there.

The firm for which he worked supplied him with a car, and Black set out. It occurred to him that another word or two with old Harris, the gardener, might prove fruitful, and as it was on his way to the West Country he stopped off at Long Common, bringing as excuse a small rose tree which he had purchased off a market gardener en route. He would tell the gardener this came from his own garden, as a small return for the advice given him the previous visit.

Black drew up outside the gardener's cottage at midday, at which hour he judged the old fellow would be home for his dinner. Unfortunately Harris was not at home. He had gone to a flower show at Alton. The married daughter came to the door, a baby in her arms, and said she had no idea when he would be back. She seemed a pleasant, friendly sort of woman. Black lit a cigarette, handed over the rose tree, and admired the baby.

"I have a youngster like that at home," he said with his usual facility for playing fictitious roles.

"Really, sir?" said the woman. "I have two others, but Roy is the baby of the family."

They exchanged baby gossip while Black smoked his cigarette. "Tell your father I was in Hythe a day or two ago," he said, "seeing my girl, who is at school there. And curiously enough I met the headmaster of St Bees, the school where Miss Mary Warner was educated—your father was telling me about it, and how angry the vicar was that his daughter caught rheumatic fever—and the headmaster remembered Miss Warner well. He insisted, after all these years, that it was not rheumatic fever, but some virus the child had picked up at home."

"Oh, really," said the woman. "Well, I suppose he had to say something for the sake of the school. Yes, that was the name. St Bees. I remember Miss Mary talking about St Bees often enough. We were much of an age, and when she was home she used to let me ride her bicycle. It seemed a great treat to me then."

"More friendly than the vicar, then," said Black. "I gather your father had no great liking for him."

The woman laughed. "No," she said, "I'm afraid nobody had much opinion of him, though I dare say he was a very good man. Miss Mary was a dear. Everyone liked her."

"You must have been sorry," said Black, "that she went down to Cornwall and never came home to say good-bye."

"Oh, I was. I never could understand it. And I wrote to her down there, but never had no answer. It hurt me quite a bit, and Mother too. So unlike Miss Mary."

Black played with the tassel of the baby's shoe. The face was puckered to cry, and Black thought this might distract him. He did not want Harris's daughter to go back inside the cottage.

"It must have been lonely at the rectory all on her own," said Black. "I expect she was glad of your company during the holidays."

"I don't think Miss Mary was ever lonely," said the woman. "She was such a friendly soul, with a word for everyone, not stuck-up like the vicar. We used to have fine games together, pretending we were Indians and such. You know what kiddies are."

"No boy friends and cinemas, then?"

"Oh no. Miss Mary wasn't that sort. The girls are terrible today, aren't they? Like young women. They chase the men."

"I bet you had admirers, both of you, for all that."

"No, really, sir, we didn't, Miss Mary was so used to boys at St Bees, she never thought them out of the ordinary. Besides, the vicar would never have allowed anything like 'admirers'."

"I suppose not. Was Miss Mary afraid of him?"

"I don't know about afraid. But she was careful not to displease him."

"Always had to be home before dark, I suppose."

"Oh yes. Miss Mary was never out after dark."

"I wish I could keep my daughter from coming back late," said Black. "In summer evenings it's sometimes nearly eleven o'clock before she is in. It's not right. Especially when you read the things that happen in the newspapers."

"Shocking, isn't it?" agreed the gardener's daughter.

"But this is a quiet neighbourhood. I don't suppose you get any bad characters around here, and didn't in those days either."

"No," said the woman, "though of course when the hoppers come it's a bit lively."

Black threw away his cigarette. It was burning his fingers. "The hoppers?" he said.

"Yes, sir. It's a great district for growing hops. And in the summer the hoppers come down and camp in the neighbourhood, and they're quite a rough crowd, from some of the worst parts in London."

"How interesting. I had no idea they grew hops in Hampshire."

"Oh yes, sir. It's been an industry for a long time."

Black dangled a flower before the baby's eyes. "I suppose you weren't allowed anywhere near them when you were young, or Miss Mary either," he said.

The woman smiled. "We weren't supposed to, but we did," she said, "and we'd have got into a proper old row if we'd been found out. I remember one time—What is it, Roy? Is it time for your nap? He's getting sleepy."

"You remember one time," said Black.

"Oh, the hoppers, yes. I remember one time we did go off to see them after supper—we'd got friendly with one of the families, you know—and they were having a celebration, what for I don't remember—someone's birthday, I suppose—and they gave me and Miss Mary beer to drink; we'd never tasted it before, and we got real tipsy. Miss Mary was worse than I was; she told me afterwards she didn't remember a thing that happened all evening—we were sitting round the tents, you know, where the people lived, and when we got home our heads were going round and round, we were quite scared. I've often thought since, whatever would the vicar have said if he'd known, and my old Dad too, for that matter. I would have got a thrashing, and Miss Mary a sermon."

"Deserved it too," said Black. "What age were you both then?"

"Oh, I was around thirteen, and Miss Mary had turned fourteen. It was the last summer holidays she ever had at the rectory. Poor Miss Mary. I often wonder what became of her. Married, no doubt, over in Canada. They say it's a lovely country."

"Yes, Canada's a fine place, by all accounts. Well, I mustn't stay here gossiping. Don't forget to give the rose tree to your father. And put that youngster to bed before he drops off in your arms."

"I will, sir, good day to you, and thank you."

"Thank you, on the contrary," thought Black. The visit had been worthwhile. Old Harris's daughter had been better value than old Harris. Hoppers and beer. Fair enough. Mr Johnson of St Bees would say conclusive. The time factor fitted too. The boys of St Bees were absolved. What a damnable thing, though. Black let in the clutch and drove off through the village of Long Common towards the west. He felt it was important to discover at what point Mary Warner had lost her memory. That she remembered nothing of what must have happened at the hop-picking celebration was plain. A reeling head, a black-out, and two scared kids making for home at top speed before they were discovered.

Johnson of St Bees, still warm in the defence of his school, had told Black that there was no doubt Mary Warner had been completely ignorant of her condition. When the matron, aghast, had discovered the fact and taxed the child, Mary Warner was bewildered. She thought the matron had gone mad. "What do you mean?" she had said. "I'm not grown-up, and I'm not married. Do you mean I'm like Mary in the Bible?" She had not the remotest idea of the facts of life.

The school doctor advised against questioning the child further. The father had been sent for. And Mary Warner was removed. That, so far as Mr Johnson and the staff of St Bees were concerned, was the end of the matter.

Black wondered what the vicar had said to his daughter. He suspected that the vicar had questioned the unfortunate child until he had given her brain fever. The shock must be enough to turn any child mental for life. Perhaps he would get the solution down at Carnleath. The only trouble was that Black did not know quite what he was looking for. The Reverend Warner must surely have changed their names.

Carnleath turned out to be a small fishing port on the south coast. It had probably enlarged itself during the past nineteen years, because there were three or four fair-sized hotels and a sprinkling of villas, and it was evident that the populace now devoted themselves to the business of catching tourists before catching fish.

Black's family, Phyllis and the boy, returned to the mythical land whence they sprang. Black was now a newly married man, and his wife, a girl of eighteen, was expecting her first baby. Black felt doubtful as he enquired for nursing homes. But he was not disappointed. There was a nursing home in Carnleath, and it did specialise in maternity cases only. Sea View, it was called. Right out on the cliff's edge, above the harbour. He backed his car against a wall, got out, went to the front door and rang the bell. He asked to see the matron. Yes, it was about booking a room for a future case.

He was shown into the matron's private sitting-room. She was small and plump and jolly, and he felt certain that he would be well advised to leave his mythical wife—Pearl, he decided to call her in a sudden flight of the imagination—in the matron's capable care.

"And when do you expect the happy event?"

No Cornish woman this, but a hearty, ringing Cockney. Black felt at home with her at once.

"In May," said Black. "My wife is with my in-laws at the moment, and so I've come on this little trip alone. She is determined to be beside the sea for the great occasion, and as we spent our honeymoon here, she feels a sentimental liking for the spot, and so do I." Black gave what he intended to be a sheepish, prospective father's smile.

The matron was undaunted. "Very nice too, Mr Black," she said, "back to the scene of the crime, eh?" She laughed heartily. "Not all my patients are so fond of the backward glance. You'd be surprised."

Black handed the matron a cigarette. She took it and puffed at it with relish.

"I hope you aren't going to shatter my illusion," he said.

"Illusions?" said the matron. "We have few illusions here. They all go west in the labour ward. What was sauce for the gander turns out to be a pain under the pinny for the goose."

Black began to feel sorry for the fictitious Pearl. "Oh well," said Black, "my wife's a plucky girl. She's not frightened. I may say, she's considerably younger than myself. Only just turned eighteen. That's the one thing that worries me about this business. It that too young to be having a baby, Matron?"

"They can't be too young," said the matron, puffing a cloud of smoke into the air. "The younger the better. Their bones aren't so set, and they're not muscle-bound. It's the old ones that give me my headaches. Come to me at thirty-five and think they're in for a picnic. We soon show 'em. Your wife play a lot of tennis?"

"Doesn't play at all."

"Good for her. Had a girl here last week, she was local champion over in Newquay, and she was so muscle-bound she was in labour for thirty-six hours. Sister and I were worn to a frazzle at the end of it."

"What about the girl?"

"Oh, she was all right once we stitched her up."

"You have had patients as young as eighteen before?" he asked.

"Younger than that," she said; "we cater for all ages here, fourteen to forty-five. And they haven't all had pleasant honeymoons. Would you like to see some of my babies? I've a little fellow born an hour ago, and Sister is just making him pretty for Mother."

Black steeled himself for the ordeal. If Matron was as forthright as this over one cigarette, how would she be after two double gins? He knew he must ask her to dinner. He went round the nursing home, saw one or two prospective mothers, saw several more whose illusions had apparently been shattered, and when he had inspected the babies, the labour ward, and the laundry, he made a silent vow to remain childless.

He booked a room with a view over the sea for Pearl, he gave the date in May—he even paid a deposit—and then he asked Matron to dine.

"That's very nice of you," she said. "I'd enjoy it. The Smuggler's Rest is only a small place, nothing to look at from outside, but the bar's the best in Carnleath."

"Then the Smuggler's Rest it shall be," said Black, and they arranged to meet at seven.

By nine-thirty, after two double gins, lobster, and a bottle of Chablis, with brandy to follow, the difficulty was not to make Matron talk, but to get her to stop. She launched into the finer sides of midwifery with a wealth of detail that nearly turned Black dizzy. He told her she should write her reminiscences. She said she would when she retired.

"No names, of course," he said, "and don't tell me all your patients have been married women, because I shan't believe you."

Matron tossed down her first brandy. "I told you before we had all sorts at Sea View," she said, "but don't let that shock you. We're very discreet."

"I'm unshockable," said Black, "and so is Pearl."

Matron smiled. "You know your onions," she said. "It's a pity all husbands don't. We'd have fewer tears at Sea View." She leant forward intimately. "You'd be staggered to know what games some people play," she said. "I don't mean the honest-to-God married people like yourself. But those who have slipped up. They come down here to get the business over, and they pretend to be above-board, and everything nice and pretty, but they can't deceive me. I've been in the game too long. We've had titled patients at Sea View, pretending to be Mrs, and their husbands think they are having a holiday in the South of France. Not a bit of it. They're having what they didn't reckon to have—at Sea View."

Black ordered another brandy. "What happens to the unwanted baby?" he asked.

"Oh, I have contacts," said Matron. "There's plenty of foster mothers in this part of the world who won't say no to twenty-five shillings a week until a child reaches school age. No questions asked. Sometimes I've seen the face of the real mother in the papers afterwards. I show it to Sister and we have a quiet laugh. 'She didn't wear that pretty smile in the labour ward,' I say to Sister. Yes, I'll write my memoirs one of these days. I dare say they'd be worth something, and they'd sell like hot cakes."

Matron took another of Black's cigarettes. "I'm still worried about my wife's age," he said. "What's the youngest you've ever had?"

Matron paused for reflection, breathing smoke into the air.

"Sixteen, fifteen," she said. "Yes, we had a fifteen-year-old once, barely fifteen, if I remember rightly. That was a sad case. Long time ago now, though."

"Tell me about it," said Black.

Matron sipped her brandy. "She came of well-to-do people too," she said; "the father would have paid anything I asked, but I'm not a grasper. I told him a sum I thought fair, and he was so pleased to dump his daughter on me, he gave me a bit extra. I had her here for five months, which is a thing I don't do as a rule, but he said it was either that or a remand home, and I felt so sorry for the poor kid I took her."

"How did it happen?" asked Black.

"Co-ed school, the father said. But I never believed that yarn. The amazing thing was that the little girl couldn't tell any of us what had happened. I generally get at the truth from my patients, but I never got it from her. She told us at Sea View that her father said it was the greatest disgrace that could ever come upon any girl, and she couldn't make it out, she said, because her father was a clergyman, and he was forever preaching what had happened to the Virgin Mary as being the most wonderful thing in the world."

The waiter came with the bill, but Black waved him away.

"You mean to say the girl thought the whole business was supernatural?" he asked.

"That's exactly what she did think," said the matron, "and nothing would shake her. We told her the facts of life, and she wouldn't believe us. She said to Sister that something horrid like that might happen to other people, but it certainly hadn't happened to her. She said she had sometimes dreamt about angels, and probably one had come in the night, when she was asleep, and that her father would be the first to say he was sorry when the baby was born, because of course it would be a new messiah. Do you know, it was really pathetic to hear her talk, she was so sure of herself. She told us she loved children and wasn't a bit afraid, and she only hoped she was really good enough to be its mother; she knew this time he really would save the world."

"What a frightful story," said Black. He ordered coffee.

Matron became more human, more understanding. She forgot to smack her lips.

"We became ever so fond of the child, Sister and I," she said, "you couldn't help it. She had such a sweet nature. And we almost came to believe in her theory ourselves. She reminded us that Mary had only been a year or so younger than she was when Jesus was born, and that Joseph had tried to hide her away because he was shocked at her having a baby too. 'You see,' she told us, 'there'll be a great star in the sky the night my baby is born,' and sure enough, there was. It was only Venus, of course, but both Sister and I were glad for the child's sake it was there. It made it easier for her, took her mind off what was happening." Matron drank her coffee and glanced at her watch. "I ought to be going," she said. "We're doing a Caesarean at eight tomorrow morning, and I must have a good night's sleep."

"Finish your story first," said Black. "What was the end of it all?"

"She had her baby, and it was a boy, and I've never seen anything so sweet as that child sitting up in bed with her baby in her arms; it might have been a doll given her for a birthday present; she was so pleased she couldn't say a word. She just said, 'Oh, Matron, oh, Matron,' over and over again, and Lord knows I'm no softie, but I nearly cried, and so did Sister. But I can tell you one thing, whoever was responsible for that bit of work was a redhead. I remember saying to the child, 'Well, he's a proper little Carrots and no mistake,' and Carrots he became to all of us, and to the poor little girl as well. I don't ever want to go through again what happened when we parted them."

"Parted them?" asked Black.

"We had to do that. The father was taking her away, to begin a new life, and of course she couldn't do that with a baby, not a child her age. We kept her and Carrots for four weeks, and even then it was too long; she'd grown too attached to him. But it was all arranged, you see; the father was to fetch her, and the baby was to go to a home, and Sister and I talked it over, and we decided the only way to do it was to tell the poor child that Carrots had died in the night. So we told her that. But it was worse even than we thought. She turned dead white, and then she screamed . . . I think I shall hear the sound of that scream to my dying day.

"It was terrible. High-pitched, queer. Then she fainted dead away, and we thought she would never come round and that she would die. We called in the doctor, which we don't do as a rule— we attend to our patients ourselves—and he said the whole thing was monstrous and that the shock of losing her baby might turn her mental. She came to, eventually. But do you know what had happened? She had lost her memory. She didn't recognise us, nor her father when he came, nor anyone. She remembered nothing of what had happened. Her memory had gone quite dead. She was well physically and mentally, but for that. The doctor said then it was the most merciful thing that could have happened. But if it ever came back, he said, it would be like waking up to hell for that poor little girl."

Black summoned the waiter and paid the bill. "I'm sorry we've ended the evening on such a note of tragedy," he said, "but thank you very much for the story all the same. And I think you should include it in your memoirs when you come to write them. By the way, what happened to the baby?"

Matron reached for her gloves and her bag. "They took him in at the St Edmund's Home at Newquay," she said. "I had a friend on the Board of Governors and got it arranged, but it was quite a business. We called him Tom Smith—it seemed a safe, sound name—but I shall always think of him as Carrots. Poor lad, he'll never know that in his mother's eyes he was destined to be the saviour of the world."

Black took Matron back to Sea View and promised to write as soon as he returned home, confirming the booking of the room. Then he ticked her and Carnleath off the list in his notebook, and beneath them wrote the words "St Edmund's Home, Newquay." It seemed a pity to come all this way to the south-west and not drive a few miles further on what would be only a matter of routine.

The matter of routine proved harder than he thought. Homes for the offspring of unmarried mothers are not usually willing to discuss the whereabouts of the children handed to their care, and the superintendent of St Edmund's Home was no exception to this rule.

"It doesn't do," he explained to Black. "The children know nothing but the home that brought them up. It would unsettle them if the parents ever tried to get in touch with them in after life. It might lead to all sorts of complications."

"I quite understand," said Black, "but in this case there could be no complications. The father was unknown, and the mother is dead."

"I have only your word for that," said the superintendent. "I'm sorry, but it's strictly against the rules to break silence. I can tell you one thing. The last we heard of the boy he was going steady, in a good job as travelling salesman. I regret I cannot tell you any more than that."

"You've told me quite enough," said Black.

He went back to his car and looked at his notes. It was not only in his mind that the superintendent's words had rung a bell, but in his notes as well.

The last person to see Lady Farren alive, except the butler, had been a travelling salesman touting orders for garden furniture.

Black drove north, to London.

The firm who made the garden furniture had its headquarters in Norwood, Middlesex. Black obtained the address by putting a call through to Sir John. The catalogue had been kept amongst all the other papers and letters belonging to Lady Farren.

"What is it? Are you on to anything?" Sir John asked over the telephone.

Black was cautious. "Just a final checkup," he said; "I believe in being thorough. I will get in touch with you again as soon as possible."

He went to see the manager of the firm, and this time Black did not disguise his identity. He gave the manager his card and explained that he was employed by Sir John Farren to enquire into the last hours of the late Lady Farren, who—doubtless the manager had seen in the newspapers—had been found shot a week before. On the morning of her death she had given an order for garden seats to a travelling salesman for this firm. Would it be possible, Black asked, to see the man?

The manager was extremely sorry, but the three salesmen were all away, and when they were travelling it was not possible to contact them. The distances they covered were large. Could Mr Black give him the name of the particular salesman he wished to question? Yes, Tom Smith. The manager consulted his book. Tom Smith was quite a young fellow. This was his first round. He would not be due back at Norwood for another five days. If Mr Black wanted to see him as soon as possible, the manager suggested he should go to his lodgings, on the evening of the fourth day, when he might have returned. He gave Black the address.

"Can you tell me," said Black, "if by any chance this young man has red hair?"

The manager smiled. "Sherlock Holmes?" he said. "Yes, Tom Smith has a shock of red hair. You could warm your hands at it."

Black thanked him and left the office.

He wondered whether he should motor down to see Sir John right away. Was there any purpose in waiting four or five days to question young Smith? The pieces of the jigsaw fitted. The story was conclusive. Lady Farren must have recognised her son, and that was that. Yet . . . had she? The butler had taken in Lady Farren's glass of milk to the drawing-room after the salesman had left, and had found her perfectly normal. The pieces fitted, but there was still one little odd-shaped bit that was missing. Black decided to wait.

On the fourth evening he went down to Norwood about half-past seven, on the chance of finding that Tom Smith had returned. His luck held. The landlady, who opened the door to him, told him that Mr Smith was having his supper, would he please come inside? She showed Black into a small sitting-room, where a young fellow, hardly more than a boy, was seated at the table eating a plateful of kippers.

"Gentleman to see you, Mr Smith," she said, and left the room.

Smith put down his knife and fork and wiped his mouth. He had a thin, rather pinched face, like a ferret, and his eyes were pale blue and close together. His red hair stuck up from his head like a brush. He was quite small in size.

"What's up?" he said. He was plainly on the defensive before Black had opened his lips to speak.

"My name is Black," said the detective pleasantly. "I'm from a private-enquiry agency, and I want to ask you a few questions, if you don't mind."

Tom Smith rose to his feet. His eyes loked smaller than ever. "What are you getting at?" he said. "I've not been doing anything."

Black lit a cigarette and sat down. "I'm not suggesting you have," he said, "and I'm not here to look at your order book, if that's what's scaring you. But I happen to know that you visited a Lady Farren on your rounds just recently, and she gave you an order for two garden seats."

"What about it?"

"That's all. Tell me what happened at the interview."

Tom Smith continued to watch Black suspiciously. "All right," he said, "let's say I did go to this Lady Farren, let's say she did give me a couple of orders; I'll make it right with the firm when I see them, if they've got wind of it. I can say I asked the cheque to be made out to me through a mistake, and it won't happen again."

Black was reminded of Miss Marsh. Reminded, too, of the Reverend Henry Warner. Even of Mr Johnson and his touchy self-defence. Why did people invariably lie when questioned about something else?

"I think," said Black, "it would be much simpler for you, and for your relations with your firm, if you told me the truth straightaway. If you do I won't report on you, either to the firm or to the Superintendent at St Edmund's."

The young man shifted uneasily from one foot to the other. "You've come from them?" he said. "I might have known it.

Always down on me, right from the start. Never had a chance, not me." A note of self-pity crept into his voice. He almost whined. The baby destined to save the world, thought Black, had obviously not made a conspicuous success of the job up to date.

"I'm not interested in your childhood," he said, "only in your very immediate past, the interview you had with Lady Farren. You may not know it, but the lady is dead."

The boy nodded. "Saw it in the evening paper," he said; "that's really what decided me to do it. She couldn't split on me."

"Do what?" asked Black.

"Spend the money," said Tom Smith, "and cross the order off my book and say nothing to no one about it. Easy done."

Black smoked his cigarette, and he had a sudden vision of crowded tents, lorries and mattresses, dumped in a field where the hops grew beside tall poles, and bursts of laughter, and the smell of beer, and a shifty-eyed, redheaded fellow like this boy, hiding behind a lorry.

"Yes," said Black, "easy done, as you say. Tell me more."

Tom Smith became more relaxed. The detective wasn't going to say anything. Not if he told the truth. All right.

"Lady Farren was on the list of the big nobs in that district," he said, "plenty of money, I was told, and she'd be sure to give me an order. So I called there, and the butler showed me in, and I gave the lady my catalogue, and she chose two seats and I asked for a cheque. She wrote it out, and I took it. No more to it than that."

"Wait a minute," said Black. "Was Lady Farren pleasant to you? Did she take any particular notice of you?"

The boy looked surprised. "Notice of me?" he said. "No, why should she? I wasn't anyone. Just a chap trying to sell her garden seats."

"What did she say to you?" persisted Black.

"She just looked through the catalogue, and I stood by waiting, and she marked two items with a pencil, and then I said would she make out the cheque to bearer—I tried it on, see; she had that dumb sort of face that's easy to fool—and she didn't bat an eye, but went to the desk and wrote out the cheque. Twenty quid it was. Ten pound a seat. And I said good morning, and she rang for the butler, and he showed me out. I went off and cashed the cheque right away. I put the money in my wallet, and even then I wasn't sure about spending it or not, but when I saw in the paper the lady was dead, I said to myself, 'Here I go.' Well, you can't blame me. It's the first chance I ever had to make a bit of money no one knew anything about."

Black extinguished his cigarette. "First chance, and you use it dishonestly," he said, "your choice, and your future. Ashamed of yourself?"

"No one's ashamed till he's caught out," said Tom Smith. And suddenly he smiled. The smile illuminated the pale ferret face, deepened the light blue eyes. The furtiveness went, and in its place shone a strange, engaging innocence. "I see now that dodge didn't work," he said. "I'll try something else next time."

"Try saving the world," said Black.

"Eh?" said Tom Smith.

Black said good-bye and wished him good luck, and as he walked away down the street he was conscious that the boy had come out on to the doorstep and was watching him.

That afternoon Black went down to report to Sir John Farren, but before being shown into the library he asked the butler to have a word with him alone. They went to the drawing-room.

"You brought the traveller into this room, and you left him with Lady Farren, then after five minutes or so Lady Farren rang and you showed the salesman out. After that, you came in again with Lady Farren's glass of milk. Is that correct?"

"Quite correct, sir," said the butler.

"When you came with the glass of milk, what was her ladyship doing?"

"She was just standing, sir, much where you are now, and she was glancing through the catalogue."

"She looked just as usual?"

"Yes, sir."

"What happened then? I've asked you this before, but I must just check again before reporting to Sir John.'

The butler considered. "I gave her ladyship the milk. I asked if there were orders for the chauffeur, and she said no, Sir John would be driving her in the afternoon. She told me she had ordered two garden seats, and she showed me them marked in the catalogue. I said they would be useful. I saw her put the catalogue down on the desk, and she walked towards the window, to drink the glass of milk."

"She said nothing else? She didn't refer to the salesman at all who had brought the catalogue?"

"No, sir. Her ladyship didn't remark on him. But I remember I did, just as I was leaving the room, but I'm sure her ladyship didn't hear what I said, because she never answered me."

"What did you say?"

"I said, joking-like, her ladyship enjoyed a bit of humour, that if the traveller called again I'd know who he was because of his hair. 'Proper little Carrots he is, and no mistake,' I said. Then I closed the door and went to my pantry."

"Thank you," said Black, "that's all."

He stood looking out across the garden. Presently Sir John came into the room.

"I expected you in the library," he said. "Have you been here long?"

"Only a few minutes," said Black.

"Well. And what's the verdict?"

"The same as before, Sir John."

"You mean, we're back where we started from? You can't show me any reason why my wife should have killed herself?"

"None at all. I have come to the conclusion that the doctor's opinion was right. A sudden impulse, owing to her condition, made Lady Farren go to the gun room, take up your revolver, and shoot herself. She was happy, contented, and, as you and everybody else knows, Sir John, she had led a blameless life. There was absolutely no motive for what she did."

"Thank God," said Sir John.

Black had never before considered himself a sentimentalist. Now he was no longer so sure.

Panic

The hotel was in one of those narrow, obscure streets that lead from the Boulevard du Montparnasse.

It was a grey, drab house, that shrank away from the pavement and flattened itself between two buildings, as if ashamed, as if conscious of its own squalor. The very sign appeared unwilling to attract attention as it swung high above the door, in faded gold letters, "Hotel"; and then lower down, humble and mean, the word "Comfort".

There seemed no purpose in its being there, no reason for its existence. There was not even a café in the street, with gay checked tableclothes spread over little tables, and a large menu, illegible but generous, to welcome passers-by. Nothing but the street and the hotel, and next door a shabby fruit shop with dusty windows; hard greengages that no one would ever buy, and sad wizened oranges. The flies settled on them wearily, too tired to move.

In the hotel no one stirred. The *patronne* sat huddled at her desk in the dark little office, her fat white face resting on her hands, her mouth open. She breathed heavily, she was nearly asleep.

Who could possibly remain awake in such weather?

Every year it was the same. The fierce, dead heat that descends on Paris like a white blanket in July, stifling the body, stifling the brain. A fly crept on to her arm and ran up her shoulder. She was aware of it in her sleep, she shook it away and woke yawning, grumbling to herself, pushing her dyed red hair from her forehead with hot sticky fingers. She fumbled about on the floor, looking for her shoes, and dragged them on, still yawning, not realising what she was doing.

"The heat has made my feet swell," she thought stupidly.

She rose from her chair and went to the door. Still not a breath of air. The sky was white, the pavement burned her shoes. She stood looking up and down the street. She could hear the clanging of trams and the screaming horns of the taxis, as they rattled and shook; part of the ceaseless traffic in the Boulevard du Montparnasse.

A taxi broke away from the block and came down the street, slowly, uncertainly, the driver looking from right to left. He drew up with a jerk before the hotel.

"Would you like to try here, M'sieu?" he asked. "It's not much of a place, but I tell you Paris is packed—packed—you'll be lucky to find anything tonight."

The sweat poured down his face. He was tired, uninterested; wouldn't these English people ever be satisfied?

The girl stumbled from the taxi and looked up at the hotel, and then at the fat, greasy *patronne*, who stood at the door, a false smile of welcome on her face.

"*Vous désirez, Madame?*" she began, her eyes closing together, her tongue running over her lips.

The girl drew away instinctively, and then laughed, in case her companion should notice.

"I don't know—what do you think, it's sordid rather, depressing."

The man made a movement of impatience.

"Of course it's sordid, these places always are. What did you expect? But we must decide somewhere."

He made no effort to conceal his irritation. Why must she persist in being tiresome? Women always wanted things to be romantic, attractive; they liked to drape the truth in pretty colours. She had been difficult all day, silent, not in the right mood. Supposing this adventure was going to be a failure?

He turned to the *patronne*. "*Vous avez une chambre pour ce soir?*" he said in his slow, careful French.

"*Entrez, Monsieur . . . On va vous trouver quelquechose. Gaston—Gaston,*" she called.

A boy in a dirty shirt appeared, wiping his hands on a towel. He took the two suitcases from the taxi. The woman went into the dark office, and came back clutching a handful of keys.

"*Une chambre avec salle de bain . . . ?*" began the girl.

"*Ah! Non, c'est impossible. On n'a pas d'eau courante ici,*" snapped the woman.

She led the way up the dingy staircase.

"What does it matter?" whispered the man fretfully. "We can't be particular . . . "

There was a strange smell in the passage, the air was full of it, it seemed to come from the woman herself. Stale scent and staler powder. The smell of people who sleep in the afternoon, who do not take off their clothes. Cigarette ash, not thrown away, and over-ripe fruit eaten in bedrooms.

The woman knocked at a door. From within came an exclamation, quickly stifled, and the sound of heavy naked feet crossing the floor. The door opened about a foot and a man's head appeared, tousled, damp.

He smiled, showing a row of gold teeth. "*Je regrette, Madame, mais je ne suis pas présentable.*"

The woman laughed. She seemed pleased, she raised an eyebrow. "*Excusez-moi, je vous croyais parti,*" she murmured, and closed the door softly. She led the way to a room at the end of the passage. "*C'est ce que nous pouvons trouver de mieux pour ce soir.*"

It was small and incredibly hot. She threw open the window, which looked upon a narrow courtyard. There were two cats in the yard, and a girl washing something under a tap. A large bed, recently made, with a heap of unnecessary bed-clothes, stood in the corner of the room. In another corner a washstand—a fat jug with a crack down the middle. There was an ugly pattern on the wallpaper, and a red carpet on the floor. The man glanced uneasily at the girl—

"Sordid, but necessary," he said, forcing a laugh. "Let's go out and get something to eat."

They had dinner at a restaurant on the Boulevard du Montparnasse. She was not hungry, she poked at her food, and then pushed away the plate with a sigh.

"But look here, you must eat," he began. "You scarcely touched anything on the train. What's the matter? You're surely not scared, you, of all people?"

"Don't be silly—of course not. I'm not hungry, that's all." She turned away and pretended to watch the people passing in front of the restaurant. He glanced at her anxiously. She looked different this evening, quite different from what she had been in London. Perhaps it was because they were alone at last. Nearly always before there had been people, and she had seemed cool, definite, provocative, with a depth of knowledge behind her eyes, a world of experience. This was what had attracted him. Tonight she looked younger, much younger, almost a child. She wouldn't drink anything either. He read the wine list very carefully. It was impossible to do this sort of thing unless one was a little drunk.

It was all being utterly different from what he had planned. Why couldn't she make an effort? Why bother to come away if this was how she was going to behave? He resented the fact that she was not being attractive to him. Her face was like any other face. He began to suspect he did not want her so very much after all. Oh! but this idiotic feeling would pass, they were both a trifle shaky, he supposed. Funny little things, women; one never knew really what they felt or why.

Funny, but necessary from time to time. It was a long while since he had been so attracted to anyone, he didn't want it to stop now, before anything had happened.

"That's the worst of being temperamental," he thought, "one's emotions are so utterly out of control."

In his mind he drew a picture of himself, odd, eccentric, a bit of a genius, driven by passion, hypnotised by this girl.

The picture intrigued. "*Garçon!*" he called, shaking the wine list. "*Garçon!*"

He was beginning to enjoy his dinner.

It was dark when they returned to the hotel. The *patronne* must have retired for the night, the little office was empty. The boy in the dirty shirt appeared from nowhere, yawning, rubbing his eyes. He watched them anxiously as they went upstairs.

"There's something evil about this hotel," whispered the girl. "I wish now we hadn't come here." She laughed, trying to pass it off as a joke. From one of the rooms they could hear the low murmur of a woman's voice, and a man's cough. Then silence. A blind rattled somewhere. Although the window was open the heat in their bedroom was unbearable. A ray of moonlight shone on the cracked water jug and a strip of the ugly wallpaper.

He sat down on a chair and began to take off his shoes. "This is a terrible place," he admitted, "but for God's sake let's try and keep our sense of humour." He wished he had drunk a little more; he still felt coldly and insanely sober.

She did not reply. She poured some water into the tooth glass and drank thirstily. Her hands trembled. She did not know why she had come, or what was going to happen, but it was too late to think about this now. She felt tired and sick, and deep down inside her something was cold with fear. Why had she come? Curiosity, adventure, a senseless spirit of bravado. He might have been a complete stranger to her.

"Supposing we're found out?" she said.

"Don't be absurd, no one will ever know, at least, not about me. Didn't you arrange everything on your side?"

Surely she hadn't forgotten, or done anything foolish.

"Of course—it's all right."

She felt as if this was happening to somebody else. This was not her. She was at home, putting the car away in the garage.

"What would happen if they found out?" he wondered uneasily. Perhaps he would be expected to marry her. It was too late now, though, trying to think this out. Why was she putting difficulties in the way? She sat down on the bed, a pale, frightened-looking child. What an impossible situation.

He crossed over to the basin and started to clean his teeth. He wanted to hit her. Damn women. Why could they never be in the right mood at the right time? He was not going to give way, though, it wouldn't be fair to himself. Coming all this way, fagging over to Paris. He supposed he must make some effort to hide his annoyance. He threw down the towel and sat beside her on the bed.

"Cold feet?" he said carelessly. "What do you generally do when you do this sort of thing? What have you done before?"

She backed away from him, smiling nervously.

"That's just it. I've never done anything like this before."

He waited, not understanding. "What on earth do you mean?" He felt the colour rise from his throat, spreading over his face. He shook her arm angrily, his face scarlet. "If you think you're going to fool me . . ."

He woke suddenly, startled, dragged from the depths of a sleep that was like death.

What was the matter? Was she dreaming aloud, a nightmare?

"What is it?" he whispered. "What is it?"

She was breathing strangely, quickly, as if suffocating, and all the while a funny little noise in her throat. He fumbled with a match, and peered into her face. It was white, ghastly, drained of all colour. Her hair was wringing wet. Her eyes stared up at him, without recognition, two pieces of glass, no light in them. There was no sound in the room but her terrible choking breathing, inevitable, persistent.

"Be quiet," he said desperately. "Be quiet, somebody will hear." He left the bed and poured some water into the tooth glass. "Drink this, darling, drink this."

The glass rattled against her teeth, the water spilt on her chin. Still she made no sign.

"What shall I do?" he thought helplessly. "What in Christ's name shall I do?" He crept to the door and listened. The passage was still dark, but a ray of daylight was creeping through an open window.

He stood in the middle of the room. He saw her stay-belt pushing underneath her chemise on the chair. Stupidly the thought ran through his mind. "Pink, why a pink stay-belt?"

He passed his hand over his forehead. His fingers were wet with sweat. He could hear himself swallow.

Suddenly the breathing stopped. Not a sound came from the bed. He stood motionless, unable to move, unable to think, listening to silence.

A grey light began to filter through the open window. The furniture took shape, he could distinguish the pattern of the wallpaper. He wondered who had chosen it, and if it had been on those walls a long, long time. His brain refused to work properly.

"It's no good standing here," he thought. "It's no good standing in the middle of the room."

She was dead, of course. He knew that. She was dead. Funny—he felt no sort of emotion. Fear had taken it all away. He leant over the bed and gazed at her. She looked pinched and small, her mouth was open. No breath came from her now, no sound. Yes, she was dead. He went over to the basin and washed his face and hands. He wondered senselessly what had killed her. Heart, perhaps, she had never looked strong. She should have told him, it was not his fault. No, of course it was not his fault. Had he killed her? He did not know enough about women. He had not realised.

"I don't know what one does quite when a person dies," he thought, drying his hands on the towel.

He was frightened because he felt no emotion. Perhaps it was repressed, stifled; perhaps something had happened to his brain. He must not allow himself to become hysterical. Supposing he laughed, supposing he laughed in the silence of this dark sinister room and woke the other people in the hotel. Supposing they crawled in at the door, queer, shadowy figures, peering over the fat shoulder of the *patronne*. The man with the gold teeth, smiling, bowing—"*Je regrette, mais je ne suis pas présentable.*" He could imagine his grey unshaven face, the grin fading away as he saw the still figure on the bed.

This was awful. He was going to laugh—he was terrified he was going to laugh.

The silly line of an old song, heard years ago, came into his brain:—"Cheer up, Jenny, you'll soon be dead—A short life but a gay one." Supposing he threw open the door and sang down the passage . . . "A short life but a gay one."[2]

An hysterical giggle rose in his throat and broke the silence of the room. The sound brought him to his senses. He must dress quickly and get away. He must not be found here with her. The police—and questions, endless questions. The truth being dragged from him, and her family arriving—an appalling inquest —scenes and questions, more questions. There would never be an end to it, never. Panic came upon him, like an unseen hand seizing him by the throat. Why had this terrible thing happened to him? Why should he have been chosen to play this part? If he could get away now, though, no one could ever know. He pulled on his clothes, his fingers slippery with sweat. There was no reason why his identity should be discovered, he had given no name. The cards still lay on the mantelpiece, waiting to be filled in. He pushed his things into his suitcase and closed the lid. Out of the tail of his eye he saw the dark outline of her body on the bed. He pretended to himself he had not seen. The idea came to him that this scene would stay for ever before his eyes. The small, hot bedroom, the dead girl on the bed, and the ugly paper on the wall behind her head. He turned away, afraid.

He crept down the stairs, his suitcase in his hand, his hat pulled over his eyes. Somewhere a clock struck the half-hour. He heard a door creak. He flattened himself against the wall, drawing in his breath.

A woman came into the top passage and stood listening. She

was holding something in her hands. Then she stole softly along the passage and went into a different room.

The man on the stairs waited, it seemed to him that his feet had turned to stone. Once more the vision of the bedroom flashed before his eyes, the silence, the dark figure on the bed.

He left the hotel and started to run. He ran down the street, and into another street, and across the boulevard, and so on into a meaningless procession of streets. Grey houses, all alike, and dreary deserted cafés. This was not the Paris he knew, it was a nightmare in his brain, it was an inferno. And all the while the patter of his feet beat time with his heart to the senseless repeating tune. "Cheer up, Jenny, you'll soon be dead—A short life but a gay one."

He could run no longer. He walked steadily, his bag in one hand, his coat over his arm. Paris awoke to another day, white, blistering, like the days that had gone before. People came into the streets. Sleepy boys rolled aside the shutters of the shops and wearily dusted the tables in the cafés.

Someone leant out of a window and shook a mattress. A woman, her hair falling about her face, brushed the steps of a house with her broom. A yellow dog stretched itself, and sniffed at a lamp-post. Traffic began to rattle over the cobble stones.

The man could go no farther. He sat down, at a table outside a café, and rested his head in his hands. He could remember nothing but that he was tired, so tired that he desired only to lay himself upon the ground and sleep, his head in the gutter.

The drowsy garçon stood before him. He heard himself ordering coffee. Trams passed by, and a few early taxis.

"A short life but a gay one. A short life but a gay one." Would the tune ever leave him? Senseless, utterly senseless. Yes, he must find some train and get away, right away. Somewhere down on the Mediterranean. He would be able to write a play there, perhaps—do a little work.

He called the garçon for his bill. He must go now and find out about trains, he would take the first one that left for the south. He fumbled in his pockets, staring at the slip of paper. Then a tight band slipped away from his head, leaving his brain clear, cold.

Something, like the clutch of a clammy hand, closed upon his heart. His back weakened. A little trickle of sweat ran down his forehead and crept upon his cheek.

He remembered that he had left his pocketbook and everything that it contained—letters, money, addresses—in the bedroom of the hotel by the Boulevard du Montparnasse.

The Supreme Artist

He came away from the stage after the final curtain, and went along to his dressing-room humming a tune to himself, thinking of nothing. The girl followed close behind, patting the lock of hair that had fallen over her face.

"You smudged your eye-black when you cried this afternoon," she told him, "it came off in streaks down the side of my neck— look how filthy it is. I suppose you must cry?"

"I don't know, I've never thought about it before," he said. "I'll try something else tonight. We might alter the whole of the last act. What about wearing a beard? I'm sure one could give an entirely different performance in a beard." He turned to the looking-glass in his room, and squinted sideways at his profile.

"I should hate you in a beard," she said, feeling his chin. "It would make you all heavy and middle-aged. Darling, promise me never to wear one?"

He picked up a hand-mirror and viewed himself from another angle. "I'm not so sure," he said doubtfully, and then called over his shoulder to his dresser, "Monkton, what about a beard for the last act?"

The man coughed politely behind his hand. "Well, sir, it's hardly for me to say, but I scarcely think it would be suitable. Not for this type of part, sir."

"P'raps you're right. Why is it I'm never allowed to do as I like—Oi, where are you going?"

She turned to him from the doorway. "Upstairs to change. Have you got the car outside?"

"Yes—want throwing out anywhere?"

"Take me back to the flat like an angel, unless you've got millions of people to see. I can easily find a bus . . ."

"Don't be a mug, of course I'll drive you anywhere. Buck up

and get your things on. Monkton, there's nobody waiting, is there?" He began taking off his coat.

"One minute, sir, excuse me, but I believe there's a lady wishes to see you. Here is her card, but she said you wouldn't know the card, sir. I said I knew you generally liked to get away quickly matinée days, and she seemed disappointed. Said she'd wait in case you could spare her a few minutes."

"Give me the card." He frowned over it, twisting it in his fingers. "Mrs John Pearce—conveys nothing to me. What's she like, Monkton?"

"Well, sir—it's rather difficult to describe. A middle-aged lady, I should say, white hair, tall—dressed almost in country clothes. A very pleasant speaking voice."

"Oh, Lord! Pour me out a drink and show her in."

He lit a cigarette, and tried to remember the second bar of the tune that was haunting him.

"Why are you so mean to me?

Why are you . . . ?"

He had forgotten all about the woman, until the door closed suddenly and she was standing there before him. She laughed at him, holding out her hands. "You haven't changed at all, have you?"

He saw someone with a mass of thick white hair under an ugly hat, someone with a bronzed, rather weather-beaten face. Her eyes were blue, and she was nice when she smiled. Her clothes were all wrong, though, her ankles thick. She obviously did not care about these things. He started back in surprise, pretending to be overwhelmed with joy and astonishment.

Of course he had no idea who she was. "My dear," he began, "but this is too marvellous. Why on earth didn't you tell me you were in front?"

It seemed as though she could not move away from the doorway, but must stand there watching him, feeling his eyes with hers, uncertain of the truth of his words.

"I didn't think you'd recognise me," she began. "I was certain you wouldn't have the remotest idea who I was. What is it—nearly thirty years? Think of all that's happened since, so much and so much . . ."

"But you're talking nonsense," he interrupted, "of course I knew you the moment you came into the room."

He racked his memory for some light out of the past. Who on earth could she be? Mrs John Pearce . . .

She loosened the scarf round her throat and sat down on the edge of the sofa. "This is the first time I've ever been brave enough to come round," she said. "I've wanted to so often, but something always prevented me, a sort of silly pride. A feeling you wouldn't know me, wouldn't remember. I come and see all your plays, you know. I'm still sentimental enough to cut out your notices and paste them in a book!"

She laughed at him, shaking her head. He made a little noise in his throat to save the necessity of words. "You see, I live right down in the country now," she went on. "It's quite an expedition to come up to London. When I do, about twice a year, I make a point of seeing you act. I don't know what it is, but the years don't make any difference to you. To me, a tired middle-aged woman in the stalls, you are always the boy I knew, funny, excited, with his hair rumpled. That's being a sentimentalist, isn't it? Can I have a cigarette?"

She reached out for the box on the table. He wondered why she gave him no clue to her personality, and why she did not even bother to mention the names of people or of places. Apparently they must have known each other absurdly well. Bronzed face, white hair, Mrs John Pearce.

"Let's see," he threw his question into the air, "let's see, how long is it really since I saw you last?"

She watched his expression with grave eyes. "I said thirty years just now, but maybe it's a little less," she answered. "Time is such a ridiculous thing. Do you know, I've only got to relax, and throw my mind back, and I can hear the sound of your cab starting, and you driving away in it, hot and furious, with me lying on my bed imagining that nobody ever got over a broken heart."

Oh! so they had been as intimate as that? Angry words—tears—and now he couldn't remember her at all . . .

"I must have behaved like a swine," he said angrily. "I can't understand how we ever came to quarrel."

She threw back her head and laughed. "You don't mean to

say you've thought it was because of a quarrel?" she asked him. "But we never had rows, you and I. You must remember that."

"No. No, of course not." He joined in her laugh, wondering whether she had noticed his slip. "I know we were the most wonderful friends in every way," he continued.

She sat silent for a minute, considering the matter, her head on one side. "That's where you're wrong," she told him. "It's because we never struck a proper basis of friendship that the whole thing finished. I think we were too young to have any judgment—too young and too selfish. No sense of values. We were like greedy children who make themselves sick with over-eating."

He agreed solemnly, watching her over the rim of his glass. So this had been a passionate affair. Thirty years ago—he cast his mind back in vain. He had an uneasy feeling that he had behaved badly to this white-haired woman who sat before him. In a moment he was acquitted, though.

"I shall never regret it," she said suddenly, "never one second. Being in love—terribly in love—is the best thing in the world, don't you think? The only moment I have sometimes regretted was sending you away as I did. We might have gone on being happy."

Then it had not been his fault after all. Presumably he had gone from her broken-hearted. It was all rather touching. Why had he such an appalling memory? He was ready to cry over his youthful tragedy.

"I nearly blew my brains out at the time," he said bitterly. "I suppose you never cared for one moment how it would affect me. I felt as if there was nothing to live for—nothing in life to hold on to."

"I guessed it would be hard at first," she smiled, "but look— you soon got over it."

He was certain he had taken months in getting over it. For all he knew this woman had blasted his whole outlook thirty years ago. They had obviously been passionately in love and she had given him the chuck, breaking his heart. He forgot her ugly hat and her tired, weatherbeaten face. He began to imagine somebody young, somebody slim. He pictured to himself all sorts of mad, impossible things.

"Those long days together," he began dreamily, "that frock you wore—and your hair brushed away from your face."

She frowned, puzzled by his words. "But we scarcely saw each other in the daytime."

"Nights, I meant," he said hurriedly. "Long, long nights. Sometimes there was a moon making patterns on the floor. You used to put your hands over your eyes to hide yourself from the light."

"Did I really?"

"Yes—you know you did. And often we'd come back hungry —neither of us with any money in our pockets. Perhaps only enough to halve a ham sandwich. And you'd be cold—I'd have to give you my coat—but you'd wrinkle up your nose in contempt, 'Who wants to get warm that way?' Then, because I loved you so much, I'd want to strangle you, and . . ."

He stopped short, dazzled by his own imagination, and a little hurt at the astonished expression on her face.

"I've forgotten all that," she told him. "I'm sure you always had plenty of money. And we never halved ham sandwiches, we nearly always dined with Mother."

He glared at her, shocked and confused. His ideas were so much more romantic. She was spoiling everything. Why must she drag in her relations?

"I have always hated your Mother," he said coldly, "we never got on. I didn't like to tell you at the time."

She stared at him blankly. "But why ever didn't you say so? You know it would have made all the difference in the world."

He brushed her statement aside. He would not talk about her Mother. He saw himself young, miserable, very much in love. This was the only thing that mattered.

"I tried drinking at first," he went on gloomily, "but it wasn't any good. I never could get your face out of my thoughts, never for a single instant, night and day. It was complete and utter hell—"

"What about your ambition, surely that gave you some sort of interest? And then when success came to you?"

"Ambition? Success?" He laughed scornfully, throwing his cigarette into the fireplace. "What were they compared with my love for you? Don't you understand that after you sent me away I was broken, done in? You took from me the only chance of happiness I ever had. I was young, I had ideals, I believed in you more than anything in the world. Then, for some reason that I shall never know, you chucked me. You didn't care what became of me, and you have the face to sit there and tell me that the fact of my being successful should have put you out of my mind. Don't you know that success has not brought one grain of happiness to me, that always in the depth of my heart I've known that you were the only thing that mattered?"

He blew his nose noisily, and poured himself out another drink. His eyes were red and his hands trembled with emotion.

She rose from the sofa and laid her hand on his shoulder. "I'd no idea you felt it in that way," she said gently. "Please, please don't reproach me like this. I believed I was doing it for your good. I thought I would be a drag on you."

He refused to be comforted. He shook his head miserably.

"You were the sweetest influence in my life—the one reason for existence," he said. He glanced down at the wedding ring on her hand, and was aware of his unreasoning jealousy. "Who is this fellow you've married, anyway?" he asked roughly. "This John Pearce—damn his eyes. So you couldn't even be faithful to one ..."

"I met him eighteen months after you went away," she answered. "John and I have been married twenty-seven years now. Four grown-up children—just think of that! We lead a very peaceful life down in Devonshire. Don't you remember how I always loved the country? That dream has come true, anyway. I have a snapshot of my youngest boy here in my bag. He's rather a darling, don't you think? He's doing so well in Burma."

He scarcely looked at the snapshot. He wasn't interested in her children, or in her house in Devonshire.

"Does your husband know about us?"

She put the photo away in her bag.

"Oh, yes! I tell him everything."

"Then he doesn't mind?"

"Why should he? He's scarcely likely to bother over something that happened thirty years ago! He's always very interested in you. We read your notices together. He's going to be terribly excited when I tell him I've been round to see you."

He did not want it to be like this. He wanted a hulking brute of a husband who treated her badly, who never understood her.

He wanted her to be lonely and unloved, leaning out of a window, watching for a star. He could not allow her to be married for twenty-seven years and have four grown-up children. She seemed to take it all for granted, too. She made no allowance for his feelings.

"So much for fidelity," he said grimly, "so much for vows and promises, and all the things that go to make up belief. We used to hold each other and whisper words like 'never' and 'forever'. Just a silly little string of lies, that's what they were. You've killed my last illusions today; you've made me feel as though nothing's worth while."

She shrugged her shoulders and began to draw the gloves on her large brown hands. "You talk as though you had never made love to other women," she laughed comfortably.

"Other women?" He waved the idea away. He would not even discuss it. In his mind he saw a meaningless procession, to all of whom he had sworn the same things. The thought irritated him. He found it unattractive. He would have liked men and women to be as birds on a tree—the male bird dumb and inconsolable on a high branch, with its mate dead at the foot of the tree. The picture saddened him. He felt unhappy for no reason. She was standing now, the ugly hat crammed over her face, the scarf pulled anyhow on her shoulder.

He caught at her hand. "I don't want you to go," he said.

She smiled and made her way to the door. "I must catch my train at Paddington, John and the children expect me. It's made me so happy coming to see you. I shall sit in the train tonight and go through it all over again. It's been a great excitement in my quiet, uneventful life, you know. God bless you, and take care of yourself. You don't know how young you've made me feel."

He looked at her white hair and the bronzed, weather-beaten face. "You're taking something away with you that belongs to me," he said. "It's something that has no name, but it means a great deal to me. I wish I knew what it was."

But this time she laughed and would not believe what he was saying. "Now you're just acting," she told him.

"No," he said, "no, that's what you don't understand."

She went from him down the passage and out of the stage door. He heard her footsteps pass along the alley outside his window.

He looked at himself in the mirror above the fireplace. He felt tired and listless.

"Monkton?" he called. "Monkton?"

When he had cleaned away his grease paint and washed, his face seemed thin and pale. There were little lines beneath his eyes. His hair was streaked with grey.

Somebody knocked at the door. It was the girl ready dressed, carrying her beret in her hand.

"Who on earth was that old lady with the white hair and the large bosom?" she asked him.

"I don't know," he said, "as a matter of fact I haven't the vaguest idea even now."

"Did she keep you ages, poor darling? What a bore for you."

He made no answer. She followed him to the car waiting in the street. When they came to a block in Piccadilly she looked at him, wondering what he was thinking about.

He was singing absently to himself, his thoughts miles away—

"Why are you so mean to me?

Why are you . . . ?"

He broke off in the middle of a bar. "Tell me," he said suddenly, "that woman—did she seem old to you, really old?"

Adieu Sagesse

Richard Ferguson was a dull man. Everybody said so. He was the sort of man whom people turned into a shop to avoid, if they saw him walking along the street: "Let's go into Smith's for a minute or we shall run into old Ferguson." They knew that, if he should meet them, he would only raise his hat and pass on. He would not attempt to fall into conversation with them. No, it was just that he was dull, deadly dull. It was a mystery to the people of Maltby how he had ever come to be manager of the Western Bank. How he had married—well, everyone had long since ceased to discuss it. They had forgotten what he had been like as a young man. He had surely never been attractive.

His wife was such a charming woman too, really charming. Always ready to entertain and join in any of the local amusements. A keen sense of humour, of course—a real Maltby sense of humour. And the three daughters—the life and soul of any party. It was a wonder that the four of them could bear to live with old Ferguson.

Oh! he was dull. People said that he was henpecked. Well, it served him right. Maltby liked a man who had some spirit. Not Ferguson, though, he hadn't an ounce. No manners either, for that matter. If he were asked to dinner, he'd sit in a chair or stand by the window and never listen to a word that was spoken. He wore a funny sort of smile all the time. Superior, perhaps. Yes, that was it, superior. Maltby resented it. What did he mean by it, sulking in a corner, smiling to himself?

Poor Mrs Ferguson. Amazing how she put up with such a stick of a man. See Mrs Ferguson at a party! Her big cheerful laugh ringing out above the others. Hear her in church on Sunday, her voice drowning the choir boys, "Praise ye the Lord." Watch Mrs Ferguson at the Maltby regatta in August. She was superb in grey satin. And she wandered to and fro on the club terrace, complete with a sunshade the same tone as her dress. She dug young Shipton in the ribs, 'Isn't it time, Jack, you thought of settling down?" A good joke this! She was thinking of Helen who was still unmarried. Never mind. Perhaps later in the summer he would take her sailing. She turned with a smile to someone else. Her daughters were bound to marry sooner or later. Such striking, amusing girls. Wonderful woman, Mrs Ferguson. Once more her laugh rang out, strong and true.

The girls were drinking tea inside the clubhouse. They whispered and nodded over their cups. "Mrs Marshall has the same dress as last year. Would you believe it? Dyed, of course." Their eyes glittered among the guests. "I swear to you, the look she gave was positively—well—you know. Do they? Oh, my dear, don't tell me."

They laughed scornfully, they shook their shoulders like so many birds ruffling and shaking their feathers. Young Shipton passed with a friend. At once the girls moved differently. They became enemies. They held venomous thoughts towards each other. He threw them a word and moved away. Young Shipton was conscious of his power.

The sun shone, the sea sparkled, the brass band played a shade too slowly. Maltby was *en fête*.

"What a success it has been. What a delicious day," the voices said to one another. And then in a minute, whispering, muttering, "What on earth had she got on her head—a tea cosy?" . . . "There must be something in it. He's never left her side all the afternoon."

Happy, brilliant Maltby.

Old Ferguson continued to turn his back on the club guests and to watch the crowd below. He puffed thoughtfully at his cigarette.

What were the thoughts of the dullest man in Maltby?

Directly beneath him was a rowing boat filled to the brim with folk. It was Sam Collins the crabber, with his family. The "family" were dressed in their best clothes. They hopped about in the boat and dangled their hands in the water. Sam's wife sat in the stern with her sister and a friend, and a friend's sister . . . "an' I said it was turrible, really, the way she was goin' on, an' her hair all over her face and rouged up something awful, ee woud'en believe it!"

Sam sat on the centre thwart, the oars in his hands. His best suit worried him considerably and he longed to take off his coat. He hated the noise and the fuss of many boats. On his face was a wistful expression. He gazed sadly towards the harbour mouth, where the jumping water told its own tale. He heaved a sigh and shook his head. "I bet there's mackrail out there."

Nobody heard him. Yes, somebody. He heard a chuckle above him. He raised his eyes and saw the bank manager leaning against the club railings. Sam flushed and then smiled a little sheepishly. They both smiled; they both looked towards the harbour mouth; they both sighed; and old Ferguson winked, positively winked, at Sam the crabber.

"He's a dull fellow," thought young Shipton, watching his back, "deadly dull."

Old Ferguson sat at his desk in the private room belonging to the manager of the Western Bank. His papers lay untouched before him; his fingers drummed on his knee. It was no use, he could not settle down to work. It was not that he was ill—not a bit of it. He'd never felt better in his life.

No, there was nothing the matter with his health. But he felt queer, damned queer. There was something at the back of his mind he wanted explained. It had been growing on him for weeks—months. Just the feeling that nothing in life really mattered.

He began to wonder why he sat here day after day, year after year. No worries, no sorrows. Even the war had left him untouched. Here he was, sixty, nearly sixty-one, with one of the best positions in Maltby, with a loving faithful wife, with three devoted daughters. What about his house, "The Chestnuts"? Hadn't he got the finest view in Maltby—one of the finest gardens? On the very top of the hill, above the town, overlooking the harbour.

There was his own particular summerhouse, at the end of the garden. He used to sit there sometimes with his telescope and watch the ships as they left the harbour. Half-a-minute . . . wait . . . he'd nearly got it . . . it swung before him out of the mist, the first moment when the queer feeling had come upon him. He had been sitting one evening long ago, last summer, in his favourite haunt. He must have dropped asleep, because in his sleep he had heard a challenge. A challenge, a call, a summons from the depths of his being, clutching at his heart, seizing his mind.

He had awakened with a start, expectant and alert. There . . . it sounded again . . . a summons! He had risen to his feet and gazed about him. And then he had realised what it had been. Merely the siren of a ship. A ship leaving port. Leaving Maltby. That was all. It happened every day. But why had it entered into his sleep? Why had it sounded to him like a call from the dead?

He remembered standing in the summerhouse, his telescope under his arm, watching the ship steam into the open sea. Three times she blew her siren—three prolonged blasts. Signal of farewell. Farewell to Maltby. Soon she had become a smudge on the horizon, then only a far faint ribbon of smoke. Farewell to Maltby.

Then the feeling had come to Ferguson. He was dead. They were all dead. Maltby was a dead city . . . worse than any visionary Pompeii. Worse than a place of ashes. The only living thing was the ship that had steamed away. She hadn't been caught. She had gone before they tried to hold her back. A dim haze on the horizon now. Never mind whither she was bound. Her siren had been a call to him, a summons to the dead from the living. Farewell to Maltby . . . Hullo! here was the rain. Splashing against his office window.

Old Ferguson turned to the papers on his desk before him. The sound brought him to his senses. What was he doing, dreaming like this in the middle of the day? The rain streamed down in the street outside, raining as it can only rain in Maltby.

Old Ferguson reached for his pen and began to write. The clock ticked solemnly on the wall before him. "With reference to your letter . . . " But before his eyes was the smudge of a ship on the horizon, and in his ears whispered the throb of the siren that called farewell.

Ferguson rose from the tea-table and wandered towards the window. It was real Maltby weather. The rain of the morning had given way to an atmosphere of general mugginess. The sun forced a half-hearted smile and there were wide patches of blue on the flat sky. Ferguson left the room muttering something about matches. In the hall he paused to listen. No one attempted to follow him. He struggled into his old tweed jacket, seized his cap from the rack and, taking his favourite stick from the stand, left the house.

Maltby lay beneath him wrapped in a faint mist. Smoke curled from the chimneys and he could hear the cries of the children as they grubbed on the bit of beach below the town quay. Old Ferguson pretended to himself that he was just going for a stroll to breathe some fresh air into his lungs. If that had been the case he would have walked along the Esplanade and probably reached the golf course.

Why, then, did he turn in precisely the opposite direction?

Make no mistake about it. Old Ferguson knew where he was going. He made straight for the mud reach at the further end of the harbour. Here was seclusion and peace. No voices to trouble him. The tide was out, and the seagulls dived in the mud, searching for fish ends.

On a low piece of ground, where the overhanging bough of a tree partially concealed it, lay a boat. At least, she looked like a boat. Maltby would have called her a tub. In her day she had been a seven-ton cutter and proud of the fact. She had never been a beauty even in her youth. She had too much beam for length and a high, ugly transom stern. Never mind about that. She was a boat, a real boat. Not merely a few planks of wood nailed together to form a pretty shape, to be painted white with a sky-blue water-line and then sailed on fine afternoons round the harbour mouth.

Old Ferguson ran his hands along her sides. He took his pen-knife from his pocket and poked at the wood. A slow smile spread over his face. It was rare for him to smile.

"She's sound," he said softly. "Sound as a bell." He looked at the faded gold lettering on her stern. *Adieu Sagesse.*

He remembered buying her ten years ago when her owner had died of 'flu. Queer sort of chap. A Frenchman who had suddenly appeared out of the blue. He had sailed into Maltby one evening on this boat, and a fortnight later he had been found, practically dead, in the cabin. Odd fellow! Must have been as mad as a hatter. And he, Ferguson, had bought the boat for a song.

Nobody had ever known where the Frenchman had come from, and the boat was not registered. It had only meant half-an-hour's dealing with the harbour authorities. Why had old Ferguson bought her? Nobody knew. He did not even know himself.

He had never had the nerve to use her, and there she had lain on the mud for—ten years.

"Such a stoopid thing to go and do," Mrs Ferguson had complained, "buying up an old tub like that. You'll be the laughing stock of the club. So unpleasant for the girls. What d'you propose to do with her now you've bought her?"

To this her husband made no reply. He scratched his head. He couldn't think of an answer. He had merely obeyed an impulse, if you like, but there it was. Something had whispered to him, like the throb of the siren—"buy her, you never know."

Ten years lying on the mud. *Adieu Sagesse!* Old Ferguson cocked his head on one side and sniffed the air. He looked just like an overgrown mongrel dog.

Somebody was coming along the beach, sinking into the mud with heavy feet. He appeared round the corner of the tree. It was Sam, the crabber. Like conspirators they smiled at one another.

"Good evening, Sam."

"Evenin', sir . . ."

Old Ferguson lit a cigarette, Sam coughed and spat behind his hand.

"I've been taking a look at the boat, Sam. She seems as sound as when she first lay here. I've been testing her hull with my knife. No soft spots."

Sam stroked his beard and winked.

"There b'aint nothin' wrong with her, sir. An' never has bin. Her only wants a coat o' paint, to be ready fur sea."

They smoked awhile in silence.

"I'd sail her to America, I wud, an' niver ship a bucket o' warter th' whole way over," boasted Sam. "Take a look at the beam of 'er," he went on. "Look at thim timbers. Ye don't foind 'em buildin' boats today like 'un."

Silence again. Then old Ferguson spoke.

"I've got the key, Sam. Let's get aboard and have a look round." He glanced over his shoulder like a guilty schoolboy.

They climbed the rickety legs, damp with seaweed, and stood on the bare deck. Ferguson stamped with his feet. "Firm as a rock," he said.

His companion was digging his knife into the mast. "She's a good spar," he muttered. "'Twould only be a matter o' scrapin' an' a coat o' varnish."

Together they lifted the dirty piece of tarpaulin that covered the hatchway. They stepped into the cockpit and Ferguson drew a key from his pocket.

The door creaked and groaned, and finally opened. Eagerly they gazed down the companion way and into the cabin. There were two long berths on either side and a swinging table in the centre. Ferguson peered into the lockers and fitted cupboards, while Sam lifted the dusty skylight. Now and again they threw remarks at one another, neither expecting a reply.

"She's scarcely damp at all, after lyin' here all these years."

"Aye—she's roomy too. I'd sail in her afore I'd set foot in one o' them big loiners."

For'ard of the cabin were the tiny galley and pantry in one, and the lavatory. Then the foc'sle and the big cabin locker.

They moved around, muttering to themselves, touching everything with inquisitive fingers. They sat down on one of the berths. Sam found a chest under the table, full of old charts. He pored over them, licking his dirty thumb.

"How long would it take to get her into shape?" said Ferguson softly, gazing up the companion way so as to avoid Sam's eyes.

Sam coughed discreetly.

"She don't want nothin' doin' to her, so far as I ken see. Mast scraping and decks. Coat o' paint all over. All her gear's good. I've seen it meself, up in Steven's loft. 'Twouldn't take no toime to rig 'er out. Could do't meself easy." He made great play of blowing his nose.

Old Ferguson whistled self-consciously. Then he rose and went on deck. They closed the skylight and locked the door, covering the hatch once more with the ragged tarpaulin. On the beach they stood and gazed at the boat. The sun had set below the hill. The tide was creeping in, sucking its way along the mud. Golden patterns formed in the water, and the air seemed filled with splendour.

A seagull lifted its wings and settled on the mast head. The two men sighed and smiled, conscious of each other's thoughts.

"I believe she'd stand any amount of bad weather," said one.

The song of the sky and sea in unison, the creaking of the mast, the rattle of the shrouds. White foam, white clouds. The world to roam in. Alone. Alone.

"Aye, she'd sail too. Like a bird she'd be," said the other.

Stinging spray and the tang of salt. Brown sails spread to the sky. A tiller that kicked like a bucking horse. A ship that laughed and shook herself from the seas like a live thing. No land . . . and a wild, wild wind.

Something distant sounded through the dusk. Sam turned his head and listened. Ferguson closed his eyes. It was the summons he knew so well. The throb of a ship's siren as she left the harbour—outward bound.

Then Sam moved awkwardly to the stern of the boat and spelt out the name in the faded gold lettering. "Niver could make head nor tail o' this, sir. Nonsense, I reckon."

"*Sagesse* is the French for wisdom. Sam. And *adieu* means farewell."

"It's turrible queer languidge these furrin chaps do speak. Farewell to wisdom, that's what he reckoned to say. Must'a bin touched. Howsumever . . . " Sam considered the matter for a moment. "Kind o' grows on ye," he admitted, "but he must a' bin touched for sartin."

Old Ferguson smiled in the darkness. He felt young and at peace. He wanted to run to the top of the hill and wave his hand. *Adieu Sagesse*. Once more the siren called from the sea. The cry of something that escapes. Grey seas, grey skies. "Good night, Sam."

"Good night, sir."[2]

"What's come over old Ferguson?" said the Club secretary one day. "I ran into him this afternoon on the golf links and the man was actually whistling to himself. He waved his stick at me and smiled all over his face. I've never been so surprised in my life. Must be goin' potty."

"If you ask me," came the voice of the Very Reverend Travers, now retired, "it's something very different, very different indeed. I hate to say this sort of thing against an old friend, and nobody respects Ferguson more than I do. But if you ask me and you really wish to have my candid opinion, it's this. The poor fellow drinks." He shook his head sorrowfully and sipped his whisky-and-soda with a thoughtful air.

"Where on earth does he get the stuff?" muttered Colonel Strong, ex-Indian army. "I've never seen him take anything but ginger ale here. He's never offered me a drink in his life."[2]

"Probably sneaks into the bar at the Queen," suggested the secretary, "and has a good old souse. Or else keeps the stuff up at his house. Jolly disgustin', if you like, a man in his position. I think people ought to be told about it."

"I'm sincerely relieved he is not on the committee," stated the Very Reverend Travers. "It would put us all in a most embarrassing position. I feel it my duty to inquire into the whole business. Delicately, of course. I shall call upon Mrs Ferguson one day this week." Incidentally he remembered the excellence of Mrs Ferguson's home-made seed cakes. Also he would be able to judge for himself the brand of Ferguson's whisky.

"Personally, I've always thought him a bit peculiar," said the secretary, following another train of thought. "Remember how he bought up that old tub ten years ago? Never even used her, as far as I know. Rather peculiar, to say the least of it. I was walking along that way about a week ago and somebody had been down there. The masts were scraped and half of one side was painted. The skylight was opened, too. I climbed up the bank to have a look. However, it's no business of mine."

The Reverend Travers coughed and blew his nose.

"I hope—er—that the boat is not being used for any—er—wrong purpose? I don't like the sound of all this at all. Has anybody noticed a light there after dark? For all we know . . . " He looked around him significantly.

Who could say there were not orgies of a Bacchanalian nature taking place even in Maltby?

"I did see him talking to that very pretty daughter of Sam the crabber," said the secretary eagerly, "only the other day. It's just come back to me. It was in rather a dark corner, by the church. Funny sort of a place to be, now I come to think of it. Secluded and all that, don't you know?"

"Decidedly!" exclaimed the clergyman.

"Did you—er—happen to overhear what he was saying to her?"

"Yes—as a matter of fact I did," admitted the secretary carelessly. "He was askin' her if she depended on old Sam for her livelihood. Rather suggestive, what?"

Colonel Strong rose from the chair, scarlet with indignation.

"Good God! That means one thing—and one thing only. The damned old satyr, he ought to be horsewhipped."

"Well, I've lived in Maltby thirty years and I've never heard of such a thing," said the Reverend Travers. He was quite overcome. He rang for the steward and ordered another whisky to calm his nerves. "To think that what we have always believed to be a respectable, god-fearing member of society should turn out such a ruffian. Drinking himself to death, and apparently debauching the youth of Maltby. And using that old hulk of his for immoral purposes. This is really very distressing."

"What are we going to do about it?" inquired the secretary, his inquisitive nose in the air.

"Don't see what we can do, short of tackling him to his face," said the Colonel gloomily.

"I suppose you wouldn't let me get hold of the girl and draw the story out of her? I don't mind gettin' in touch with her." The secretary was perhaps too eager to make himself of use.

"Certainly not," Travers replied with great dignity. "At any rate, not at present. The unfortunate girl would probably start a scandal. We must have no scandal in Maltby."

"No—no—of course not," agreed the others hastily. "Because if there is something I abhor and detest," declared Colonel Strong, Indian Army, now retired, "it's anything in the nature of gossip or scandal."

If the members of the Maltby Yacht Club had taken the trouble to find out, they would have discovered that the manager of the Western Bank had been in the habit, during the last week, of locking himself in his office every evening and examining a number of titles, documents and deeds. His behaviour was, to say the least of it, suspicious. If he was not gambling in secret with the precious bonds entrusted to him by the worthy inhabitants of Maltby, then he must be preparing to decamp with their worldly goods.

Could it be that old Ferguson, the dullest man in Maltby, was a crook, a swindler, in short, a criminal of the deepest dye? It looked extremely like it. And yet, if the said members had possessed the powers of invisibility, and had stolen into the manager's room and glanced over his shoulders as he read his documents, they would have been baffled and intrigued. It seemed that he was examining the exact state of his own private finances, with a view to making a settlement on his wife and three daughters. Yet, in spite of his sixty years, old Ferguson looked strong and healthy. He had surely many more years to live.

Could it be that he was a victim to some deadly illness, and expected death at any moment? The suspense would have proved too much for the members of the club. For not only was the manager arranging his own affairs, but also those of a certain Sam Collins, crabber. Yes, he was actually declaring a certain sum to be paid quarterly to Martha Collins, wife of Sam Collins, and those dependent on him.

Ah! Maltby, what sinister secrets are these? Gentlemen of the Yacht Club, what is going on under your very eyes!

On Wednesday evening, old Ferguson leant back in his chair with a sigh of satisfaction. His papers lay before him on his desk, neatly docketed and labelled. His work was finished. All was now in order. Nothing more remained to be done. He gazed round at the familiar walls. The heavy roll-top desk, the books of reference, the plain brown walls, the map in the corner. Strange that after so many years he should feel no affection for them—no regret.

He rose and stretched himself. He straightened his tie and looked in the little mirror by the mantelpiece.

"You're sixty," he told himself. "Nearly sixty-one, and a damned ridiculous old fool."

And then he laughed aloud. Twenty minutes later Ferguson was standing by his boat on the mud flats near the harbour mouth. What a change three weeks had made in her appearance. The mast was scraped and varnished, the hull painted, the decks scrubbed. The rigging had been set up and the mainsail bent. A dingy brown sail if you like, patchy in places, but strong. Below, everything was in order. There were cushions in the cabin, a clock, an oil stove. Even the cupboards were filled. The little pantry was stocked with crockery. Ferguson peered into every corner. No—nothing had been forgotten.

"Sam," he called softly, "Sam, where are you hiding?"

An edge of beard appeared round the foc'sle door.

"Here I be, sor," said a hoarse voice. "Jest seein' all were ship-shape an' Bristol fashion."

His wife would have sighed at Sam's appearance. His jersey was spotted with tar, his sea boots coated with grime and filth. A disreputable old sou'wester was stuck on the back of his head. From his mouth hung the fag end of a cigarette.

"Where's your Sunday suit, Sam?" said Ferguson, winking an eye.

"Good Lard, sir! You'm surely not going' to ask me that?" Sam's face was a study of despair. "Why, sir, I've got rid of 'un over to Maltby, quiet like. I was'n goin' to refoose good money. As it es, I reckon that chap got et turrible cheap."

"Never mind, Sam, the days of tight collars are over. No more beastly suits for either of us."

They climbed on deck.

"What time's high water?"

" 'Bout 'ard-an-hour, sir, and we'll get it two foot higher tomorrow, d'un ee forget it."

"D'you think she'll lift, man?"

"Aye, like a bird. Her won't be no trouble."

"Right, Sam, I don't think there's anything more, then. I'll be here without fail. No regrets, eh?"

Sam spat into the water.

"What about the weather?"

"Wind's backing. We'll have it strong from the sou'west, I shouldn't wonder. She'll stand it. It'd take more'n a summer breeze to put her down."

"I believe it would, Sam."

Ferguson scrambled into the little dinghy. The letters on the boat's stern were no longer faded. They stared out in bold relief, challenging the world. *Adieu Sagesse!* The two men smiled at one another, saying not a word.

"Until tomorrow, Sam."

"Aye, aye, sir."

Ferguson climbed the steep hill that led to his house, "The Chestnuts". The sun was setting behind the distant hills. Dark orange, sombre, while the grey clouds gathered. A steady wash ran past the harbour mouth.

Rain and wind, what did it matter? Beneath him lay Maltby, secure and snug. He hated her general air of self-righteousness. The prim aspect of the houses, the narrow gardens with their stiff flowers, their shingle paths. The elderly spinsters who peered from the closed windows; the retired officers who stumped up and down the Esplanade. The people who formed the congregation in church, the members of the club, the inquisitive shopkeepers, the officious harbour authorities—all those who had robbed Maltby of her living soul, and stamped her with the death's-head seal—"A seaside town." How he hated them.

Only the gulls were true, and the quiet, grave waters of the harbour. The spirit that still lurked beneath the cobbled stones of the market square; the smoke that curled from the few huddled cottages; the call of the rooks at evening; the tall silent trees on the hillside; the calm beauty of the sea after the sun had set; the soft white mists that came with the rain in summer—only these remained.

Wherever he went, he would carry in his soul a love for these things—but Maltby was dead. No regret, no fear. Something lay before him that was splendid, intoxicating, immense. The call rose strong within him, supreme. The call of life itself. And he, sixty-one, stood on the threshold of his dream.

He threw back his head and laughed. He was old, old, but nothing mattered. Nobody cared. The world was his.

His last evening. It was typical of his life. He remembered that Travers was coming to dinner. He thought of the group seated round the table in the dining-room. Helen's new dress. The parlourmaid's heavy breathing as she handed the vegetables. The most comfortable house in Maltby. "Well, you can have it. You can have the lot," he cried aloud.

Adieu Sagesse! As he entered the house he heard the sound of his wife's loud laugh coming from the drawing-room. One of the girls had started the noisy gramophone. On the hall table lay the black hat of the Very Reverend Travers. Old Ferguson glanced at it with a glint in his eye and made for the drawing-room. He was going to enjoy himself for the first and last time in Maltby.

"Now, Richard, what in the world have you been doin'? The gong will sound in a minute. You knew perfectly well Mr Travers was comin' to dinner." Mrs Ferguson frowned at her husband impatiently.

"I know. That's why I came in so late. I waited till the last possible moment," replied old Ferguson cheerfully.

Mrs Ferguson opened her mouth in astonishment, while the girls turned round from the gramophone and gazed at their father. As for the Very Reverend Travers, he drew out a large handkerchief from his pocket and proceeded to blow his nose. How extremely awkward and distressing, the wretched fellow was drunk already.

"How are you, Ferguson?" he inquired, ignoring his host's unfortunate remark. "I don't seem to have seen you about lately —except of course in church on Sunday."

"I don't know if it's the approach of autumn," declared old Ferguson with an innocent smile, "but certainly these last Sundays I've slept sounder in church than I've ever slept in my life. And you too, my dear," he added, turning to his wife, "I noticed that it was only Mrs Druce's voice singing 'Peace, perfect peace', that roused you at all after the sermon last Sunday."

Mrs Ferguson turned a deep purple, the girls coughed, and the Reverend Travers bent down and pretended to stroke the spaniel's ears.

At that moment the gong sounded and the agitated hostess led the way into the dining-room.

As he entered the room the clergyman glanced surreptitiously at the sideboard. Alas! It was as he had feared. The whisky decanter was half-empty. Of course, his host was on the verge of delirium tremens; probably kept the drink locked up in his room.

The party seated themselves at the table. Everyone appeared to be nervous and ill at ease, except old Ferguson who had never been in a better humour in his life.

The soup was handed in silence. No one seemed willing to start speaking. The minutes passed. The noise of people eating became intense.

Towards the end of the meal the clergyman remembered his promise to the members of the club, to find out the meaning of Ferguson's sinister behaviour.

"It's curious how the young people of Maltby have changed," he began, as he carefully peeled his pear. "They seem to think of little but their appearance. I was walking along the High Street this afternoon and really, to see some of the girls from the shops, you'd imagine they were dressed for the theatre. No sleeves, silk stockings, their faces powdered and painted. Sometimes I doubt their respectability."

"Oh, come Mr Travers, you're exaggeratin'," Mrs Ferguson exclaimed. "They merely believe in fresh air. Short sleeves hurt nobody. Though I must say I hate to see girls of that class apein' their betters. We shall have them trying to join the golf and the tennis club, unless we keep them in their places."

"Would it matter if they did?" asked her husband.

"Matter? My dear Richard, what a thing to say. I, for one, should never want to play a game again if I had to mix with them."

"I don't approve of all these modern ways," said Mr Travers. Wasn't he going to be offered any port? Really, his host's manners were atrocious. "Life was far more romantic when I was a boy. I doubt even if these games improve your appearance, as people try to make out. A womanly woman has sweeter qualities than all these sturdy modern creatures. By the way, that little May Collins, old Sam's youngest daughter, is a pretty type of girl." He stole a stealthy look at his host.

"I know her well," replied Ferguson. "She's a very charming girl. I've found her an excellent job at Penleath. I'm even thinking of settling some money on her."

The clergyman turned scarlet with embarrassment. His eyes glistened behind his spectacles. Really, his host was going a little too fast.

"Richard is jokin', of course, Mr Travers," said Mrs Ferguson in icy tones. "Would you care for some grapes? They come from our own vines."

"No, thank you, dear lady."

The girls gazed stonily before them. What on earth had happened to father?

"Yes, as I was saying," continued their guest awkwardly, "it's scarcely a romantic period."

"I agree, Mr Travers," broke in Helen in a sullen voice. "Men, for instance, are quite hopeless nowadays. Years ago, I believe, if a man was attracted to a girl, he sent her flowers and things. Now he doesn't even bother to remember a promise to play a round of golf, or anything else." She laughed scornfully. "I despise men!" she added.

"In my opinion, girls don't make the most of their chances. Things were very different in the old days," retorted her mother.

"There's a jolly sight too much competition, I consider," muttered one of the girls.

Helen glared at her sister.

"Hum! It's all very sad," sighed the Reverend Travers, wiping his mouth with his napkin. "The present age is far from ideal. Don't you agree with me, Ferguson?"

"No, Travers, not at all. I think it's a great age."

The family looked at him in astonishment. Most extraordinary for father to venture such an opinion.

"May we ask why, Richard?" asked his wife, raising her eyebrows.

Old Ferguson waited a moment before replying. Then he turned to the clergyman with a bland smile.

"There's a general lack of morality I find extremely pleasant," he said.

There was a minute's horrified silence.

The Very Reverend Travers was entirely speechless. He could only stare and blink his eyes. Then Mrs Ferguson rose majestically from the table, followed by the three girls.

"Wait a moment," cried her husband. "I've got something to say to you all. You think I'm mad and off my head. Well, perhaps you're right. But I'm proud of it and, if I'm mad, then I'm going to commit the most sublime piece of folly that ever came into a madman's head.

"I'm starting out on a great adventure. I've had to wait sixty years for it, but it's not too late. What comes of it I neither know nor care. There's something in the quality of the unknown that holds more beauty than the Peace of God. One thing I know full well, and that is, if I pass away, Maltby will not pass away. You will live here, year after year, happy in your supreme self-righteousness. The congregation will continue to sleep in church on Sundays and to discuss their duty towards their neighbour during the week. You girls will marry, if your mother works hard enough, and you in your turn will produce sons and daughters to the everlasting glory of Maltby.

"They will sail their little boats on fine afternoons in the summer and hack round the golf course in the winter. I sincerely hope the annual balls will always be successful. I trust the Borough Council will gain their wish to erect what they term 'a smart promenade to attract visitors'! I shall be bitterly disappointed if my wife gives up the bridge parties that have made her so famous and which, incidentally, have added not inconsiderably to her private income.

"I shall feel I have failed as a father should my daughters forsake their very excellent habit of following young men who have no use for them. May gossip, back-biting and slander continue to be the mainstay of the club, and may members make up in argument the points they lose in sailing. As for the retired, worthy representative of the Church of England, I pray that his profound spiritual inclination, his devotion to the God of Whisky may remain as fervid and as unremitting as it is at present."

He turned in the doorway and reached for his old tweed jacket and cap that were hanging on the stand in the hall. He paused a moment to light his pipe. Then he smiled, winked his pale blue eye and bowed to the group in the dining-room.

"Good night to you all."

The front door banged and he was gone in the darkness.

Seven o'clock and a grey morning. The wind was blowing strong from the south-west, with a hint of rain behind it. No anger in it yet, for the gale signal was not hoisted on the top of Castle Hill.

The trees shivered and swayed, the rough harbour water sucked and splashed against the steps of the houses. The little boats rocked at their moorings. Grey clouds flew low on the wind-streaked sky, and high in the east gleamed a wild-wet sun.

A small black boat with patched brown sails was beating her way out of the harbour. Her lee gunwale was awash, but she faced her way through the heavy seas like a seagull bred to the wind.

Holding to the mast was a figure in a torn yellow oilskin much too big for him, a sou-wester on his head and a smile on his face that reached from ear to ear. Seated at the tiller was somebody in a faded blue shirt and an old tweed jacket. His grey hair was wet with spray, but he laughed as he shook it off.

"Aren't you going to say good-bye to Maltby, Sam?"

The figure in the yellow oilskin spat into the water. It was his supreme gesture.

The mast creaked, the wind screamed and whistled in the rigging, and the boat rose and fell through the waves with a heavy ponderous sigh.

Behind lay Maltby, wrapped in her morning mist.

The man at the tiller never once looked round. Before him stretched the open sea, mournful, terrible, mysterious. The call rose within him and became part of him forever. Grey skies—grey seas.

Adieu Sagesse.

Fairy Tale

The room was hardly more than a garret. High up, at the very top of the building, there was nothing between it and the sky but a thin roof, and the walls were all outside walls, exposed to every breath of air. There was one large window on the left, and through this could be seen the ugly chimney-pots and the slate roofs of other houses, stretching for ever, as far as the eye could reach, with no trees to break the monotony, and a ceaseless stream of smoke rising from the chimneys into the leaden sky.

Because of its nearness to the roof, in summer the heat was unbearable, but now it was winter, and even with the window tightly shut the icy cold air from outside penetrated the room. The atmosphere was freezing, even the walls and the bare boards of the floor were chilled—it was as if the room could never be warm again, not until the spring came once more and the sun shone.

Opposite the window, beside the door leading into the tiny bedroom, was a fireplace where no fire was laid. A little bundle of sticks stood in the grate, waiting their turn, kept preciously until the cold should prove beyond human endurance, when they would be kindled two by two, the poor flame showing a pretence at heat.

The walls of the room were brown, and high up by the ceiling large discoloured stains marked where the damp had forced an entrance.

The furniture was scanty. A table in the middle of the room, rickety on three legs, and two chairs, while near the fireplace was a large mat worn threadbare and a bench which seemed a rough imitation of a sofa, covered as it was by an old rug and boasting a faded velvet cushion. Close to the door leading to the landing there was a cupboard half open, and on the shelf stood a loaf of bread.

From the bedroom came the sound of a woman coughing,

irritating, persistent, a dry hard cough repeated at regular intervals, and this would be followed by a sigh of exasperation, suggesting mingled fatigue and distress. Once she raised her voice and called to the room: "Aren't you back yet? Is there nobody there?" And she would realise by the silence that the room was empty, and then she would cough again. Because of her coughing she did not hear the sound of a low knocking at the door, and not until the door opened and someone stood inside the room could she have realised that she was no longer alone.

"Is that you?" she called. "Are you back at last?" The intruder waited a moment before he answered. He was an old man with a long shabby coat reaching almost to his ankles. His hands, wrapped in thick woollen mittens, were folded over his full protruding belly.

He shrugged his shoulders, passing his tongue over his lips. "It is I, madam," he said, turning his head in her direction, " 'ave you not been expecting me all the day?" He smiled as he heard her stifled exclamation. "No, your 'usband he 'as not returned," he said, "maybe he will not come for a long while. But that makes not the leetlest bit of difference to me, no. You know why I 'ave come."

He waited, and then her voice came to him, tearful, hurried, with a suggestion of fear.

"I tell you I haven't got the money. It's no use. Even if you stand there and threaten me with murder, I can't give it to you. Why can't you wait—why can't you give us a little while longer? It can't mean much to you—to wait. He will be home soon, he may give it to you then. But I can't do anything, weak and helpless here."

The man's eyes narrowed, he glanced around the room as though seeking some solution, he even peered into the cupboard, bare save for the loaf of bread.

"I cannot wait any more," he said harshly. "I tell you last time, today was the limit of my patience. This morning the money was due—out of the goodness of my heart I wait till now. How do you think I am to live? I must 'ave now what you owe. I do not go away till you give it to me."

"But wouldn't I keep my promise if I had the money?" she cried. "There is nothing here, I tell you, nothing in either of the rooms. I haven't eaten all day—there's a stale loaf in the cupboard for my husband when he returns. What can I do? In bed, sick—"

The man spread out his hands. "I could let these rooms for double the sum you owe to me. Even now there are people ready to pay me, who wait only to take possession. I cannot any more afford to give the charity to paupers. You will either give me that money or I put you out in the street."

He could hear her crying in the adjoining room.

"You wouldn't do that?" she cried. "Not even the most brutal of men would act in such a way. I'm helpless here. For pity's sake wait until my husband returns."

"Your husband will not pay me," said the man, "he is a gambler, a waster, a good-for-nothing. He plays cards while you cry for food. Why should I be kinder to you than he? No—I will not wait. I shall call my son to aid me—we shall put these sticks of furniture into the street and you too—on the doorstep. There you can wait for your husband." He stood on the threshold of the bedroom, watching her eyes.

"Get up," he said, "it is all pretence, this illness. It is part of your deceit. Put on your clothes."

There was quiet for a minute. Then she stood beside the bed, a thin shawl over her shoulders, leaning against the framework to give herself strength to stand.

She spoke pleadingly, the terror rising in her voice. "No, no! You cannot do this, you cannot! My husband will kill you— you're a devil, wicked inhuman!" She was choked by a paroxysm of coughing.

"Put on your clothes," he said.

She leant back, panting, exhausted. "Stop!" she said. "I've lied to you. I have some money. But nobody knows—I haven't told a soul, not even my husband. Because if he had known he would have gambled it away. So I kept it from him, hidden, my last wretched little stock, saved for such a moment as this. I've prayed to God the moment would never come. But you've won—you've beaten me."

He did not move; he suspected she was lying. "Show me your hiding-place," he said.

"Go to the fireplace," she told him. "You will find a loose tile under the grate. Rock it slowly from side to side and it will come away in your hands. Feel down into the hole and you will touch a small wooden box. The money is in the box."

Still incredulous, shrugging his shoulders, the man obeyed her directions, and kneeling beside the fireplace he felt for the loose tile as she had told him. After working at it for a moment it came away, and, uttering an exclamation of surprise, he put in his hand and drew out a wooden box.

"You 'ave spoken the truth for once," he said. "How does it open?" He turned the box over in his hands.

"Bring it to me," she said, her voice shaking. "I have a little key that will fit it."

He went into the bedroom. There was a pause while she struggled with the lock.

"It must be jammed somehow," she began; and then she called out in horror, realising the truth. "Good God!" she cried. "The lock is broken—it's been forced open. There is no money inside. It's gone—stolen!"

The sound of his voice rose above hers, furious, and high pitched. "You lie!" he screamed. "There was never money there. You wish to play me a trick—you think to deceive me. Liar, liar!"

"I swear I told the truth!" she said in terror. "My husband must have discovered it—he has stolen the money!"

The man came out of the bedroom, his face scarlet, shaking his fist in the air.

"You go out into the street," he shouted. "This is the end; you go now, this minute. By force I will make you—I will fetch my son!"

He flung open the door, crashed it behind him. From where she lay, exhausted, across the bed, she could hear the sound of his footsteps clattering down the stairs. He must have been interrupted halfway, because there rose the clamour of voices in argument, the noise of men shouting, and then a sudden silence.

"What is it?" she cried. "What is it?"

A light footstep sounded on the landing outside, then the door opened once more and a man came into the room. He wore a coat buttoned up to his chin, and a cap on the back of his head. Round his throat was knotted a rough scarf. He came in on tiptoe, a smile on his face.

"What's the matter?" he said. "I could hear you calling as I came up the stairs. Is your cough worse?"

Her only answer was a torrent of weeping.

"You've stolen my money," she sobbed. "Like a thief you

took it, never telling me, creeping out of the house. And there's nothing left, nothing. He's been up here, threatening me. It's the end. There's only the streets left for us now!"

Still he smiled, his eyes dancing. "Yes, I took the money," he said. "I was a thief, I stole it. Aren't you going to forgive me?"

He heard her sigh, he heard her move restlessly.

"What have you done with it?" she asked wearily.

"I took it weeks ago," he confessed. "I put it in a lottery."

He rubbed his hands in delight as he listened to her exclamation of dismay.

"But you are mad!" she cried. "You have no sense of anything at all. Don't you realise it was the only thing that stood between us and starvation?"

"I know," he said. "I took a gamble—and I lost. It's no use going over it all now. I've just been talking to the old chap below. We can stay for tonight, so you needn't worry any more. Tomorrow something may turn up—who knows?" He looked through the bedroom door, laughing at her.

"You're hopeless," she said, "hopeless."

"I know I am," he said, "and you don't mind, really, do you? You wouldn't have me any different?"

He must have made her smile, for she answered: "No, I wouldn't change you for anyone in the world."

He came back into the room and stood looking about him as though it were strange to him.

"D'you know what we're going to do?" he said. "We're going to play a game of pretence. Somehow this last night has got to be passed, and as there's nothing to eat but a stale loaf, and it's too cold to sleep, it's not going to be very cheerful. So we'll pretend to ourselves we've won the lottery—and I'll make up for you a story of all the things we would do."

He cocked his head on one side, waiting for her reply.

"You're a boy," she told him; "you're nothing but a little child."

"Very well," he said, "but you've got to listen to my story."

He tiptoed across the room and threw open the window. He leant far out, beckoning down into the street. Then he drew back—he listened—but she had not heard. He opened the door on to the passage and waited.

"What are you doing?" she called.

"I'm just thinking how to start my story," he said. As he spoke he moved aside from the door, and with his finger on his lips he admitted some half-dozen men into the room. They trod softly, in stockinged feet, their arms laden with packages, and as he moved amongst them, signing directions, he continued his rapid monologue to the bedroom.

"I think we'd begin with a fire, don't you?" he called, and as he pointed to the grate a man knelt down and proceeded to stack the fireplace with logs, and lumps of coal, and paper, to which he put a match. "Yes, we'd begin with a fire, and soon it would be burning brightly, throwing tongues of light on to the ceiling, filling the room with warmth. And as there is something so luxurious about a fire, we would think to ourselves that we ought to do away with our sticks of furniture, and arrange the room in a new way."

While he was speaking the men, following his orders, carried the rickety table and chairs, the poor bench, the cupboard, the torn mat, out on to the landing, and brought back with them, swiftly, as though by magic, the things he was describing to her.

"At last we could afford some curtains," he said, "heavy blue velvet curtains, reaching to the floor. The pole is there all ready, it doesn't take a moment to hang them in place.

"And we'd want a blue carpet to match. You know, those carpets that cover a whole room, and when you step on to it your feet seem to sink right into it. We'd lay that right across the floor, and it would be exactly the same colour as the curtains. Then— well, let's admit it—we just couldn't bear to live any longer with these stained, brown walls. It takes a long while to have the room repapered, we'd have to make shift with something. I have it! Screens. We'd place screens against the walls, right round the room, and they would keep out the draught too. Don't you think it a good idea?"

And the curtains were hung, and the carpet was laid, and the screens were standing against the walls.

"Next we'd have to think about the furniture," he said. "I rather fancy one of those long, low divans next to the fireplace. You would be able to rest there, you see, propped up by cushions, and I should sit in a large armchair opposite you, so as to be near whenever you wanted anything. At the end you would have a bookcase packed tight with books, close against the screen, and whenever you cared to read you would only have to stretch out an arm. Do you like that? Aren't you pleased?"

Like a miracle the room was being transformed under his directions, and he stood rocking on his heels, pointing here, pointing there.

"I must say I am pleased with our dining-room table," he said. "It's a genuine antique, and so are the chairs that go with it. We've got rather a superior dresser as well. You once told me you would love to have a dresser full of pots and pans.

"The thing that worried me most was the lighting. You see, up in this garret we aren't fitted with plugs for electricity. We haven't any gas either. D'you know what I think would be the best thing to have—in fact, the only way to get over it at all? Old standing lamps, and instead of electric light we'll have candles. You've no idea how nice it's going to look. There won't be a glare at all, but a soft shaded light. We'll have one lamp in a corner of the room and another by your divan. And on the dining-room table we'll have six tall candles.

"I tell you there's never been such a room as this." He had taken off his cap and coat by now, the scarf, too, was gone. Underneath he had been wearing a new suit of clothes. He ran his fingers through his hair.

"We'll hang a mirror over the mantelpiece, on the nail where we used to stick last year's calendar," he said, "and for ornaments —upon my soul, I don't think we can do better than a Dresden shepherd and shepherdess."

He stepped back from the fireplace, he glanced at the whole effect—the room was furnished.

"Nothing matters, now, but the fact that I'm ravenously hungry," he said. "We shall have to set the table for dinner. Plates, knives and forks, glasses. I don't mind admitting our dinner service is pretty good. What are we going to eat, though, that's the main thing. I'd like—I'd like—by Jove, what would I like? Roast chicken? Any objection to roast chicken? No, passed, settled. Right we'll have roast chicken. It smells good, it smells damned good. And the vegetables aren't so dusty, either.

"I think we might pile the table high with fruit—peaches, grapes, tangerines, bananas, every sort of fruit under the sun. We'll drink champagne, of course. Let's be gluttons while we can. And—I say, you said just now I was a child. Well, would you think it terrible if I went on being a child and we had crackers? After all, it is a sort of a fête, and we ought to celebrate. Besides, they look so jolly on the table. There. I don't know that I can think of anything else.

"Wait a minute, keep quiet. I may have forgotten the most important thing of all. Yes, I knew it. The most important. We've just got to fill the room with flowers. Wherever there's any space we'll put flowers. Roses are still your favourite, aren't they? There are so many roses in the room that I'm practically suffocated. It's like a garden that will never come true."

He paused, he looked round the room once more. No, there was nothing to add now. Everything had been arranged and placed as he had described. The room was ready for her. He nodded to the men, and they went from the door gently, on tiptoe, just as they had come in.

"That's the end of the story," he said softly. For a moment there was no answer, and he heard her catch her breath, as though she would prevent herself from crying.

"It was beautiful," she said at last, "beautiful. How did you think of it? Did it all just come into your mind as you said it? I feel as though I'd woken up from a lovely dream. And I wanted the dream to go on—and on. It was cruel of you in a way, wasn't it?"

"Perhaps it was," he said.

"Your voice sounded happy and gay as you were telling me," she said, "and I pictured you standing in the middle of that bare, lonely room, your hands in your pockets, your collar turned up because of the cold. I was wondering, would it be very terrible to light those few sticks and make a tiny, tiny fire?"

"They couldn't make any difference to this temperature," he said, his eyes laughing.

"No," she sighed. "I suppose not." She was silent for a moment, then she said: "Are you frightfully hungry?"

"Frightfully," he nodded.

"What about the remains of the loaf of bread?" she asked him.

"I shan't eat anything unless you come and join me," he told her.

"It's so freezing in there," she said, "and I'm so empty. I want food so much that the bread will choke me after the story you've been telling me."

She was ready to break down again.

"Please come," he said, "even if the room is cold, even if there's nothing but half a loaf of bread and we're starving, and miserable, and the old chap is going to fling us into the streets, can't we be happy together?"

He waited, and then he said: "Besides, you haven't forgiven me yet for stealing your money, and throwing it away in a lottery."

Then her voice called to him, gentle, tired: "I'll come."

He could hear her getting out of bed and fumbling for her shoes, the bed shaking slightly as she leant against it.

"D'you want any help?" he asked.

"I think I can manage," she said. "I didn't realise I should feel so weak. And I'm frightened of the cold. Shall I get a terrible shock when I come in?"

"I'm afraid you will," he said.

She sighed, he heard her walk slowly across the bedroom towards the door.

"Wait a minute," he said. "Tell me first you aren't angry with me any more! Tell me you've forgiven me?"

He heard her laugh helplessly.

"You know I've forgiven you," she said.

And she came into the room.

The Rendezvous

Robert Scrivener noted, with some slight irritation, that his secretary had her eye upon the clock. He had made no engagements for the evening, in view of his early departure the following morning for Geneva, and she knew this, therefore her preoccupation with the passing of time could not be on his account. No doubt she had what was vulgarly called "a date". A secretary had no business with "dates" when her employer, a writer of Robert Scrivener's standing, had a mass of correspondence to clear before leaving the country.

"Judith," he said at last, raising his horn-rimmed spectacles and balancing them on his forehead, "you keep looking at the clock. Are you, for some reason, in a hurry?"

She had the grace to blush. "It's all right," she said quickly, "it's only that I'm going to the theatre later, and I rather wanted to change first."

So typical of the girl's mentality. To arrange a visit to the theatre on the one day of the week when she was likely to be kept late. He stared at her, baffled by her stupidity.

"What an odd thing to do," he said, "to choose tonight of all nights to go to the theatre. Does that mean you want to go at once, and leave these letters until I return from Geneva?"

She had flushed all over her face. Most unbecoming. "Of course not," she said. "I'm really in no hurry. It was just . . ."

"Youthful impatience to be free of your fetters," he declared, "to be done with all this tedious nonsense. I quite understand. May I go on? I'll make my letters as brief as possible."

He replaced his spectacles, and continued dictating his letters in measured tones. Robert Scrivener was a writer of renown and great integrity. He had first attracted notice in the literary world by his reviews in a liberal weekly, and later in a Sunday newspaper. These reviews showed him to be a man of wide culture; given neither to wild enthusiasm nor to damning condemnation, he showed appreciation of the finer, more polished writings of his contemporaries, of the scholarly biographies, of the books of travel in countries less known to the general reader. In fiction he was careful to praise books which were unlikely to sell, but which showed some constructive approach to world problems.

During the war—poor eyesight kept him from active service— he continued his literary criticism, with a slight bias towards the Left in politics, but he gave his services to the censorship department of the War Office, and received a small decoration in recompense. The war over, he published a novel that was instantly successful.

Fortune Favours the Brave was the story of a soldier who, horrified by war and its consequences, holds a spearhead on the Italian front against tremendous odds, and is subsequently captured. He tries to escape three times, but each attempt proves abortive. Finally he catches bubonic plague and dies, but not before giving a message on freedom to his fellow prisoners which is a model of exquisite prose, and for which Scrivener himself received an Italian decoration. The novel was, indeed, an amazing and deeply moving piece of work, coming as it did from someone who had never in all his life seen a shot fired.

His success was not a flash in the pan. The novel that succeeded the war book, entitled *Madrigal,* had for protagonist a man who, pursued by women, can find no peace or harmony within himself until he has acceded to their demands, and so impoverished his own spiritual integrity. Scrivener himself was unmarried, and was not known to possess intimate friends of the opposite sex, but his second novel also was widely acclaimed. Here at last was someone who might restore some sort of standard to English fiction. Other novels followed, all exquisitely written, all throwing into relief the problems that so beset mankind during the present century, and Scrivener's income began to approach five figures.

Robert Scrivener did not permit himself to be spoilt by his success, and he was careful to tell his friends that he would never be tempted by offers from Hollywood to prostitute his work upon the screen. As a matter of fact no such offer came, but this was beside the point. Had it come, Robert Scrivener would have turned it down. He concentrated almost entirely upon his literary work, but he also gave lectures, and appeared from time to time on brains trusts. He had a good appearance and an agreeable speaking voice, and to those television viewers who were ignorant of his work as novelist and critic he suggested the law, a distinguished barrister, or even a youngish judge. Scrivener knew this, and was not displeased. In fact, he was determined to touch lightly on certain aspects of the law, as it concerned writers, during his forthcoming series of lectures at Geneva; but mostly he would concern himself with the integrity of the writer's Self and how, once dedicated to the perfecting of the written word, no writer who respected his profession should swerve from the high standard he had set himself.

Robert Scrivener continued to dictate his letters; although he was careful not to prolong the dictation, there was a certain deliberation in his voice, a formality of delivery, that warned the girl he considered her evening a breach of faith. Finally he removed his spectacles and sighed.

"That will be all, Judith," he said. "Don't let me detain you a moment longer."

The secretary, still uncomfortable, felt she had ruined Robert Scrivener's evening. "I'll get them typed at once," she said, pushing back her chair, and then, before leaving the room, remembered a letter, still unopened, on his desk. "I'm afraid I forgot to tell you about the one from Switzerland," she said. "It's there, on your blotter. It must be from that fan who keeps bothering you about some poem you promised to criticise. I think I recognise the handwriting."

Scrivener glanced at the envelope. "Very probably," he said. "In any case it can wait. I would not dream of letting you be late for the theatre."

His secretary left the room, and immediately she had gone Scrivener reached for the letter. How careless of him, he thought, as he slit the envelope with a paper knife, not to glance through the pile before starting to dictate. He might have known there would be a letter, and even the scribbled "Personal" would not keep it sacred from the prying eyes of Judith.

Some few months previously Robert Scrivener had received a letter from a reader praising three poems that had appeared in a new quarterly. Nowadays he did not often contribute verse to literary periodicals, and when he did so it was as a special favour, an intimate revelation, so he thought, of his more personal feelings, which he would have hesitated to make public but for his duty to Art and Letters. The editor of the quarterly, whose own book of verse had recently been praised by Scrivener in the Sunday newspaper for which he wrote, was pleased to publish his more famous colleague's group of poems.

The writer of this letter said that never had any poems, save those of Rimbaud and Rilke, made such an instant and profound impression upon him: his world, literally, had changed. The depth of wisdom, the cosmic understanding, the sheer tragedy of outlook—the poet, as it were, looking out upon a doomed world with a wry smile, yet giving this same world his benison— these things had made the reader review the whole of life in its totality, personal problems were forgotten, in a word he was reborn.

Robert Scrivener answered the letter. The signature was ambiguous, A. Limoges, and the address Zürich. Scrivener visualised a professor of psychology, or if not a professor—for surely such a one would have letters after his name—possibly a student, at any rate someone of great sensibility and intelligence.

A week later he received an acknowledgement. The writer had not slept all night after receiving his letter, but had walked the streets of Zürich. Scrivener replied a second time. He might not have done so had he not also received that day a press-cutting from some obscure newspaper in the United States disparaging his last novel, *Taurus*, which, anticipating A.I.D., showed how the self-sacrifice of one man could be responsible for the birth of thousands. The reviewer called the novel "pretentious nonsense", and advised the author to inject himself with some genuine bull's blood. Scrivener threw the press-cutting into the waste paper basket; nevertheless the review pricked, and it was a relief to turn to the letter from A. Limoges. This time he let himself go, and discoursed for two pages on suffering, the inner man, and the existentialist approach.

There was silence for a week, and then a modest note came containing a poem by A. Limoges and asking for criticism. Scrivener read the poem indulgently. It was not bad. A little influenced, of course, by everything A. Limoges had ever read, but even so there was nothing glaringly faulty about it. Scrivener wrote back, enclosing his own signed photograph, and dismissed the fellow, the "fan" as Judith insisted on calling him, from his mind. He was surprised to receive by return of post the photograph of a girl, signed Annette Limoges, and he realised, with a slight shock, that his correspondent and admirer was neither a professor of psychology nor a student, but sold nylon stockings in a large store in Zürich.

Scrivener's first reaction was to tear the photograph in two and throw it, with the letter, into the fire. Then the eyes of the girl, very large and liquid, stared up at him reproachfully. She was certainly lovely. Nothing cheap about her, or vulgar, and the letter enclosed with the photograph said something about a father, now dead, who had been a colonel in the French Army. Scrivener locked the letter and photograph in a drawer in his desk where the inquisitive hands of Judith could not rummage, and it was only when yet another epistle came, apologising for the presumption of sending her photograph, and declaring that the sender was so overcome by Scrivener's own photograph that she had, for the second time, walked the streets of Zürich by night, that the renowned author of *Fortune Favours the Brave* decided to acknowledge it.

It was following upon this exchange of photographs that a weekly correspondence was set up between Robert Scrivener and Annette Limoges. It made, so he told himself, a relaxation from the work he was engaged upon, a biography of Swedenborg. His letters varied. At times serious, at times amusing, he formed the habit of treating his unknown correspondent as a form of peg on which to hang his theories and his moods. A week that had gone well reflected itself the following weekend in the letter to Annette Limoges. The letter would be confident, even gay, containing scraps of gossip about his friends of whom the sales girl in the Zürich store had never heard. A week that had gone badly, with only a few pages of manuscript covered, resulted in a certain asperity of outlook, or perhaps a tirade against his muse which had, for the time, forsaken him. The letters he received in return invariably commented on his feelings and his moods, making Scrivener feel that here, at last, was someone who understood, someone who, while making no sort of interference in his life, had yet become part of it, absorbing his confidences as blotting-paper absorbed the ink-blobs from his pen. Annette Limoges lived, it would seem, only to retain what Scrivener cared to send her, passing chills in London were her concern in Zürich, his laughter at noon her solace at midnight, his thoughts, his whims, his attitudes her spiritual food.

It did not occur to Robert Scrivener, when he accepted the engagement to give two lectures at Geneva, that this might give him an opportunity to meet Annette Limoges in person. He wrote and told her of his forthcoming visit, as he told her all his plans, but with no other thought in mind. It was Annette—and by now they were Annette and Robert—who wrote in great excitement saying that the dates he had booked for the lectures in Geneva happened, by a miracle, to coincide with her own vacation, and it would be the simplest thing in the world to take the train to Geneva and meet him at last.

Now it happened that Scrivener had, that particular week, attended the wedding of a friend and fellow-author, a widower, who had suddenly decided to marry again. Although Scrivener had gone to the wedding in a spirit of mockery he found himself, during the reception, with the tables turned. The elderly groom, his young bride at his side, twitted him, Robert Scrivener, with being an old maid. There were standers-by who laughed. He even overheard a guest murmur something offensive to the effect that experts who wrote books called *Taurus* should practise what they preached. When he shook hands with his old friend, whose books he despised—they sold in ridiculous numbers—and congratulated him, his friend smiled, almost as if he were sorry for Scrivener, and said, "Don't you envy me, going off to Majorca with this?" And he looked at his bride and laughed.

The episode rankled: it was almost as though there was some disagreeable suggestion afoot that he, Robert Scrivener, was a fake, without the wide experience of life that his novels appeared to possess. Boldly he took up his pen and wrote, there and then, to Annette Limoges suggesting that she should come down to Geneva to meet him, and that he would reserve the necessary accommodation.

As the time for the encounter drew near Robert Scrivener was aware of mounting excitement. He felt ten, twenty years younger, and found it almost impossible to concentrate on his notes for the forthcoming lectures. The integrity of the writer, the perfection of the written word, these things took second place when he thought of the two connecting rooms at the Hotel Mirabelle,

Geneva—he had been careful to make the reservations himself—
and on this last night, before departure, he allowed himself the
luxury of imagining the first meeting: Annette radiant and a
little shy, smiling at him across a dinner table set on a terrace.
The lecture was not until the following night, and his earliest
engagement was luncheon with the Swiss man of letters who was
organising the tour, therefore the first evening would be set aside
for Annette alone. The letter he now opened, which had escaped
the vigilant eye of Judith, was an ecstatic note telling him she
would arrive in Geneva first, possibly the day before, and would
be waiting at the airport to meet him. "If I'm not there," she said,
"it will mean I don't want to embarrass you before the officials,
and you will then find me at the hotel." This showed her discre-
tion; she was not going to put herself forward in any way. And
then . . . Image succeeded image, and Robert Scrivener could
hardly wait for the necessary hours to pass before he left London
airport for Geneva.

The flight to Geneva was luckily smooth—Scrivener disliked
bumps, and a rough trip might have brought on migraine—and
as the aircraft taxied up the landing strip he looked out of the
window eagerly for a young girlish figure with a cloud of light
brown hair. The time was late afternoon; the sun blazed, the lake
was a dazzling blue. A crowd of people had gathered behind the
reception barrier to greet their friends, but he could see no one
resembling the photograph that he now knew so well.

Scrivener went through customs, collected his baggage and
hailed a porter. No official advanced to welcome him. This did
not bother him, although it might have been courteous. As for
Annette, she had warned him she might not come. It was disappointing, but discreet. The porter summoned a taxi, and very
soon it drew up before the hotel Mirabelle, gay and inviting in
the bright sun, its windows and terrace overlooking the blue lake.
Scrivener's bags were seized by a page, and he went to sign the
register and collect his key.

It was a moment of apprehension. He had a foreboding that
after all Annette Limoges might not have come. Something
could have prevented her. Some mishap in Zürich. He heard
himself asking in an unsteady voice if there was any message for
him. The concierge turned to a pigeon-hole and produced an
envelope; it was in her handwriting. He stepped aside and opened

it. The message was brief. She had arrived safely, actually she had been in Geneva two days. It had turned so hot in Zürich, and her holiday had started, so it seemed foolish not to take the opportunity and give herself an extra day. The rooms were wonderful. The flowers he had ordered to welcome her were exquisite, Geneva itself a paradise. She had gone to bathe, but would be back at the hotel directly. Scrivener followed the page upstairs.

The first thing he did, after glancing round his room and appreciating the window and the balcony, with the view over the lake, was to try the communicating door. It was locked. However, that could easily be remedied. Feeling a little foolish, he put his eye to the key-hole. He could see nothing. He straightened himself and began to unpack. He had a bath, changed, and went out on to the balcony. The waiters were already on the terrace serving drinks. Beyond the terrace was the promenade, and beyond the promenade the lake. In the far distance he could see diving-boards, and boats, and collections of happy bathers sitting about bronzed and idle, or with bobbing heads in the still water.

Scrivener telephoned for his floor waiter to bring him a martini, and as he sipped it, standing there on the balcony looking down on the terrace, his anticipation of what the hours would bring him grew into a fever of impatience. Why was she late? It was not thus that he had imagined the start of their evening.

Too agitated to remain on the balcony, he went back into his room, and flinging himself in a chair began to read over the notes for his lecture. It was no use, though. He could not concentrate. Then he had the idea that she might, after all, have arrived back at the hotel and gone to her room, lacking the courage to let him know. He crossed the room and tapped on the door. There was no answer. Possibly she was in her bath. He seized the telephone and asked to be put through to the room next door. There was silence, and after a moment or two the voice at the switch-board informed him that room 28—his own room was 27—was unoccupied.

"Unoccupied?" he said. "But there must be some mistake. I want to speak to a Mademoiselle Limoges, who has taken room 28."

'Monsieur is mistaken," replied the voice. "Mademoiselle Limoges occupies room 50, on the floor above."

Scrivener controlled himself with difficulty. The fools at the reception must have made some idiotic mistake. He had distinctly ordered the two communicating rooms. The mistake could no doubt be set right, but perhaps not tonight. He asked, with shaking voice, to be put through to room 50. The inevitable ringing tone followed, with the inevitable no reply. Scrivener swore, and replaced the receiver. Then he went down to the terrace and ordered another martini. People came out on to the terrace, in couples or in groups, some to drink and some to dine, and Robert Scrivener sat at his solitary table with nothing to do but watch the door leading into the Mirabelle restaurant. Even the solace of lighting a cigarette was denied him; he was a non-smoker. A third martini did little to calm him; being a moderate drinker at all times, this sudden taking of spirits produced an intensity of fever. It occurred to him that some disaster might have overtaken her, cramp in the lake, anything, and it was only a matter of time before a grave reception clerk would appear through the restaurant door to break the news.

Twice the waiter had come to his table with the menu and had been waved away. Then, as he downed his last martini, he saw advancing towards him, half-screened by a group of people dressed for dinner, someone in striped jeans and sandals, a vivid emerald shirt, and yes, it was her, it was Annette Limoges. She raised her hand and waved, and blew a kiss. Scrivener stood up. She was by his side, taller than he had expected, darker, the hair still damp from her swim and dishevelled, but lovely, undeniably lovely, people at the next table were staring at her.

"Can you ever forgive me?" she said, and the voice, attractive with its slight accent, was soft and low.

"Forgive you?" he said. "Of course I forgive you. Waiter . . . " and he turned to summon a passing waiter for another martini, but she put her hand on his arm. "No . . . no . . . " she said quickly, "you surely don't think I'm going to sit down like this? I'll fly upstairs and change. I'll be ten minutes. Order me a Cinzano."

She was gone before he had time to assimilate anything that had happened. He sat down again and began to crumble a roll, thrusting small pieces of it into his mouth. The photograph had led him to expect something attractive and warm, but the reality far surpassed the photograph, and indeed the images conjured in imagination. In fact . . . he was bowled over. He had seen himself

being indulgent, a little patronising, while she sat listening with
rapt eyes to his conversation, but now he was not so sure;
hypnotised by the striped jeans and the emerald shirt he felt
suddenly at a loss, callow, as awkward as an undergraduate
ordering his first dinner.

He was considering the menu in consultation with the maître
d'hôtel when she returned—better than her word, the minutes
were seven. She had changed into a strapless frock of some sort
of spotted material, showing to great advantage the already
bronzed arms and shoulders. The light brown hair, worn long
when she first appeared, was now twisted into a knot behind her
head, very chic, very becoming, and the touch of green eye-
shadow made the eyes themselves seem even larger and more
lustrous. Scrivener felt himself outdistanced. Her appearance
warranted a tuxedo, a button-hole, and his grey suit somehow
seemed out of place, more fitted to a doctor, a lawyer.

"You can't imagine," she said, as she sat down, "what it means
to me to do this. After the long hours in that terrible store, where
I care for no one and no one cares for me, to be transplanted, by
the wave of a magician's wand. And you are the magician, you,
sitting there in front of me, just as I imagined. Robert. Robert
Scrivener."

He smiled, and made a little gesture of deprecation. "The
Cinzano," he said, "is it iced enough for you, is it how you like
it?"

"Perfect." She embraced him with her smile. "But then,
everything is perfect. Geneva, the hotel, the lake; and you."

The waiter was at his elbow again, and Scrivener had to take
his eyes away from Annette Limoges and concentrate upon
another perfection, the final decision of what they should eat and
drink. It seemed to him immensely important that he should not
fail her in this, that their first dinner together should be as
momentous as everything else had been to her.

"You are quite sure that is what you would like?" he asked for
the third time, over-anxious in his desire to please, and she
nodded, and the waiter bowed and disappeared.

"Well . . . " Robert Scrivener looked across the table at his
correspondent over so many months, to whom, indeed, he had
bared his heart, released his innermost thoughts, and he found

himself inarticulate, the fine phrases that rolled from his pen with such ease were non-existent.

"The wonderful thing about this," said the girl, "is that we know each other already. We don't have to break any ice. We might have been having dinner together night after night."

He wished he felt the same. The one thing that troubled him at that moment was that they had never dined before.

"I know," he lied, "it makes all the difference."

"Usually," said Annette, "there is some sort of restraint when two people meet for the first time. But not with us. You know that you can tell me everything. I know the same."

She had finished her Cinzano and was looking about her for another. Feverishly, he summoned the waiter.

"Another Cinzano for Mademoiselle," he said. It was all very well on paper, alone in his study, with a glance perhaps at the photograph, but now in reality, faced with this vision, with that face, those eyes, those lips, how much simpler it would be if they did not have to talk, did not even have to endure the performance of this dinner, but could go upstairs and let nature take its course. Forget conversation. Forget everything.

The business of eating helped, and with the wine, the blessed wine, his self-confidence returned, his aplomb, and he could not have seemed dull to her or disappointing because she laughed and smiled, accepting his smallest remarks as witticisms; it was just a momentary phase, he realised, that sensation of his own dumb idiocy. At any rate, she had not noticed it. Little flattering phrases fell from her tongue like crumbs of comfort. She asked him about the lectures he was to give, about the biography he was writing, every remark she made proving how often she must read his letters, and when the ritual of the dinner was over, and they sat over their coffee and liqueurs, Robert Scrivener felt himself bathing, as it were, in a kind of luminous warmth. He was being nourished and caressed by someone who was half the figment of his imagination and half the bodily presence of this beautiful entity before him.

"You know," he said, and he was aware now that his words were a little slurred, "you know, my dear, the fools have made a mistake about our rooms."

"A mistake?" She looked up at him puzzled.

"Yes. I'm on the first floor. You are on the second."

"Oh, but that's my fault." She smiled across at him. "When I arrived I was on the first floor, number 28 I think it was, but it was such a little cubby-hole of a room I asked to have it changed. Now I have a beauty. With a wonderful view both ways."

"Ah! That explains it."

He pretended to understand, but in truth he was taken aback. From what he had been able to glimpse of the room next to his—from the closed window on the balcony—it had not been a cubby-hole at all, but exactly similar to his. He had made a point of ordering communicating rooms of the same size.

"I hope they've given you a quiet room," she said. "You'll be working, probably, last thing at night and first thing in the morning. That's your usual routine, isn't it?"

"I don't work on holiday," he said.

"But the lectures," she said, "do you mean they are quite ready, no final polishing to give?"

"Any polishing," he told her, "will be done on the platform, as I speak."

She was surely being a little obtuse. He might have thought it natural modesty had she been shy, but she was so certain of herself, with such innate sophistication, that this supposition that he would be working in the evening struck him as strange. He wondered whether he should be blunt, announce, with a laugh, "If there is one thing I detest, it's walking about hotel passages in a dressing-gown," when she suddenly put out her hand across the table and took his. "This is the most wonderful part of all," she said, "that I can say anything to you, just anything. As though you were my twin. Other people think of you as Robert Scrivener, but not me."

The warmth held him deliciously. So much promise in the voice, such subtle strength in the pressure of the hand. After all, did it matter so much about the room on the second floor? The actual fact of separation might make the going to and fro the more intriguing.

"It's exciting," she said, "to be so terribly in love."

He returned the pressure of her hand, wondering how best to manoeuvre their departure from the terrace. Perhaps a stroll by the lake for ten minutes or so, and then . . .

"It happened so suddenly," she said, "you know how it is, it must have happened to you a dozen times, with your experience. You know how in *Madrigal* you made Davina walk into a restaurant and lose all acount of time, and space. It was like that with me. Directly I saw Alberto come out of the bathing-hut yesterday I knew I was finished."

Scrivener let his hand stay where it was, in hers, but he felt his body stiffen.

"Alberto," he repeated.

"Yes," she said, "Alberto. It sounds like a hairdresser, doesn't it? In point of fact he's the bathing attendant on the Mirabelle plage, and the handsomest thing you've ever seen. Bronzed, a sort of sun-god. We took one look at each other, and there it was." She laughed, and squeezed his hand again. "I said I had no towel," she went on, "so we got into conversation, and then—he acts as swimming instructor too—he came in the water with me. Of course I swim like a fish, but it was fun to pretend, and it looked better, because of the other swimmers. Oh, Robert, I can't tell you how wonderful it was. I spent the rest of the day down there, on the plage, and again today, and of course that was the reason for my being late for dinner. I told him all about you and he was so impressed, he was quite embarrassed that you might be here waiting for me. I said he needn't worry. Robert Scrivener isn't an ordinary man, I said. He's the most intuitive, the most understanding person in the whole world. That's why he is famous."

She withdrew her hand to light another cigarette, and he made a pretence of swallowing the dregs of liqueur left in his glass. Whatever happened she must learn nothing from his face or from his voice.

"How very amusing," he said.

She wrinkled her nose as he lit her cigarette. "But I don't behave like this as a rule," she told him. "I'm very good, very sedate. This is just one of those things. As I said to Alberto this evening, 'How Robert is going to mock me when I tell him what has happened.' Alberto was not so sure. He thought you might be offended."

It was Scrivener's turn to laugh. The laugh sounded natural, but the effort he put into it cost him ten years.

"Offended?" he said. "Why on earth should I be offended?"

"Why indeed? It's just one more tiny bit of experience for

Robert, I said to Alberto. No, what is so wonderful for me is that you've made the meeting possible. Here I am, in this heavenly hotel, having the time of my life, and it's all owing to you."

Ironic phrases rose to Scrivener's lips. Bitter reflections such as, "Glad to be of use," or "Always willing to oblige," but he had the strength of mind to smother them. To show the faintest shadow of annoyance would be to lose face.

"Do I meet the paragon?" he asked lightly.

"But of course," she said. "As a matter of fact I told him to be at the bar near the railway station at precisely ten o'clock. Which it is now. We agreed the railway station was best, because no one would recognise us there, and it's always crowded. You see, if it was known that the bathing-attendant from the plage was having a wild affair with one of the hotel visitors my beautiful Alberto might lose his job."

And rightly, thought Robert Scrivener. A dull anger had succeeded the first feeling of shock, but an anger which he could not utilise. The futility, the indignity of the evening ahead over-shadowed action. One jibe and he was lost. One slip, and his writer's integrity, the possession he had come to Geneva to lecture on, the balance, the understanding, would be forever blemished.

"I'm ready if you are," said Scrivener, and she rose at once— no attempt for courtesy's sake to disguise her eagerness—and led the way from the terrace through the restaurant, a sensuous, alluring figure, cool and lovely in the strapless frock, primed for the bathing-attendant, but not for him.

The terrible thing was that there was no redress. To feign sudden fatigue, the excuse of work, indigestion, any of these excuses meant total loss of prestige. What above all caused him anguish was the consciousness of his own letters, week after week, the letters of a friend, a confidant, baring his soul.

"Don't mind if Alberto's shy," she said as they walked through the streets, humid now that darkness had fallen, languorous with the softness of velvet, "he's only twenty-two, my age, and he won't know what to say to you. Naturally he wants to come to the lecture tomorrow. We thought we'd go together. He's never met a well-known writer before."

"Have you?" The retort shot from him like a bullet from a

rifle, but she was too happy, or too temporarily insensitive, to seize his tone.

"In Zürich, sometimes," she replied, "but I'm generally too tired in the evenings to go out and enjoy myself."

"Yes. Selling stockings must be an exhausting business." How apt, how cutting, could it be said; but pride forbade.

They came to a garish bar, fronting the wide street by the station, and Annette Limoges, confident and gay, pushed her way through the knots of laughing people. "I hope you won't be recognised," said Annette. "It would be too bad if the evening was spoilt by some wretched official coming up and button-holing you."

Robert Scrivener felt it would be his one salvation. He would have given much for some member of the Society of International Letters to approach him at that moment, to touch his arm with reverence, some stranger, however heavy, however deadly dull, to approach him and say, "It's Robert Scrivener, isn't it? We've been trying to get you at the Mirabelle. Do join us in a drink." Then, only then, after some such bald encounter, could he look across at Annette Limoges and say, "My dear, do you mind? Run along and find your Alberto. I have to join these friends." Pride would then be salvaged, the wreckage of morale restored. Nothing of the sort happened. Annette led him to a corner of the bar, where, sitting upright on a high stool, sat a bronzed young man with a great mop of curling hair. Good-looking, perhaps, in a flashy sort of way, but the ring on the little finger made Scrivener flinch. And Annette . . . Annette, who had seemed so entirely in place on the terrace of the Hotel Mirabelle, so full of *savoir faire,* so desirable and truly lovely, seemed suddenly to lose caste before his eyes. The wiggle that she gave as she sighted Alberto—for Alberto it must be—was frankly . . . common.

"Hullo, darling," she said, and the darling was an offence to Scrivener, an outrage, "here we are. I want you to meet Mr Robert Scrivener."

The young man put out his hand, and Scrivener touched it as he would an unclean substance.

"Pleased to meet you," said Alberto, sliding from his stool, and then the three of them stood there, falsely smiling, and Scrivener, the host, ordered the round of drinks.

They sat at a small table, and the older man, who earlier that evening had been the girl's proud escort, the cynosure of other men's envious eyes, must now play the role of indulgent uncle or—worse—plain gooseberry. It seemed to Robert Scrivener that his sense of inferiority was deepened by an instinctive feeling that the bathing-attendant was aware of his discomfiture, and as embarrassed as he was himself. A real vulgarian could have been despised, but Alberto, as retiring as Annette Limoges was brazen, kept his eyes fixed on his glass of beer which apparently satisfied his modest wants; now and again fluttering his long lashes and glancing sideways at Scrivener with a semblance of apology.

The writer knew—and it was this knowledge that only made degradation more profound—that should Annette leave them for the space of a few minutes he could turn to Alberto and pass a note for a few thousand francs across the table, and the bathing-attendant would understand his meaning without a word in reply. He would just disappear. Once out of the way the girl would be Scrivener's once more. The shocking truth was that could this only be achieved Scrivener would still be willing to blot out from immediate resentment the events of the past two days, such was the fascination of the sales girl from Zürich. Scrivener was not so blind as to assume that his own physical charms could be as compelling as those of Alberto; nevertheless the girl had come to Geneva to meet him, she was his guest, the guest of someone renowned in the international world of letters, who must surely command adulation from the most beautiful women in the world. But could he? Here was the secret stab. Everywhere there were men at this moment acting the part of husband or lover; sometimes they paid for the privilege, sometimes the services of their companion were given free, but in either case contact did at least take place. Yet Robert Scrivener, known the world over for his masterly diagnosis of the problems of the human heart, was obliged to seek out a shop-girl from a Zürich store who could not even wait for his custom.

"I tell you what, Robert," said Annette, breaking in upon his bitter train of thought, "if you don't have any engagement before the lecture tomorrow evening we could all three of us spend the day in the mountains. You could hire a car, and we could take a picnic. I'm sure the Mirabelle would put us up a packed lunch."

Oddly enough, this had originally been Scrivener's plan. Before the advent of the bathing-attendant. He had visualised a drive to the mountains, or an expedition across the lake, after his luncheon with the Swiss men of letters.

"I'm afraid," said Scrivener, "that I am booked for luncheon."

"Oh, what a bother," said Annette, "but I suppose we could go without you. Alberto will be free after twelve o'clock." She squeezed the hand of the bathing-attendant, as she had squeezed Scrivener's at dinner. "Darling," she said, "you'd like that, wouldn't you? Robert would arrange a car for us, and we could stay out until it was time to come back for the lecture. Then we could all dine afterwards."

Alberto, his bronzed skin flushing, looked apologetically at his host. "Perhaps Mr Scrivener has other plans," he demurred.

"Oh no," said Annette Limoges, "you haven't, have you, Robert?"

The writer felt a sudden irritation at the constant use of his Christian name. Never had the surname Scrivener sounded so sweet in his ears, so full of dignity. He tried to remember when he had first given permission to the correspondent in Zürich to call him Robert, but it was too many months ago, they had slipped into the habit without realising.

"I have no plans at all," he said, "I am in Geneva to deliver two lectures. I'm really in the hands of the authorities concerned."

"Well, we can always arrange details in the morning," said Annette. "The thing is for us all to be happy. Alberto hasn't read *Taurus* yet, have you, Alberto, so he doesn't know that wonderful passage where Mark explains his philosophy of life—I'm going to buy him a copy tomorrow and you'll autograph it for him, won't you, Robert?"

"I shall be delighted," said Scrivener, and with the gallantry of Sir Philip Sidney he ordered another beer for the bathing-attendant. The endless evening wound to its close. The bar emptied. And long before this, had it not been for fate and Alberto, Scrivener and Annette Limoges would have been clasped together in heaven knows what sweet, prolonged embrace in room 27 or 50 of the hotel Mirabelle.

"The bar-tender," said Scrivener, "looks as if he wants to get rid of us." The three inseparables rose to their feet, Scrivener paid the bill for the final round of drinks, and they proceeded back to the hotel, Annette between the writer and the bathing-attendant, holding an arm of each.

"This is what I call heaven," she said, "to be with the two men in the world who mean most to me."

Neither of her escorts answered. Whether coals of fire were heaped upon Alberto's head Scrivener neither knew nor cared. He himself was reminded of the remark of an Irish groom to the ecstatic purchaser of an unridable horse, "Faith, you're easy pleased."

Outside the steps of the Mirabelle Annette paused. She dropped the arm of Scrivener, but still held that of Alberto.

"I'll walk with Alberto to the end of the promenade," she said, and Scrivener saw her glance towards the pontoons bordering the lake where stood the line of bathing-huts, discreetly dark and silent, to which the attendant very probably possessed the key.

"Then I will bid you both goodnight," said Scrivener.

Annette Limoges embraced him with her smile. "It's been a wonderful evening," she said, "I don't know how I'm going to thank you."

Nor do I, thought Scrivener. Raising his hand in a salute of farewell, half benevolent, half fascist, he turned his back on both of them, and entering the hotel Mirabelle was borne upstairs to room number 27 by a yawning page. His bed was turned down, his pyjamas laid out upon the cover. How neat, how smooth, how virginal the room! The suit he had discarded hanging in the wardrobe, the notes for his lectures folded on the table. Switching on the bedside lamp he saw that the time, by his travelling-clock, was a quarter to two. He crossed to the window and with a determined gesture drew the curtains close. He picked up the Penguin Turgenief he had been reading in the aeroplane and put it, with his spectacles, upon his pillow. Soberly, he undressed.

Scrivener did not see Annette Limoges until late the next morning. He telephoned her room at ten, and the sleepy voice that answered him was too heavy, too drugged with the delights of the preceding night, to make itself understood. Curtly he rang off, telling her he would ring again at eleven. He did so, having by that time bathed and dressed himself, breakfasted, and been out for a short walk. This time there was no reply, and the switchboard operator suggested that the inmate of room 50 was probably in her bath. Scrivener was due to be collected by his Swiss man of letters at midday, therefore he was ready and waiting in the hall of the hotel Mirabelle at five minutes to the hour. At precisely three minutes to twelve Annette Limoges came out of the lift, dressed in her striped jeans and sandals and emerald shirt. Her hair was loose upon her shoulders. Her lips were a vivid red. She looked like a ripe peach that had just been plucked, and not, alas, by Scrivener.

"It's all arranged," she said, with a huge smile. "I've ordered the car. I'm picking Alberto up at half-past twelve."

As she was speaking a stout man in a grey suit, carrying a homberg hat, entered the hotel. He moved ponderously towards Scrivener.

"Mr Robert Scrivener?" he enquired, his accent Swiss-German, his manner affable. "I am pleased to present myself, Fritz Lieber, secretary of the International Society of Letters. Welcome to Geneva."

"Thank you," said Scrivener, and after a moment's hesitation, "this is Mademoiselle Limoges." The stout man bowed.

"It's too bad, Herr Lieber, that you are taking Mr Scrivener off to a solemn lunch," announced Annette gaily, "we had it all fixed for a day in the mountains."

Herr Lieber, puzzled, turned to the writer for confirmation. "I hope there has not been some misunderstanding," he began, and Scrivener, embarrassed, waved his hand. "No, no, of course not, our luncheon was arranged many weeks ago."

His companion for the day, anxious for the International Society of Letters to be all-inclusive in hospitality, murmured something about any friend of the guest of honour being welcome at the luncheon table. Robert Scrivener, seeing a momentary hesitation in Annette's eye, quickly interposed. He sensed that such an invitation must also include the bathing-attendant.

"Mademoiselle Limoges has already made other arrangements," he said, and turning to Annette, "I shall see you when I return. If you are back before me, leave a message at the desk." Fearful that she might suggest a change of plans involving Alberto, he forced a genial smile upon the representative of the International Society and added, "Shall we go?"

As they stepped into the waiting car and drove away, Scrivener caught a glimpse of the distant mountains, the peaks snow-capped in spite of summer, and he thought of what might have been on some sun-baked plateau, or perhaps beside a glacial stream, but instead the formal luncheon inside the airless restaurant of a rival hotel. Guest of honour indeed, but the sales-girl from Zürich and Alberto of the Geneva bathing-plage would enjoy, at his expense, the more varied delicacies of the afternoon.

"I regret very much," began Herr Lieber, "that you did not tell me there would be others in your party. It would have been so simple to extend the invitation. The young lady . . . did you say, your niece . . . ?"

"An acquaintance only," said Scrivener coldly.

"Please to pardon me. The young lady, Mademoiselle Limoges, will surely require tickets for the lecture this evening, and tickets too for anyone else you care to bring?"

"I believe," said Scrivener, "that Mademoiselle Limoges has already booked her tickets."

"Good. Excellent. There will be refreshments afterwards, of course, Mr Scrivener, I must apologise for certain difficulties that have arisen, I was unable to warn you in time, but owing to many people being on holiday at the moment and certain other factors beyond our control, we were unsuccessful in selling many tickets for the second lecture you were kind enough to suggest giving. For the first we are fully booked, but for the second . . . " he broke off, pink with embarrassment, and blinking behind his spectacles.

"I quite understand," said Scrivener. "You would prefer to cancel the second lecture?"

"That is, of course, for you to say," said Herr Lieber quickly. "It is just that the hall might be almost empty, it would not be very agreeable for you, Mr Scrivener, and a waste of your valuable time."

"You must cancel it, of course," replied Scrivener, and he was aware of the expression of relief on his companion's face.

They arrived at the hotel, and within a few moments he was the centre of an earnest group of men and women, some twenty-five or thirty in number, to all of whom he was introduced before they filed into the restaurant towards a long table set at the end of the room, decorated with the flags of many nations.

Generally Robert Scrivener was pleased to discuss the merits of his novels with strangers. The finer passages of *Madrigal*, the philosophy of *Taurus,* even the possibly out-moded theme of his first success *Fortune Favours the Brave,* these things made contact, as a rule, between himself and the less well-endowed members of the reading public. Today, for no fit reason that he could give himself, the subject was dull as ashes. Why profess himself grateful to the pince-nez'd lady on his right for being able to quote a whole paragraph from *Jason* without hesitation, and how did it profit him to know that the learned gentleman on his left had read *Taurus* a dozen times and himself proposed to lecture upon it, granted Scrivener's permission, to the university at Basle the coming winter? He heard himself answer courtesy with courtesy, platitude with platitude, and he ate his way through course after course of rich, substantial food, but his mind and his heart were elsewhere. Upon what ice-blue peak, he wondered, did the luscious entity of Annette Limoges disport itself with the sun-bronzed Alberto, what mountain strawberries fell into their mouths, what melting snow, what kisses?

"Yes, indeed," he answered his hostess on the right, "it is up to all of us, as writers, to fight the commonplace where we find it, to do battle continually against those philistines who would drag us all to their own level of mediocrity. I hope to touch on this very subject in my lecture tonight."

He shook his head as the waiter offered him a second helping of roast pork—strange choice for a June luncheon—and bent his ear to the neighbour on his left, who declared that the cinema had destroyed the values of the western world.

"Even in Geneva here," declared his neighbour, "where we like to pride ourselves on gathering into our midst the best brains of Europe, your second lecture, Mr Scrivener, must be abandoned through lack of demand for tickets. Yet two streets away the people fight to get into some nonsense from Hollywood. I call it murder of the intellect. There is no other word for it."

"No other word," agreed Scrivener, and glancing furtively at his watch he saw that the hands already stood at half-past two, and the luncheon had been in progress since half-past twelve.

His entertainers did not release him until after five in the afternoon. The luncheon over, he must visit the headquarters of the International Society of Letters and examine the array of manuscripts in their possession, usually kept behind glass, but today spread open upon a table in his honour. There were portraits, too, of other famous members of the Society, not present, unfortunately, to welcome Scrivener, but their letters of regret for absence were all read. Tea was produced at four, with luncheon not yet forgotten or digested, and with tea came a formal line of new arrivals, not considered of sufficient standing to attend the luncheon yet every one anxious to shake the hand of Robert Scrivener. It was nearing half-past five when, warned that he had but two hours' respite before his lecture, due to start at half-past seven, the writer returned to the Hotel Mirabelle.

The first thing he noticed on asking for his key was that it had gone. He was told that Mademoiselle Limoges had asked for it about an hour before, and, since it had not been given back, must doubtless still be there. Scrivener summoned the lift and hurried along the corridor to his room. Annette was lying on the balcony, changed from her jeans into brief enticing shorts. Large black glasses protected her from the sun.

"Hullo," she called, as Scrivener entered the room, "we've had a wonderful day. Alberto's only just gone, but he'll be back again directly." Indeed, about his neat room were traces of recent occupation other than his own. A pullover flung on the bed. A tray of drinks. His books moved. And worse still, on the bathroom floor a wet towel.

"I thought you were going to the mountains?" he said, too taken aback to protest at this invasion of his room.

"We never went," replied Annette. "We lunched just outside Geneva, and then decided, as it was so hot, to go and bathe instead. The car took us to an enchanting spot Alberto knows, about fifteen miles along the lake. Then we came back here. I couldn't ask him up to my room, it would have looked odd, but I knew you wouldn't mind if we came up here instead. Alberto had a bath, and now he has gone off to change for your lecture."

She removed her black sun-glasses and smiled up at him.

"I thought," said Scrivener, "that you did not care to invite your friend into the hotel for fear it should get him into trouble with the management?"

"Had he come to my room yes," answered Annette. "I would never have suggested that. But as you can well imagine, Mr Robert Scrivener can do no wrong. There are notices everywhere in the entrance hall about your lecture. Alberto and I are dying for it."

Dying, observed Scrivener to himself, so much that he could not even pick up the bath-towel from the floor or stand the cork-mat to dry. The splodgy marks of wet feet were still upon it. And the soap, the cake of soap he had brought from London, had been left in the bath. It protruded, half-consumed, from the gaping waste-hole. Murderous rage gripped Scrivener. It rose in his throat and nearly choked him. He turned away from the bath-room and went to the balcony and stared down at Annette Limoges, who was intent on anointing her toe-nails a vivid puce.

"You know what," she suggested, dipping the brush in the bottle of scented varnish, "how would it be if the three of us went dancing, when your lecture's over? There's a wonderful place, Alberto tells me, the other side of the lake, where one can dine and dance outside, and watch the flood-lighting and the fountain."

"You've spilt some varnish on the balcony," said Scrivener.

"Have I? Never mind, the *femme-de-chambre* will wipe it off. Well, what do you say to my idea? You'd like some gaiety, wouldn't you, after the mental strain of the lecture?"

"Mental strain!" echoed Scrivener. "Mental strain . . . !" The laugh that came from him held an hysterical note.

Annette Limoges glanced up at him, surprised. "What is it?" she said. "Is anything the matter?"

And even now, he thought, even now, if she would only dismiss the bathing attendant for this once, he could forget his rage, forget her intolerable presumption and impertinence, swallow pride, swallow indignity, and be ready to continue where they had so disastrously left off.

"You're not nervous, are you?" asked Annette. "I assure you, there's no need to be. Only the people in the first six rows will hear what you say anyway. The acoustics are very bad, Alberto says. He knows someone who cleans the lecture hall."

Robert Scrivener clenched his fists. It seemed to him that there were two alternatives. One was to murder her at once. The other to seize her from the balcony and carry her to his bed. He lacked the courage to do either. The third alternative, miserable as it was, was the only course now open. He turned away from her, and, going into his bathroom, slammed the door and locked it. Presently he heard her knock. He took no notice and proceeded to run both taps. Then he sat with folded arms until the sound of a distant door told him that she had gone away. Scrivener then prepared himself for the lecture.

Punctually to the minute, at seven precisely, his host of the day arrived at the hotel to bear him away. Bulging from his stiff shirt front like a pouter pigeon, Herr Lieber once again expressed his apologies for the fact that the idea of the second lecture the following day must be abandoned, blaming, as had the neighbour at luncheon, the pull of the cinema over potential listeners.

"They are queuing in hundreds for this film across the way," he observed, "my wife and daughter have been twice. I never go to the cinema myelf. Of course, when we arranged your lecture we did not know what was to be shown at the Elysée."

Had they known, wondered Scrivener, would they have written to him cancelling the first lecture as they had done the second? His thesis was ruined, as it was. The two lectures, planned to present a cohesive world—on the theme of the essential purity of the poet, and his cosmic significance acting as counter-point to the novelist's duty to mankind—these headings that he had worked upon before leaving London had to be abandoned, or rather embodied into a single credo that would send his audience forth informed and satisfied. The task, he felt, was impossible.

As he sat on the platform, listening to the introduction of his person by the president of the International Society of Letters and looking down upon the rows of earnest faces, it seemed to Robert Scrivener that all he had worked for hitherto had been in vain. *Fortune Favours the Brave, Madrigal, Taurus, Jason,* all beng lauded at this moment by the president of the Society, and presumably familiar to the audience below, had been set at naught through a sequence of events which he had been powerless to control. His journey to Geneva had been ill-starred, and even now, when he should be gathering the threads of his wasted material together, part of his mental process was composing a telegram to Judith, warning her that after all he would be returning to London the following day. For what use was it now to consider getting hold of a car and driving up the Rhone valley, if the hoped-for-companion of his travels was not worthy of her hire?

"And so I have much pleasure in introducing the famous novelist, poet and critic, Mr Robert Scrivener." The president of the Society bowed towards him, and Scrivener rose to his feet.

Integrity, he supposed afterwards, integrity and training brought him through the ordeal. The appreciative silence of the audience, interrupted only occasionally by the coughing of those who should have remained in sanatoriums, and the generous applause at the conclusion, followed by a buzz of conversation and the congratulations of fellow members of the Society upon the platform with him, these tributes proved to him that he had not failed. He was, however, exhausted. He had spent himself for literature. Not for his own fame had he stood there for the full seventy minutes of his lecture, but to place on its true pedestal, out of reach of the vulgar, the trivial-minded, the prostitutes of art, the sacred vessel he had dared to call his Muse. Let the lesser breed defile it if they so willed, the essence would remain untouched in the hands of himself and others like him.

Almost fainting as the result of his own eloquence, Scrivener allowed himself to be led into the room behind the platform, where he was given chicken sandwiches and sweet champagne. This, he understood, was the culmination of hospitality that had begun for him that morning at half-past twelve. When he had sufficiently cooled his parched throat, and shaken the remaining hands extended to him, he would be a free man, without even a car or Herr Lieber at his disposal. For this, he was grateful. Further expressions of international goodwill would have slain him. He made ready, therefore, for his departure, giving as excuse a belated supper with friends who awaited him even now at the hotel Mirabelle.

Just as he was about to leave, a note was put into his hands by Herr Lieber. Scrivener recognised the handwriting of Annette Limoges, and put the note into his pocket. A final hand-shake, a final bow, and he made his escape from the Society of International Letters.

A steady rain was falling when he came out into the street. One of those brooding thunderstorms that hover over the Jura and finally break upon the lake of Geneva had evidently burst during the course of his lecture. Here was the aftermath. And he could see no taxis. He stood for a moment, looking to right and left, and then remembered the note in his pocket.

"Dearest Robert," he read, "you were marvellous. Alberto is quite overwhelmed. We left early, so as not to be trampled in the crush. I expect you will be having supper with the Society and won't be back at the hotel until after midnight, so this is just to let you know I shall take Alberto up to your room and we will have supper there, as we are both feeling too tired to dance. Looking forward to seeing you later on, and congratulations once again, fond love, Annette. P.S. You had better knock on the door before coming in!"

Robert Scrivener crumpled the note in his hand and dropped it down a convenient drain. Then, with his collar turned up, he hurried along the street to find a taxi. But if he found one, he wondered, where should he go? Annette and Alberto were even now making free of room number 27. His head low, because of the rain, he found himself brought to a standstill by a crowd of people. Were they all looking for taxis too? Glancing about him he realised that he had, through the mischance of not looking where he was going, got himself jammed into a cinema queue, and now, unable either to proceed further or break from it, he was forced to advance with the queue towards the auditorium. The one advantage in this form of motion was that he was now sheltered from the rain. Slowly but steadily he was borne towards the box-office. Useless to try to explain that he had no wish to visit the cinema; simpler to let circumstance defeat him. He wanted, above all, to sit down, to relax.

Scrivener felt in his pocket for change, and as he passed the box-office exchanged his few hundred francs for the small slip given him in return. He was propelled on once more, and, stumbling in the darkness over legs that seemed thrust out purposely to trip him, blinded by a torch flashed in his eyes, he groped his way to the humble seat answering to the number on his ticket. The picture, whatever it was, had begun. Galloping horses chased one another across a wide screen. Music sobbed from the sound-track. Robert Scrivener was very tired. The sweet champagne had numbed, for the moment, his taut nerves, and a sad self-pity, a nostalgic *à quoi bon*, had turned his mood to one of resignation.

He sat back on his hard cheap seat, hemmed in and breathed upon by his neighbours, and lifted his eyes to the screen. Little by little the thread of the story became plain. The leading character was a man of middle-age whose life had turned sour and who, in a moment of drunken folly, had killed his wife. He then fell in love with his step-daughter. As Scrivener followed the dénouement and watched the leading character, who might have been himself, wander across an endless prairie, deserted not only by his step-daughter but by his horses too, he was aware of a terrible sensation of despair. Tears came into his eyes and began to roll slowly down his cheeks. This wretched man was himself. The step-daughter was Annette Limoges. And the horses, the horses which the man had driven with such confidence and power at the beginning of the story and which now ran from him, scattering with thundering hooves across the wild prairie, these horses symbolised for Scrivener those works that he had written and that were now lost to him, lost across the wasted years of his own dull, empty life.

He sat there in the cheap cinema sat and wept. He had no interest now in the past or in the future. The thought of the return flight to London, the resumption of his biography of Swedenborg, was odious to him. He took out his handkerchief and blew his nose, as indeed did those around him, while the words *The End* flashed upon the screen. Only then, reading through the titles repeated before him, did he realise that what he had been seeing, and what had moved him so much, was the adaptation of that best-selling novel he had always despised, that unworthy pot-boiler written a year or so ago by the fellow-writer whose wedding he had attended such a short time before. Robert Scrivener replaced his handkerchief and, rising to his feet, shuffled his way through the departing queue, and so out into the damp streets of Geneva. His cup was full.

La Sainte-Vierge

It was hot and sultry, that oppressive kind of heat where there is no air, no life. The trees were motionless and dull, their drooping leaves colourless with summer dust. The ditches smelt of dead ferns and long-dried mud, and the grasses of the fields were blistered and brown. The village seemed asleep. No one stirred among the few scattered cottages on the hill-side; strange, uneven cottages, huddled together for fear of loneliness, with white walls and no windows, and small gardens massed with orange flowers.

A greater silence still filled the fields, where the pale corn lay heaped in awkward stacks, left by some neglectful labourer. Not even a breeze stirred the heather on the hills, lonely treeless hills, whose only dwellers were a host of bees and a few lizards. Below them the wide sea stretched like a sheet of ice into eternity, a chart of silver crinkled by the sun.

Away from the hills, towards the scattered houses, was a narrow, muddy lane leading to nowhere. At first it seemed one of those shy, twisting lanes, tempting to explore, that finish in a distant village or an unknown beach, but this one dissolved into a straggling path that soon lost itself among tall weeds. In a sheltered corner of the lane Marie was washing her linen in a pool.

The water looked like a basin of spilt milk, white with soft soap, and the clothes lay limp upon the slippery stones. Marie scrubbed hard, scornful of the heat, her black hair screwed behind her head in a tight knot; now and again she brushed away with an impatient hand the streaks of perspiration that trickled from her forehead.

Her face was thin and childish, rather plain and pathetic, and though she was twenty-three she looked little more than seventeen. There were tired lines under her eyes, and her hands were rough and uncared for. She was a typical Breton peasant, hard-working and reserved, whose only beauty was her youth, which would quickly pass. When the Breton women sorrow they show no grief upon their faces, they would rather die than let their tears be seen; thus Marie bore no outward trace of the pain that was in her heart.

She was thinking of Jean, her husband. She lived for him; there was nothing else in her life. She was a woman who would love but once, and give everything. There was no part of her body and soul that did not belong to him; she had no thought and no wish beyond his happiness. He was her lover and her child. Yet she never told him this, she did not even understand it herself. She was ignorant and unintelligent; it was only her heart that knew.

"He is going away from me," she was thinking, "he is going in his boat on that terrible sea. Only a year ago now since my brother was drowned in the sudden gale that came after the hot weather. I am afraid, so terribly afraid. Jean is ashamed of me; he thinks I am not fit to be the wife of a fisherman. I cannot help it. The coast is dangerous, more dangerous than anywhere else in Brittany. And these storms—the mists—the odd currents. Jean is rash and he loves danger, he does not mind. If he could be safe and return to me unharmed, I would work my fingers to the bone."

Every few months Marie would go through this agony, when Jean and the other fishermen went to sea and stayed for ten days without sight of land. The weather was uncertain and storms were frequent; the frail boats stood very little chance against a heavy sea. "I must not let him see I am afraid," she said to herself. "He cannot understand it, and I irritate him."

She paused in her work and sank back upon her heels. Her throat was dry, and she had an aching, sick feeling below her heart. It would be terrible to be alone without him, worse than it had ever been before. Something was going to happen. If only she had not the feeling that something was going to happen. The sun shone down upon her uncovered head, and she was aware of her great weariness.

There was no one near her, and through the trees the village looked dusty and lifeless. The linen lay in an untidy heap by her side. What did it matter whether it was clean or dirty?

She closed her eyes, and was filled with a sense of unbelievable loneliness. "Jean," she whispered, "Jean."²

From across the fields came the sound of the chapel bell striking the hour. Marie sat up and listened, and over her face came a strange smile, a smile in which hope and shame were mingled. She had suddenly remembered the Sainte-Vierge. In her mind she saw the figure in the chapel, Notre Dame des Bonnes Nouvelles, with the infant Jesus in her arms.

"I will go this evening," she thought. "When it is dark I will go to the Sainte-Vierge and tell her my trouble. I shall ask her to watch over Jean when he is at sea." She rose to her feet and began to lay her washing in the basket.

Her memory of the chapel had stopped the sick feeling in her heart, and as she walked through the fields and the village she was conscious only of her weariness. When she had left her basket in the cottage Marie went down the hill to the harbour, where she hoped to find Jean.

She walked towards a group of men who were standing on the edge of the quay, by a heap of old nets and discarded sails. Jean was among them, laughing and talking. Marie felt so proud as she looked at him. He was a good head taller than any of the others, with great broad shoulders and a mass of dark hair.

She ran forward, waving her hand. Jean's eyes narrowed as he saw her, and he muttered a curse under his breath. "Shut your mouths," he said to the other men, "here comes the child." They laughed awkwardly, and some of them began to move away.

"What are you doing down here?" asked Jean.

"It is settled, then, that you sail," said Marie breathlessly. "What time do you leave?"

"At midnight, so as to catch the tide," he replied. "But listen here, I must have supper early tonight, there are a lot of things I have to do. Jacques here wants me to help him with his boat."

He winked at the young fisherman next to him, who carefully avoided Marie's eye.

"Yes," said the lad, "that's right," and strolled away towards the beach. Marie did not notice anything, but the sick feeling had begun again in her heart.

"Come away," she said to Jean, "I have something to tell you." He followed her rather unwillingly up the hill.

They paused halfway, and turned back to look at the sea. The heat of the afternoon had passed, and in about four hours' time the sun would sink below the horizon. The sea shone like splintered silver, while westwards beyond the beacon streams of burnt clouds were massing in a purple haze. Down in the bay some children were bathing, and the sound of their voices and splashes floated up to the hill. The gulls wheeled and screamed around the harbour, searching for food.

Marie turned away, and climbed towards the village. She had a vivid mental picture of the sea, and was aware that it was the last time she would look at it with Jean. Subconsciously, in the depths of her being, she consecrated the spot. Jean spat out the fag end of his cigarette; he was not thinking of anything.

Theirs was the last cottage beyond the village shop—a funny little white place with a prim garden. Marie went straight to the living-room, and began to lay the supper things on the table. She went about her work mechanically; she had no idea what she was doing. There was only one thought in her mind—in a few hours he would be gone.

Jean's shadow loomed in the doorway. "You were wanting to tell me something?" he asked. Marie did not answer for a moment. Her love for him was so great that she felt it would choke her if she spoke. She wanted to kneel at his feet, to bury her head against him, to implore him to stay with her. If only he would understand to what depths of degradation she would sink for his sake. Everything she had ever felt for him came back to her at this moment. Yet she said nothing, and no sign appeared on her stolid little face.

"What is it?" he asked again.

"It is nothing," she answered slowly, "nothing. The Curé was here today, and hoped you would see him before you go."

She turned to pick up a plate, conscious of the lie, conscious of her failure. He would never know now.

"I will see," said Jean, "but I don't think there will be any time. This boat of Jacques'—and the nets." He left the rest unfinished, and went out into the garden.

The next few hours passed rapidly. After supper Marie washed up the dishes and put away her clean linen. Then she had her mending to do, mostly things for Jean.

She worked until it became too dark to see, for she was very thrifty and would not use a lamp. At ten o'clock Jean came in to say good-bye. "May I come with you and help Jacques with his boat?" she asked.

"No, no, you will be in the way," he replied quickly. "We cannot work and talk as well."

"But I will not say a word."

"No, I won't have you come. You are tired, too; it is this heat. If I know that you are here in bed I shall be happy, and think about you."

He put his arms round her and kissed her gently. Marie closed her eyes. It was the end of everything. "You will be careful, you will come back to me?" She clung to him like a child.

"Are you mad, you silly girl?" he said, and he laughed as he shut the door and left her. For a few minutes Marie stood motionless in the middle of the room. Then she went to the window and looked out, but he was already out of sight. It was a beautiful evening, very clear and bright, for there was a full moon.

Marie sat down by the window, her hands in her lap. She felt as if she were living in a dream. "I think I must be ill," she said to herself. "I've never felt like this before."

There were no tears on her cheeks, only deep shadows in her eyes. Slowly she rose to her feet, and after putting a shawl round her head and over her shoulders she opened the door and stepped outside. There was no one about, and everything was quite still. Marie slipped through the garden and crossed the lane. In a few minutes she was running across the field that led to the chapel.

The Chapel des Bonnes Nouvelles was very old, and was no longer used for services. The door remained open day and night, so that the peasants could go in and pray when they wanted, for they always felt a little in awe of the new church at the end of the village.

Marie pushed open the creaking door, then paused to listen. The chapel was quite deserted. Through the low window by the altar the moon shone now and again, lighting the nave. There had probably been no one inside for days. A few leaves lay on the rough stone floor, where they had blown in from the open door. The white-washed walls were grimy, and great cobwebs hung from the rafters in the roof.

Hanging by nails on the wall, on either side of the altar, were gifts presented by the peasants who had prayed there: roughly carved models of ships, pathetic little toy boats, brightly coloured balls, and strings of glass and wooden beads. They had lain there many years, perhaps, and were covered in dust. There were even a few wedding wreaths, now old and faded, given by the brides of long ago. All over the walls were inscriptions written in pencil, prayers and thanksgivings to Notre Dame des Bonnes Nouvelles, *"Mère, priez pour nous"*, *"Notre Dame des Bonnes Nouvelles, sauvez mon fils qui est sur mer."*

Marie went slowly to the rails and knelt down. The altar was bare of flowers, and alone in the centre stood the figure of the Sainte-Vierge. Her golden crown was crooked on her head, and covered in cobwebs. Her right arm had been lost, and in the other she held the little figure of the infant Jesus, who had no fingers on His hands. Her robe had once been blue, but the colour had come off long ago, and it was now a dirty brown. Her face was round and expressionless, the face of a cheap doll. She had large blue eyes that looked vacantly before her, while her scarlet cheeks clashed with her cracked painted lips. Her mouth was set in a silly smile, and the plaster was coming off at the corners. Round her neck she wore string upon string of glass beads, the offerings of the fishermen, and someone had even hung a wreath over her baby's head. It dangled sideways and hid his face.

Marie knelt by the rails and gazed at the Sainte-Vierge. The figure was the most beautiful and sacred thing in her life. She did not notice the dust and the broken plaster, the toppling crown and the silly painted smile—to Marie she was the fulfiller of all prayers, the divine mother of the fishermen. As she knelt she prayed, not in words but in the thoughts that wandered at will through her mind, and her prayers were all for Jean, for his safety and his return.

"Oh! Mother," she said, "if it is wrong for me to love him so much, then punish me as you will, but bring him safely back to me. He is young and brave, yet helpless as a child, he would not understand death. I care not if my heart breaks, nor if he should cease to love me and should ill-treat me, it is only his happiness I ask, and that he shall never know pain or hardship."

A fly settled on the nose of the Sainte-Vierge, and brushed a scrap of coloured plaster off her cheek.

"I have put all my trust in you," said Marie, "and I know that you will watch over him when he is at sea. Though waves rise up and threaten his boat, if you protect him I shall have no fear. I will bring fresh flowers every morning and lay them at the feet of the little Jesus. When I am working in the day I will sing songs and be gay, and these will be prayers to you for his safety. Oh! Mother, if you could only show me by a sign that all will be well!"

A drip of water from the roof fell down upon the Sainte-Vierge and left a dirty streak across her left eye.

It was very dark now. Away across the fields a woman was calling to a child. A faint breeze stirred in the trees, and far in the distance the waves broke dully on the shingle beach.

Marie gazed upon the figure until she dropped from weariness, and everything was blurred and strange before her eyes. The walls of the chapel lay in shadow; even the altar sank into nothingness. All that remained was the image of the Sainte-Vierge, her face lit up by a chance ray of moonlight. And as Marie watched the figure it seemed to her that the cracked, painted smile became a thing of beauty, and that the doll's eyes looked down upon her with tenderness and love. The tawdry crown shone in the darkness, and Marie was filled with awe and wonder.

She did not know that it shone only by the light of the moon. She lifted up her arms and said: "Mother of pity, show me a sign that you have heard my prayers." Then she closed her eyes and waited. It seemed an eternity that she knelt there, her head bowed in her hands.

Slowly she was aware of a feeling of peace and great comfort, as if the place were sanctified by the presence of something holy. She felt that if she opened her eyes she would look upon a vision. Yet she was afraid to obey her impulse, lest the thing she would see should blind her with its beauty. The longing grew stronger and stronger within her, until she was forced to give way. Unconscious of her surroundings, unconscious of what she was doing, Marie opened her eyes. The low window beside the altar was filled with the pale light of the moon, and just outside she saw the vision.

She saw Jean kneeling upon the grass, gazing at something, and there was a smile on his face, and slowly from the ground rose a figure which Marie could not see distinctly, for it was in shadow, but it was the figure of a woman. She watched her place two hands on Jean's shoulders, as if she were blessing him, and he buried his head in the folds of her gown. Only for a moment they remained like this, and then a cloud passed over the face of the moon, and the chapel was filled with darkness.

Marie closed her eyes and sank to the ground in worship. She had seen the blessed vision of the Sainte-Vierge. She had prayed for a sign, and it had been given her, Notre Dame des Bonnes Nouvelles had appeared unto her, and with her own hands had blessed Jean, and assured him of her love and protection. There was no longer fear in Marie's heart; she felt she would never be afraid again. She had put all her faith in the Sainte-Vierge, and her prayers had been answered.

She rose unsteadily from the ground and found her way to the door. Once more she turned, and looked for the last time at the figure on the altar. It was in shadow now, and the crown was no longer gold. Marie smiled and bowed her head: she knew that no one else would ever see what she had seen. In the chapel the Sainte-Vierge still smiled her painted smile, and the vacant blue eyes gazed into nothing. The faded wreath slipped a little over the ear of the infant Jesus.

Marie stepped out into the evening. She was very tired and could scarcely see where she was going, but her heart was at peace and she was filled with a great happiness.

In the corner of the narrow field, sheltered by the chapel window, Jean whispered his desire to the sister of Jacques the fisherman.

Leading Lady

He stood in the passage, his hat on the back of his head, a cigar hanging from his mouth. He pulled out an enormous watch and stamped his foot impatiently.

"Look here," he shouted, for all the world to hear, "I'm not accustomed to be kept waiting. Doesn't Miss Fabian know I've arrived? What the hell is everybody doing?"

The doorkeeper peered at him timidly. "I'm sorry, sir; it will only be a few moments. What name was it, sir?"

Damn it all, this fellow hadn't even recognised him! He looked at the doorkeeper steadily, waited so that he should grasp the full significance of his reply.

"Paul Haynes," he said superbly, and turned away. A frightened dresser appeared at the bottom of the stairs.

"Will you please come this way, sir?" She knew who he was all right. Hers was the proper subservient attitude to take. Good God, once he got this theatre under his control he'd change the whole damn staff. The doorkeeper would be the first to get the sack.

He strode after the dresser along the passage, swaying from side to side like a turkey-cock, spilling ash as he went. He stood on the threshold of the dressing-room, his legs wide apart, his hat still on the back of his head.

She was sitting before the looking-glass, patting her hair into place. She turned round with a little cry of distress.

"Oh, but can you ever forgive me for having kept you waiting? Those appalling film people never leave me alone for a moment—keep pestering me to go to Hollywood and offering me stupendous sums. Lewisheim has been on the telephone for twenty minutes." She waited a moment to allow her words to sink into the man's brain. She murmured something unnecessary to her dresser, and then turned back to him with a smile. "However, let's forget about that—it's something quite apart. Now, please sit down—forgive this untidiness everywhere, but you know what it is, the last few days of a long run. First of all, I must tell you, I went yesterday afternoon to see your new revue. Oh, it's the most marvellous thing I've ever seen—but the most. I can't speak about it. I've never enjoyed anything so much. Those girls—the whole production! Of course you're an absolute genius; there's no one to touch you!" She shrugged her shoulders almost impatiently.

He did not attempt to conceal his smile of satisfaction. So she liked it? H'm. Lewisheim's productions would never hold a candle to his. This woman had sense, after all. She was looking more beautiful than ever, too. Pity, perhaps, she wore so little jewellery. Only a chain round her neck. It wasn't impressive; much too simple altogether. He would like to see her in a mass of diamonds.

"Yes, it's a good show, and I don't mind admitting it," he said loudly, blowing a great cloud of smoke into her face.

Her manners were exquisite; she didn't even wave it away with her hand.

"I spend more money on my productions than any other manager in London," he went on. "None of your skimpy, shoddy stuff for me. No painted scenery."

She made a little sound in her throat and shook her head for sympathy.

"Where you spend money you draw money," he announced, "and that's always the way I do things. If you and I put on this play of yours together, I'm going to see that you have the very best of everything. No—don't thank me." He spread out his large fat hand. "You're a business woman, you know what you're about when you join forces with me. My dear, you're going to have a real big success, and you're going to make a packet of money."

She said nothing for a moment. What a conceited fool the man was! Talking to her as if she were some pathetic little actress striking out on her first venture. He didn't know anything about the theatre either. Because he was rich he managed to surround himself with people who did, that was all. He was lucky, and they flattered him, but it was only his money they wanted. Then she leant back in her chair, as if defeated.

"I think you are quite the most wonderful man I know," she

said softly. He looked at her, and put away his cigar. Once more he bent towards her.

"I'm going to tell you something," he began in a slow, impressive tone, "and it's something that I don't say to many people, because I'm a very difficult man." He waited a moment as though to prepare her for some stupendous announcement. Then: "I like you," he said. "I like you very much," he went on. "There's no nonsense about you. You look a man straight in the face and tell him the truth. I'm a great believer in truth myself. If I say a thing I mean it. If I didn't like you, I'd be perfectly frank and tell you so. My frankness brings me many enemies, but I'm not afraid of any of 'em. They know what to expect. In fact, the words 'to be frank as Paul Haynes' have become a common expression, so they tell me. If a fellow wants to hear the truth about himself, or someone else, let him come along to me."

"Oh, but I admire you for that," she broke in impulsively. "It shows such strength of mind, and such a superb indifference to what the world thinks of you. They matter so little, don't they?— all the people we meet in this profession. I have my few friends— my books, my child." She turned with a wistful smile at the photograph on her dressing-table. Half-unconsciously she pushed the snapshot of a famous boxer out of sight behind a powder-box.

"You are quite unique, my dear," he continued. "If you were not, I shouldn't be sitting here now. You know I've got a whole lot of ideas about the theatre that I think would interest you. I'm a bit of an idealist in my way, you know."

The fatuity of this man! She glanced at her watch, shading her eyes with her hand.

"Tell me about yourself," she begged.

"I want to change the present conditions," he shouted. "I want to get a different atmosphere into the theatre altogether, and by heaven I'm going to do it. I've started with my own revues, and I want to do the same with the straight plays. Do you know my revues are the cleanest in England? There's not a single line in my new show that would make a man blush. But that's not the point; that's not what I'm getting at. I'm going to put a stop to what goes on behind the scenes—all these dirty little love affairs, all this promiscuous stuff in dressing-rooms. I'm going to make it my business to find out the private life of every actor and actress who works for me. I'll make a clean sweep of the rotters. I'm a powerful man. If I find out that any man or woman hasn't got a fit record, I'll see to it they don't get another job on a London stage."

He leant back, exhausted with his eloquence.

"Of course, you're quite right," she said, without hesitating. "I suppose I'm weak. But I shut my eyes to things. And I hate to get anyone into trouble."

He went on, pleased with her reply. "Do you know, you are one of the few actresses who have never been divorced. Of course, you're a widow, but even if your husband had lived, it would have made no difference. Someone told me that five years ago, when you went about a lot with John What's-his-name—the fellow who left his wife and went out to Australia. Whether it's true or not, you showed great wisdom in cutting him out of your life. They tell me he's gone entirely to pieces—out of work, drinks like a fish. Now that's the type of thing I'm going to put a stop to; and I want you on my side. You and I together, my dear, will be practically an unbreakable force. What do you think?"

She looked him straight in the eyes. "I agree with every word you say," she told him.

He took her hand and patted it. "Partners—what?" he said, controlling his smile. "About the cast," he went on, clearing his throat. "We've decided on everyone, I think, except the other man. Is there anyone you fancy for that part?"

She began to polish her nails carelessly.

"You know Bobby Carson, the boy who has been playing my brother in the present play? He's really charming, and very capable. Not a bit expensive either."

"H'm. It requires more than capability, you know. It's a striking emotional part. The second act is almost entirely in his hands, if you remember. I don't care a damn about the expense. Now, the chap I want in the part is this young Martin Wilton. Have you seen him?"

"No." She turned to the dressing-table, frowning ever so slightly.

"His play comes off next week, so we might be able to get him. Come along Friday afternoon; they have a matinée. I think he's the finest natural actor I've seen for years. Quite young, quite unspoilt. Doesn't know how good he is. See what you think of him, anyway. He can rehearse the part on trial."

"Yes, yes, of course." She had heard too much already of this Martin Wilton. People were raving about him. The critics were almost nauseating in their praise.

"Friday, then," she smiled. "How exciting! I shall adore it."

A few minutes later, Haynes leant back in his taxi with a smile of satisfaction. He decided he had made a great impression on her. Well, it was not surprising. After all, he was rich; he had brains; he was under sixty. He felt that she had probably never met anyone quite like him before. He admitted that her husband had been a remarkable man, but no doubt very dull to live with, always wrapped up in his work, seeing her only as a character in one of his plays. He couldn't have known how to make a woman happy. Good thing he had died when he did.

Idly he wondered whether she was lonely. You never heard her name coupled with anyone—not since that fellow went to Australia, all of which was undoubtedly malicious gossip. Well, she had seen eye to eye with him over his ideas for the theatre. It was a wonderful scheme of his, to launch a great purity campaign. With the *Daily Recorder* to back him up, he would get tremendous publicity. He would be known as the Man Who Cleaned Up the English Stage. And Mary Fabian would help. Her beauty and his brains would make a great combination. He supposed she must be well in the thirties by now, with a child growing big. She wasn't everybody's money. Jove, what a figure, though! He would like to see her in a diamond necklace and with a little less on. This next play was going to be enjoyable in many ways . . .

Back in the dressing-room, Mary Fabian was cursing him for having kept her so long after the performance. He hadn't even apologised. What an appalling man! All that frightful twaddle about his clean revues, while he smacked his lips at her as though she were butchers' meat.

"Tell Mr Carson I'm alone now," she said to her dresser.

It was past midnight, and she wanted her supper. She threw off her clothes impatiently, and began brushing her hair behind her ears.

"Bobby," she called through the wall. "Bobby, my sweet."

*

She sat in the stalls on Friday afternoon without moving a muscle of her face. She was alone, after all; Paul Haynes had been called to Manchester. She thanked heaven for his absence. She could not have borne with his enthusiastic remarks, his eager concentration upon the stage. She drew her fur coat more closely around her; she buried herself in it as though she did not wish to be seen.

This Martin Wilton was good, far too good. His personality stuck out a mile, with his vivid face and tawny hair. Not her type at all, of course; but that was not the point. Even had he been attractive to her, she would not have considered him. Not for a moment. It was much too dangerous. It would be fatal to have him in the new play; he would run away with it entirely. She would become a secondary figure, her part would not matter at all.

And she had reached an awkward moment in her career. The slightest slip, the smallest mistake, and attention would be drawn away from her. People would say she was becoming monotonous, she was overplaying herself. No, this boy was too good. Already she could imagine the first night, with Martin Wilton getting the applause. She would have to stand in the background and efface herself, pushing him forward with a smile. And the papers next morning would be a paean of praise. "Mr Martin Wilton gave the finest performance of the evening." And so on, and so on . . .

Something had got to be done. He must be prevented at all costs from playing the part. She would have to be careful, though; it was not going to be easy.

Mechanically she wrote a note to Martin Wilton after the matinée.

"Your performance quite marvellous. Never seen anything like it. I want you to come and be with me in my next play. Will send it along for you to read tonight. Wonderful part for you. Forgive me for not coming round. I've got to dash away."

She felt she could not face the boy now, and his probable insufferable conceit. She drove home, racking her brains for some solution to the problem.

On the morning of the first rehearsal, when Martin Wilton was to read the part for the first time, she received a wire from Haynes. "Detained Manchester. Impossible to attend rehearsal. Rely on judgment entirely *re* Wilton."

She crushed the wire in her hand and went on to the stage, sensing victory.

"Mr Haynes is in Manchester, and can't get away for the rehearsal. Is everybody here? Then we'll begin at once."

At eight o'clock, when they had finished for the day, she flung herself down in her chair, exhausted. Things had gone exactly as she had feared; the boy had been wonderful—never seemed to make a mistake, and his technique was uncanny. How she hated him!

She sat in front of the mirror and began to make up her face very carefully. She cast her mind back to the night last week when Paul Haynes had voiced his grotesque plans for delving into the private lives of actors and actresses, and the germ of an idea came into her mind. "Will you tell Mr Wilton I should like to see him?" she said to her dresser.

In a few minutes the boy knocked at her door. "May I come in?" he said shyly. She gave him a dazzling smile; she held out her hands. "We've got so much to discuss," she told him. "Are you doing anything this evening?"

The boy flushed all over his face. "As a matter of fact, I was going back to my wife, but if it's important I can easily ring her up."

She gave a litle cry of astonishment. "Married!—but you're far too young. What do you mean by it?" She shook her head at him in mock reproof. "Ask her to spare you for a few hours," she pleaded. "We've got to talk about this second act."

In half-an-hour they were having dinner together in her flat. At first he was painfully shy, he would scarcely say a word. Completely unselfconscious on the stage, in private life he was nervous, clumsy, aware of his hands and feet. She pretended not to notice; she smiled encouragement, she spoke softly, using all her old tricks mechanically. Soon he began to warm to the influence of the room, her voice, the excellent food, and his second glass of burgundy. He could scarcely believe he was sitting here alone with Mary Fabian.

She sat with her face in her hands, a cigarette between her lips. The fire cast great shadows on the ceiling, and played about her profile. Her hair shone dully like an old coin. She was so human, so open with him; and he loved the room, with the heavy curtains, the shaded light, and the smell of the queer stuff she burnt on the fire. He was happy and at peace; she seemed to understand him so well. He had never found anyone who could listen to him like this, not even his wife.

"I want you to sit by the fire, and smoke a cigarette, and tell me all about yourself," she had said.

He found himself speaking to her as if he had known her for years, explaining all the worry of those early years, how he had fought and struggled with his family.

"You seem to understand things about me that nobody else has ever dreamt existed," he said. "The serious side of me. What I really feel about life. Because I do feel things, you know, tremendously. People have often told me that when they first meet me I seem horribly shy. All my life it's been the same. My mother, bless her, could never understand my passion for the stage. You're so awfully sympathetic." He gazed at her with worship in his eyes. "You'll think me absurd," he went on, gaining confidence, "but the one ambition of my life, ever since I first went on the stage, was to act with you. I've dreamt of it for years, grinding away in the provinces."

"No, no—you're joking!" she smiled.

"I promise you it's absolutely true. I saw you first about five years ago, and I remember thinking to myself: 'There is somebody worth while, who spends her time giving happiness to other people.' Oh, you were simply wonderful. You became my ideal, my sort of guiding star, my good angel. I judged everything by what I imagined your standard to be. I guessed you would never put up with the second-rate in life, or in acting. You would only accept the best. I love it more than anything in the world—the theatre, I mean."

She stirred slightly, and reached for his hand. "You dear," she murmured; "you dear quixotic person." Then she leant back in her chair, pillowing her cheek against a cushion.

If he went on much longer she felt she would scream. It was incredible that anyone should talk so much. What a fool he was! She turned her rising yawn into a smile. "You know, you remind me of myself," she told him. "Oh yes, quite a lot. All your ideals and beliefs. I so appreciate your outlook on life. All for Art, and the world well lost. Ah, how well I understand! I adore my work passionately. I couldn't live without it. One doesn't care about money, people, or success—it's just the longing to achieve something, isn't it?"

"Yes, yes!" he said eagerly, the light of a fanatic in his eyes.

"To create a living character out of a mass of words, to breathe life into it, to—to—" She made a little gesture with her hands, uncertain how to continue. "Oh, how marvellously you understand!" she ended, and: "We're going to be such friends, you and I."

She slipped from her chair to the floor, crouching, her hands spread to the blaze of the fire. Her head was aching; she had had a tiring day. She was longing to go to bed and to sleep. What on earth was he talking about now?

"Hamlet," he was saying. "I want to play Hamlet as no one has ever dared to play it before. There is something terrific about him, misunderstood, suppressed. You remember, in the beginning of Act Three, when he is with Ophelia, when she starts, 'My lord, I have remembrances of yours,' you know . . ."

"Yes, wonderful, wonderful!" she murmured. O God, not Shakespeare, not at this hour! She made no attempt to listen. She was wondering what time Paul Haynes arrived back from Manchester. He was certain to ring her up. The boy mustn't be here then.

"It will almost break my heart if I don't play this part with you," said Martin Wilton. "It's the chance of a lifetime. It's going to be hell until it's settled. Supposing Haynes thinks I'm no good?"

She broke from her thoughts with an effort. "Of course, you are young," she said gently, "a little too young. Personally, I think it makes the part all the more sympathetic, and I shall tell him so. Paul Haynes is a very difficult man, but I think I can persuade him. Unless he gets some absurd idea into his head. He's very thick-headed and obstinate, and once he has made up his mind, nothing in the world will make him change it. But I am sure he will like you; he is bound to agree with me."

He seized hold of her hands and kissed them. "You are being an angel to me," he said, flushing. "I can't ever forget this."

She smiled at him sadly; she ran her hand through his hair. "You remind me of someone I used to be fond of . . . " she began, and then broke off, as though emotionally moved. He cursed himself for his lack of tact. Of course, her husband was dead. It must be terrible for her. How brave she was, facing life alone like that! No one to look after her.

"You must go soon," she whispered. "It's getting late. And I've got to say good-night to my little girl. She won't sleep until I've tucked her up myself." The child was with a nurse in lodgings on the East Coast, but he would never know that. He had probably seen pictures of her soon after she was widowed, holding the child in her arms. When she had appeared the first time after her husband's death, in one of his plays, carefully made up, allowing herself to look a little wan and pale, the audience had gone nearly mad. The publicity had helped her enormously at the time.

"She is the only thing I have left," she said gently.

He stroked her hand awkwardly, like a clumsy animal. "I wish I could help," he began. "I hate to think of you like this . . . I had no idea . . . " He fumbled with the bangle on her wrist. She seemed very young suddenly, very pathetic. He wished he knew how to comfort her. The world who watched her act would never guess that off the stage she was this sweet, simple woman, broken-hearted, her life empty.

"It's all right," she was saying, "but sometimes one gets so frightfully lonely . . . "

Awkwardly he put his arm round her, patting her shoulder as though she was a child. She reached for her scrap of a handkerchief, turning her face from him, blowing her nose and laughing shakily.

"I feel so ashamed," she said. "I've never let this happen before."

He brushed the top of her head with his lips, at a loss for words, and then, impulsively, "Look here—you ought to meet my wife; she's the most sympathetic person in the world. I know you'd like her; she has a sort of gift for killing depression; she's an absolute angel. We've only got a tiny flat in a mews, but she'd adore to meet you. Come round now—it's not too late. She said she would go to a film when I rang her before dinner, but she'll be back by twelve. And we've got some wonderful records I'd love you to hear. A Beethoven concerto, Cesar Franck . . . "

"No, no, you mustn't tempt me like that; it isn't fair. I've been foolish tonight. I can't understand myself. And I should love to meet your wife, some other time . . . But I'm tired now; we are both tired; and you must go. Bless you for being so sweet to me."

"Good Lord! I've done nothing. I've just blundered on about myself. It's been the most marvellous evening. You've brought back all my old ideals and faith in the theatre; you've made me feel that everything's worth while. Any success I make I shall owe to you."

He stumbled out of the flat, not looking where he was going, his head in the clouds, his mind filled with the glorious, impossible future.

Thanking God she was alone at last, she sank into a chair, a cushion behind her head, a cigarette between her lips. Five minutes after he had gone the telephone rang. It was Paul Haynes.

"Hullo," he said. "I'm only this minute back from Manchester. Have you gone to bed or can I slip round for two minutes?"

"No, I'd love to see you," she lied. "Come along at once."

She powdered her face a little whiter than usual, using no colour, but shadowing her eyes. She looked very beautiful, but tired, strained.

"Now, I'm not going to keep you up," he said, as soon as he came into the room. "You've had a long day, and so have I. We can't afford to burn the candle at both ends in our profession, eh? Got to have beauty sleep." He smiled broadly, showing large gums. "Well, just tell me how it went. Everything go off all right without me?"

"Marvellous—considering. You know what first rehearsals are."

"Tell me—how did they all seem?"

"Splendid, on the whole. I don't think we need make any changes."

"And what about young Martin Wilton? Is he going to be good?"

"He was very much all there. Knew exactly what to do. He won't require much producing. His technique is marvellous in anyone so young. I can't understand where he's learnt it all."

"He's not too young, is he?"

"No—not really, I don't think. I hope not. We don't want to make a blunder, though. Oh, how I wish you'd been there!"

"Yes. I could have told you what I thought as soon as I'd

clapped eyes on him. How did he strike you personally? Did he seem a nice chap?—not conceited? Will you like having him in the theatre?"

She did not reply for a moment, and then laughed a little self-consciously. "He's very good at his job—I've said so already. What more can I say?"

"Look here, you're keeping something back. Don't pretend with me. Part of our bargain is to tell the truth. Martin Wilton was rude, bad-mannered?"

"No, no. Please don't ask me any more. Let's forget about him."

"I don't forget, and I shall worry you until I've had this out with you. Come on, my dear; what was the trouble?"

"It's so unfair to the boy," she protested. "He probably didn't realise what he was doing. He's young, and I suppose mixes with a crowd of awful people. I know the type—half-drunk and very promiscuous."

"What are you driving at? Wasn't he sober? What did he do to upset you?"

"Well, he—he tried to make the most violent love to me, that's all." She laughed and shrugged her shoulders.

Paul Haynes looked at her in amazement. "Good God! what on earth do you mean?"

"My dear, I assure you I was never more embarrassed in my life. Those sort of things don't happen to me. However, let's forget it."

"No, by heaven, we won't forget it," he said savagely. "I want to get to the bottom of this. What did he do, the little swine?"

"I asked him back here to talk over the second act and he stayed on and seemed to expect dinner. Perhaps he drank a little too much—I don't know. But he started talking the most frightful nonsense about being here alone with me, and said he'd been waiting for this for years. He tried to kiss me, and was, well, rather rough. I was so surprised that I wasn't prepared, you see, and—Oh, I hate telling you all this!"

"Go on," he said.

"I think he must be very unbalanced and rather peculiar. So many young men are, nowadays, don't you think? I feel so sorry for his poor little wife."

"Do you mean the little rat is married?"

"Yes—that's the awful part about it. He seized hold of me and said would I go to his flat—his wife was out—wouldn't be back till late. He was quite uncontrolled; it was revolting. Finally, I quietened him down and managed to get him away. He'd been gone only a few minutes when you rang up. That's why I'm looking so exhausted. I suppose he lost his head for the moment— probably took advantage of my being here alone. Promise me not to think any more about it."

"I'm very sorry," he said slowly. "But you remember what I told you the other day? It's just that type of thing I'm out to smash. It's vicious and disgusting. How he dared try it on with you, that's what gets me! He's probably stiff with drugs. An out-and-out rotter. And to think I was going to offer him the chance of his life! But, my dear, you weren't going to tell me. That's carrying chivalry a bit too far, isn't it?"

"But I hate making trouble," she broke in.

"Trouble? Don't talk such nonsense. If I let that boy play the part it would go against all my principles; it's one of my great ambitions to break up that gang of degenerates and I'm going to start right now. Young Mr Wilton is going to get the surprise of his life. He'll be finished in six months. As for the part, I'd rather give it to a stage-hand than to him."

She shook her head hopelessly. He moved towards the door.

"Well, you're dead-beat, my dear, and must go to bed. You've been through a very trying time."

Then, as he reached for his hat, "What's the name of the chap who played your brother?"

"What?" she said carelessly. "Oh, Bobby Carson. Why?"

"We'll get on to him in the morning. Tell him to be down at the theatre for rehearsal at eleven o'clock sharp. Good-night, my dear."

Escort

There is nothing remarkable about the *Ravenswing*, I can promise you that. She is between six and seven thousand tons, was built in 1926, and belongs to the Condor Line, port of register Hull. You can look her up in Lloyd's, if you have a mind. There is little to distinguish her from hundreds of other tramp steamers of her particular tonnage. She had sailed that same route and travelled those same waters for the three years I served in her, and she was on the job some time before that. No doubt she will continue to do so for many years more, and will eventually end her days peacefully on the mud as her predecessor, the old *Gullswing*, did before her; unless the U-boats get her first.

She has escaped them once, but next time we may not have our escort. Perhaps I had better make it clear, too, that I myself am not a fanciful man. My name is William Blunt, and I have the reputation of living up to it. I never have stood for nonsense of any sort, and have no time for superstition. My father was a Nonconformist minister, and maybe that had something to do with it. I tell you this to prove my reliability, but, for that matter, you can ask anyone in Hull. And now, having introduced myself and the ship, I can get on with my story.

We were homeward bound from a Scandinavian port in the early part of the autumn. I won't give you the name of the port—the censor might stop me—but we had already made the trip there and back three times since the outbreak of war. The convoy system had not started in those first days, and the strain on the captain and myself was severe. I don't want you to infer that we were windy, or the crew either, but the North Sea in wartime is not a bed of roses, and I'll leave it at that.

When we left port, that October afternoon, I couldn't help thinking that it seemed a hell of a long way home, and it didn't put me in what you would call a rollicking humour when our little Scandinavian pilot told us with a grin that a Grimsby ship, six hours ahead of us, had been sunk without warning. The Nazi government had been giving out on the wireless, he said, that the North Sea could be called the German Ocean, and the British Fleet couldn't do anything about it. It was all right for the pilot: he wasn't coming with us. He waved a cheerful farewell as he climbed over the side, and soon his boat was a black speck bobbing astern of us at the harbour entrance, and we were heading for the open sea, our course laid for home.

It was about three o'clock in the afternoon, the sea was very still and grey, and I remember thinking to myself that a periscope wouldn't be easy to miss; at least we would have fair warning, unless the glass fell and it began to blow. However, it did the nerves no good to envisage something that was not going to happen, and I was pretty short with the first engineer when he started talking about the submarine danger, and why the hell didn't the Admiralty do something about it?

"Your job is to keep the old *Ravenswing* full steam ahead for home and beauty, isn't it?" I said. "If Winston Churchill wants your advice, no doubt he'll send for you." He had no answer to that, and I lit my pipe and went on to the bridge to take over from the captain.

I suppose I'm not out-of-the-way observant about my fellow-men, and I certainly didn't notice then that there was anything wrong with the captain. He was never much of a talker at any time. The fact that he went to his cabin at once meant little or nothing. I knew he was close at hand, if anything unusual should happen.

It turned very cold after nightfall, and later a thin rain began to fall. The ship rolled slightly as she met the longer seas. The sky was overcast with the rain, and there were no stars. The autumn nights were always black, of course, in northern waters, but this night the darkness seemed intensified. There would be small chance of sighting a periscope, I thought, under these conditions, and it might well be that we should receive no other intimation than the shock of the explosion. Someone said the other day that the U-boats carried a new type of torpedo, supercharged, and that explained why the ships attacked sank so swiftly.

The *Ravenswing* would founder in three or four minutes, if she was hit right amidships, and it might be that we should never even sight the craft that sank us. The submarine would vanish in the darkness; they would not bother to pick up survivors. They couldn't see them if they wanted to, not in this darkness. I glanced at the chap at the wheel; he was a little Welshman from Cardiff, and he had a trick of sucking his false teeth and clicking them back again every few minutes. We stood a pretty equal chance, he and I, standing side by side together on the bridge. It was then I turned suddenly and saw the captain standing in the entrance to his cabin. He was holding on for support, his face was very flushed, and he was breathing heavily.

"Is anything wrong, sir?" I said.

"This damn pain in my side," he gasped. "Started it yesterday, and thought I'd strained myself. Now I'm doubled up with the bloody thing. Got any aspirin?" Aspirin my foot, I thought. If he hasn't got acute appendicitis, I'll eat my hat. I'd seen a man attacked like that before; he'd been rushed to hospital and operated on in less than two hours. They'd taken an appendix out of him swollen as big as a fist.

"Have you a thermometer there?" I asked the captain.

"Yes," he said. "What the hell's the use of that? I haven't got a temperature. I've strained myself, I tell you. I want some aspirin."

I took his temperature. It was a hundred and four. The sweat was pouring down his forehead. I put my hand on his stomach and it was rigid, like a brick wall. I helped him on his berth and covered him up with blankets. Then I made him drink half a glass of brandy neat. It may be the worst thing you can do for appendicitis, but when you're hundreds of miles from a surgeon and in the middle of the North Sea in wartime you're apt to take chances.

The brandy helped to dull the pain a little, and that was the only thing that mattered. Whatever the result to the captain, it had but one result for me. I was in command of the *Ravenswing* from now on, and mine was the responsibility of bringing her home through those submarine-infested waters. I, William Blunt, had got to see this through.

It was bitter cold. All feeling had long since left my hands and feet. I was conscious of a dull pain in those parts of my body where my hands and feet should have been. But the effect was curiously impersonal. The pain might have belonged to someone else, the sick captain himself even, back there in his cabin, lying moaning and helpless as I had left him last, some forty-eight hours before. He was not my charge; I could do nothing for him. The steward nursed him with brandy and aspirin, and I remember feeling surprised, in a detached sort of way, that he didn't die.

"You ought to get some sleep. You can't carry on like this. Why don't you get some sleep?"

Sleep. That was the trouble. What was I doing at that moment but rocking on my two feet on the borderline of oblivion, with the ship in my charge, and this voice in my left ear the sound that brought me to my senses? It was Carter, the second mate. His face looked pinched and anxious.

"Supposing you get knocked up?" he was saying. "What am I going to do? Why don't you think of me?"

I told him to go to hell, and stamped down the bridge to bring the life back to my numbed feet, and to disguise the fact from Carter that sleep had nearly been victorious.

"What else do you think has kept me on the bridge for forty-eight hours but the thought of you," I said, "and the neat way you let the stern hawser drop adrift, with the second tug alongside, last time we were in Hull? Get me a cup of tea and a sandwich, and shut your bloody mouth."

My words must have relieved him, for he grinned back at me and shot down the ladder like a Jack-in-the-Box. I held on to the bridge and stared ahead, sweeping the horizon for what seemed like the hundred thousandth time, and seeing always the same blank face of the sea, slate grey and still. There were low-banked clouds to the westward, whether mist or rain I could not tell, but they gathered slowly without wind and the glass held steady, while there was a certain smell about the air, warning of fog. I swallowed my cup of tea and made short work of a sandwich, and I was feeling in my pocket for my pipe and a box of matches when the thing happened for which, I suppose, I had consciously been training myself since the captain went sick some forty-eight hours before.

"Object to port. Three-quarters of a mile to a mile distant. Looks like a periscope."

The words came from the lookout on the fo'c's'le head, and so flashed back to the watch on deck. As I snatched my glasses I caught a glimpse of the faces of the men lining the ship's side, curiously uniform they were, half-eager, half-defiant.

Yes. There she was. No doubt now. A tiny grey line, like a needle, away there on our port bow, leaving a narrow wake behind her like a jagged ripple. Once again I was aware of Carter beside me, tense, expectant, and I noticed that his hands trembled slightly as he lifted the glasses in his turn. I gave the necessary alteration in our course and took up my glasses once more. Now the periscope was right ahead, and for a few minutes or so the thin line continued on its way as though indifferent to our manoeuvre: then, as I had feared, the submarine altered course, even as we had done, and the periscope bore down upon us, this time to starboard.

"She's seen us," said Carter.

"Yes," I said. He looked up at me, his brown eyes troubled like a spaniel puppy's. We altered course again and increased our speed, this time bringing our stern to the thin grey needle, so that for a moment it seemed as though the gap between us would be widened and she would pass away behind us, but, swift and relentless, she bore up again on our quarter, and little Carter began to swear, fluently and passionately, the futility of words a sop to his fear. I sympathised, seeing in a flash, as the proverbial drowning man is said to do, an episode in my own childhood when my father lectured me for lying; and even as I remembered this picture of a long-forgotten past I spoke down the mouth-tube to the engine room once more and ordered yet another alteration in our speed.

The watch below had now all hurriedly joined those on deck. They lined the side of the ship, as though hypnotised by the unwavering grey line that crept closer, ever closer.

"She's breaking surface," said Carter. "Watch that line of foam."

The periscope had come abeam of us and drawn ahead. It was now a little over a mile distant, on our port bow. Carter was right. She was breaking surface, even as he said. We could see the still water become troubled, and then slowly, inevitably, the squat conning tower appeared and the long lean form rose from the depths like a black slug, the water streaming from its decks.

"The bastards," whispered Carter to himself, "the filthy, stinking bastards."

The men clustered together below me on the deck watched the submarine with a strange indifference, like spectators at some show with which they had no concern. I saw one fellow point out some technical detail of the submarine to the man by his side, and then light a cigarette. His companion laughed and spat over the side of the ship into the water. I wondered how many of them could swim.

I gave the final order to the engine-room, then ordered all hands on deck to boat stations. My next order would depend on the commander of the submarine.

"They'll shell the boats," said Carter. "They won't let us get away, they'll shell the boats."

"Oh, for God's sake," I began, the pallor of his face begetting in me a furious senseless anger, when suddenly I caught sight of the wall of fog that was rolling down upon us from astern. I swung Carter round by the shoulders to meet it. "Look there," I said, "look there," and his jaw dropped and he grinned stupidly. Already the visibility around us was no more than a cable's length on either side, and the first drifting vapour stung us with its cold, sour smell. Above us the air was thick and clammy. In a moment our after-shrouds were lost to sight. I heard one fellow strike up the opening chorus of a comic song in a high falsetto voice, and he was immediately cursed to silence by his companion. Ahead of us lay the submarine, dark and immobile, the decks as yet unmanned and her long snout caught unexpectedly in a sudden shaft of light. Then the white fog that enveloped us crept forward and beyond, the sky descended, and our world was blotted out.

It wanted two minutes to midnight. I crouched low under cover of the bridge and flashed a torch on to my watch. No bell had been sounded since the submarine had first been sighted, some eight hours earlier. We waited. Darkness had travelled with the fog, and night had fallen early. There was silence everywhere, but for the creaking of the ship as she rolled in the swell and the thud of water slapping her sides as she lay over, first on one side, then the other. Still we waited. The cold was no longer so intense as it had been. There was a moist, clammy feeling in the air. The men talked in hushed whispers beneath the bridge. We went on waiting. Once I entered the cabin where the captain lay sick, and flashed my torch on to him. His face was flushed and puffy. His breathing was heavy and slow. He was sleeping fitfully, moaning now and again, and once he opened his eyes, but he did not recognise me. I went back to the bridge. The fog had lifted slightly, and I could see our forward-shrouds and the fo'c'sle head. I went down on to the deck and leant over the ship's side. The tide was running strongly to the south. It had turned three hours before, and for the fourth time that evening I began to calculate our drift. I was turning to the ladder to climb to the bridge once more when I heard footsteps running along the deck, and a man cannoned into me.

"Fog's lifting astern," he said breathlessly, "and there's something coming up on our starboard quarter."

I ran back along the deck with him. A group of men were clustered at the ship's side, talking eagerly. "It's a ship all right, sir," said one. "Looks like a Finnish barque. I can see her canvas."

I peered into the darkness with them. Yes, there she was, about a hundred yards distant, and bearing down upon us. A great three-masted vessel, with a cloud of canvas aloft. It was too late in the year for grain-ships. What the hell was she doing in these waters in wartime? Unless she was carrying timber. Had she seen us, though? That was the point. Here we were, without lights, skulking in the trough of the sea because of that damned submarine, and now risking almost certain collision with some old timber-ship.

If only I could be certain that the tide and the fog had put up a number of miles between us and the enemy. She was coming up fast, the old-timer, God knows where she found her wind—there was none on my left cheek that would blow out a candle. If she passed us at this rate there would be fifty yards to spare, no more, and with that hell-ship waiting yonder in the darkness somewhere the Finn would go straight to kingdom come.

"All right," I said, "she's seen us; she's bearing away." I could only make out her outline in the darkness as she travelled past abeam. A great high-sided vessel she was, in ballast probably, or there would never have been so much of her out of the water. I'd forgotten they had such bulky afterdecks. Her spars were not the clean things I remembered either; these were a mass of rigging, and the yards of extraordinary length, necessary, no doubt, for all that bunch of canvas.

"She's not going to pass us," said somebody, and I heard the blocks rattle and jump, and the rigging slat, as the great yards swung over. And was that faint high note, curious and immeasurably distant, the pipe of a boatswain's whistle? But the fog vapour was drifting down on us again, and the ship was hidden. We strained our eyes in the darkness, seeing nothing, and I was about to turn back to the bridge again when a thin call came to us across the water.

"Are you in distress?" came the hail. Whether her nationality was Finnish or not, at least her officer spoke good English, even if his phrasing was a little unusual. I was wary, though, and I did not answer. There was a pause, and then the voice travelled across to us once more. "What ship are you, and where are you bound?"

And then, before I could stop him, one of our fellows bellowed out: "There's an enemy submarine come to the surface about half-a-mile ahead of us." Someone smothered the idiot a minute too late and, for better or worse, our flag had been admitted.

We waited. None of us moved a finger. All was silent. Presently we heard a splash of oars and the low murmur of voices. They were sending a boat across to us from the barque. There was something furtive and strange about the whole business. I was suspicious. I did not like it. I felt for the hard butt of my revolver, and was reassured. The sound of oars drew nearer. A long, low boat like a West Country gig drew out of the shadows, manned by half-a-dozen men. There was a fellow with a lantern in the bows. Someone, an officer I presumed, stood up in the stern. It was too dark to see his face. The boat pulled up beneath us and the men rested on their oars.

"Captain's compliments, gentlemen, and do you desire an escort?" inquired the officer.

"What the hell!" began one of our men, but I cursed him to quiet. I leaned over the side, shading my eyes from the light of the boat's lantern.

"Who are you?" I said.

"Lieutenant Arthur Mildmay, at your service, sir," replied the voice.

There was nothing foreign in his intonation, I could swear to that, but again I was struck by his phraseology. No snottie in the Navy ever talked like this. The Admiralty might have bought up a Finnish barque, of course, and armed her, as Von Luckner did in the last war, but the idea seemed unlikely.

"Are you camouflaged?" I asked.

"I beg your pardon?" he replied in some surprise. Then his English was not so fluent as I thought. Once again I felt for my revolver. "You're not trying to make a fool of me by any chance, are you?" I said sarcastically.

"Not in the least," replied the voice. "I repeat, the captain sends his compliments, and as you gave him to understand we are in the immediate vicinity of the enemy, he desires me to offer you his protection. Our orders are to escort any merchant ships we find to a port of safety."

"And who issued those orders?" I said.

"His Majesty King George, of course," replied the voice.

It was then, I think, that I felt for the first time a curious chill of fear. I remember swallowing hard. My throat felt dry, and I could not answer at once. I looked hard at the men around me, and they wore, one and all, a silly, dumb, unbelieving expression.

"He says the King sent him," said the fellow beside me, and then his voice trailed away uncertainly, and he fell silent.

I heard Carter tap me on the shoulder. "Send them away," he whispered. "There's something wrong; it's a trap."

The man kneeling in the bows of the gig flashed his lantern in my face, blinding me. The young lieutenant stepped across the thwarts and took the lantern from him. "Why not come aboard and speak to the captain yourself, if you are in doubt?" he said.

Still I could not see his face, but he wore some sort of cloak round his shoulders, and the hand that held the lantern was long and slim. The light that dazzled me brought a pain across my eyes so severe that for a few moments I could neither speak nor think, and then, to my surprise, I heard myself answer: "Very well, make room for me, then, in your boat."

Carter laid his hand on my arm. "You're crazy," he said. "You can't leave the ship."

I shook him off, obstinate for no reason, determined on my venture. "You're in charge, Carter," I said. "I shan't be long away. Let me go, you damn fool."

I ordered the ladder over the side, and wondered, with a certain irritation, why the stupid fellows gaped at me as they obeyed. I had that funny reckless feeling which comes upon you when you're half-drunk, and I wondered if the reason for it was my lack of sleep for over forty-eight hours.

I landed with a thud in the gig and stumbled to the stern beside the officer. The men bent to their oars, and the boat began to creep across the water to the barque. It was bitter cold. The clammy

mugginess was gone. I turned up the collar of my coat and tried
to catch a closer glimpse of my companion, but it was black as
pitch in the boat and his features were completely hidden from
me.

I felt the seat under me with my hand. It was like ice, freezing
to the touch, and I plunged my hands deep in my pockets. The
cold seemed to penetrate my greatcoat and find my flesh. My
teeth chattered and I could not stop them. The chap in front of
me, bending his oar, was a great burly brute, with shoulders
like an ox. His sleeves were rolled up above his elbows, his arms
were bare. He was whistling softly between his teeth.

"You don't feel the cold, then?" I asked.

He did not answer, and I leant forward and looked into his
face. He stared at me as though I did not exist, and went on
whistling between his teeth. His eyes were deep set, sunken in his
head. His cheekbones were very prominent and high. He wore a
queer stovepipe of a hat, shiny and black.

"Look here," I said, tapping him on the knee, "I'm not here to
be fooled, I can tell you that."

And then the lieutenant, as he styled himself, stood up beside
me in the stern. "Ship ahoy," he called, his two hands to his
mouth, and, looking up, I saw we were already beneath the
barque, her great sides towering above us. A lantern appeared on
the bulwark by the ladder, and again my eyes were dazzled by
the sickly yellow light.

The lieutenant swung on to the ladder and I followed him,
hand over fist, breathing hard, for the bitter cold caught at me
and seemed to strike right down into my throat. I paused when I
reached the deck, with a stitch in my side like a kicking horse, and
in the queer half-light that came from the flickering lanterns I saw
that this was no Finnish barque with a load of timber, no grain-
ship in ballast, but a raider bristling with guns. Her decks were
cleared for action, and the men were there ready at their stations.
There was much activity and shouting, and a voice from for'ard
calling out orders in a thin, high voice. There seemed to be a haze
of smoke thick in the air, and a heavy sour stench, and with it all
the cold dank chill I could not explain.

"What is it?" I called. "What's the game?" No one answered.
Figures brushed past me, shouting and laughing at one another. A
lad of about thirteen ran by, with a short blue jacket and long

white trousers, while close beside me, crouching by his gun, was a great bearded fellow like my oarsman of the gig, with a striped stocking cap upon his head. Once again, above the hum and confusion, I heard the thin, shrill piping of the boatswain's whistle and, turning, I saw a crowd of jostling men running barefooted to the afterdeck, and I caught the gleam of steel in their hands.

"The captain will see you, if you come aft," said the lieutenant. I followed him, angry and bewildered. Carter was right, I had been fooled; and yet, as I stumbled in the wake of the lieutenant, I heard English voices shouting on the deck, and funny unfamiliar English oaths.

We pushed through the door of the afterdeck, and the musty rank smell became sourer and more intense. It was darker still. Blinking, I found myself at the entrance of a large cabin, lit only by flickering lantern light, and in the centre of the cabin was a long table, and a man was sitting there in a funny high-backed chair. Three or four other men stood behind him, but the lantern light shone on his face alone. He was very thin, very pale, and his hair was ashen grey. I saw by the patch he wore that he had lost the sight of one eye, but the other eye looked through me in the cold abstracted way of someone who would get his business done and has little time to spare.

"Your name, my man?" he said, tapping with his hand upon the table before him.

"William Blunt, sir," I said, and I found myself standing to attention with my cap in my hands, my throat as dry as a bone, and that same funny chill of fear in my heart.

"You report there is an enemy vessel close at hand, I understand?"

"Yes, sir," I said. "A submarine came to the surface about a mile distant from us, some hours ago. She had been following us for half-an-hour before she broke surface. Luckily the fog came down and hid us. That was at about half-past four in the afternoon. Since then we have not attempted to steam, but have drifted without lights."

He listened to me in silence. The figures behind him did not move. There was something sinister in their immobility and his, as though my words meant nothing to them, as though they did not believe me or did not understand.

"I shall be glad to offer you my assistance, Mr Blunt," he said at last. I stood awkwardly, still turning my cap in my hands. He did not mean to make game of me, I realized that, but what use was his ship to me?

"I don't quite see," I began, but he held up his hand. "The enemy will not attack you while you are under my protection," he said. "If you care to accept my escort, I shall be very pleased to give you safe conduct to England. The fog has lifted, and luckily the wind is with us."

I swallowed hard. I did not know what to say.

"We steam at eleven knots," I said awkwardly, and when he did not reply I stepped forward to his table, thinking he had not heard. "Supposing the blighter is still there?" I said. "He'll get the pair of us. She'll blow up like matchwood, this ship of yours. You stand even less chance than us."

The man seated by the table leant back in his chair. I saw him smile. "I've never run from a Frenchman yet," he said.

Once again I heard the boatswain's whistle, and the patter of bare feet overhead upon the deck. The lanterns swayed in a current of air from the swinging door. The cabin seemed very musty, very dark. I felt faint and queer, and something like a sob rose in my throat which I could not control.

"I'd like your escort," I stammered, and even as I spoke he rose in his chair and leant towards me. I saw the faded blue of his coat, and the ribbon across it. I saw his pale face very close, and the one blue eye. I saw him smile, and I felt the strength of the hand that held mine and saved me from falling.

They must have carried me to the boat and down the ladder, for when I opened my eyes again, with a queer dull ache at the back of my head, I was at the foot of my own gangway, and my own chaps were hauling me aboard. I could just hear the splash of oars as the gig pulled away back to the barque.

"Thank God you're back!" said Carter. "What the devil did they do to you? You're as white as chalk. Were they Finns or Boche?"

"Neither," I said curtly. "They're English, like ourselves. I saw the captain. I've accepted his escort home."

"Have you gone raving mad?" said Carter.

I did not answer, I went up to the bridge and gave orders for steaming. Yes, the fog was lifting, and above my head I could see the first pale glimmer of a star. I listened, well content, to the familiar noises of the ship as we got under way again. The throb of the screws, the thrash of the propeller. The relief was tremendous. No more silence, no more inactivity. The strain was broken and the men were themselves again, cheerful, cracking jokes at one another. The cold had vanished, and the curious dead fatigue that had been part of my mind and body for so long. The warmth was coming back to my hands and feet.

Slowly we began to draw ahead once more, ploughing our way in the swell, while to starboard of us, some hundred yards distant, came our escort, the white foam hissing from her bows, her cloud of canvas billowing to a wind that none of us could feel. I saw the helmsman beside me glance at her out of the tail of his eye, and when he thought I was not looking he wet his finger and held it in the air. Then his eye met mine, and fell again, and he whistled a song to show he did not care. I wondered if he thought me as mad as Carter did. Once I went in to see the captain. The steward was with him, and when I entered he switched on the lamp above the captain's berth.

"His fever's down," he said. "He's sleeping naturally at last. I don't think we're going to lose him, after all."

"No, I guess he'll be all right," I said.

I went back to the bridge, whistling the song I had heard from the sailor in the gig. It was a jaunty, lilting tune, familiar in a rum sort of way, but I could not put a name to it. The fog had cleared entirely, and the sky was ablaze with stars. We were steaming now at our full rate of knots, but still our escort kept abeam, and sometimes, if anything, she drew just a fraction ahead.

Whether the submarine was on the surface still, or whether she had dived, I neither knew nor cared, for I was full of the confidence which I had lacked before and which, after a while, seemed to possess the helmsman in his turn, so that he grinned at me, jerking his head at our escort, and said, "There don't seem to be no flies on Nancy, do there?" and fell, as I did, to whistling that nameless jaunty tune. Only Carter remained aloof. His fear had given way to sulky silence, and at last, sick of the sight of his moody face staring through the chartroom window, I ordered him below, and was aware of a new sense of freedom and relief when he had gone.

So the night wore on, and we, plunging and rolling in the wake of our escort, saw never a sight of periscope or lean grey hull again. At last the sky lightened to the eastward, and low down on the horizon appeared the streaky pallid dawn. Five bells struck, and away ahead of us, faint as a whisper, came the answering pipe of a boatswain's whistle. I think I was the only one that heard it. Then I heard the weak, tired voice of the captain calling me from his cabin. I went to him at once. He was propped up against his pillows, and I could tell from his face he was as weak as a rat, but his temperature was normal, even as the steward had said.

"Where are we, Blunt?" he said. "What's happened?"

"We'll be safely berthed before the people ashore have rung for breakfast," I said. "The coast's ahead of us now."

"What's the date, man?" he asked. I told him.

"We've made good time," he said. I agreed.

"I shan't forget what you've done, Blunt," he said. "I'll speak to the owners about you. You'll be getting promotion for this."

"Promotion my backside," I said. "It's not me that needs thanking, but our escort away on the starboard bow."

"Escort?" he said, staring at me. "What escort? Are we travelling with a bloody convoy?"

Then I told him the story, starting with the submarine, and the fog, and so on to the coming of the barque herself, and my own visit aboard her, not missing out an account of my own nerves and jumpiness, either. He listened to me, dazed and bewildered on his pillow.

"What's the name of your barque?" he said slowly, when I had finished.

I smote my hand on my knee. "It may be Old Harry for all I know; I never asked them," I said, and I began whistling the tune that the fellow had sung as he bent to his oars in the gig.

"I can't make it out," said the captain. "You know as well as I do there aren't any sailing ships left on the British register."

I shrugged my shoulders. Why the hell couldn't he accept the escort as naturally as the men and I had done?

"Get me a drink and stop whistling that confounded jig," said the captain. I laughed, and gave him his glass.

"What's wrong with it?" I said.

"It's *Lilliburlero*, centuries old. What makes you whistle that?"

I stared back at him, and I was not laughing any longer. "I don't know," I said, "I don't know."

He drank thirstily, watching me over the rim of his glass. "Where's your precious escort now?" he said.

"On the starboard bow," I repeated, and I went forward to the bridge again and gazed seaward, where I knew her to be.

The sun, like a great red globe, was topping the horizon, and the night clouds were scudding to the west. Far ahead lay the coast of England. But our escort had gone.

I turned to the fellow steering. "When did she go?" I asked.

"Beg pardon, sir?" he said.

"The sailing ship. What's happened to her?" I repeated.

The man looked puzzled, and cocked his eye at me curiously. "I've seen no sailing ship," he said. "There's a destroyer been abeam of us some time. She must have come up with us under cover of darkness. I've only noticed her since the sun rose."

I snatched up my glasses and looked to the west. The fellow was not dreaming. There was a destroyer with us, as he said. She plunged into the long seas, churning up the water and chucking it from her like a great white wall of foam. I watched her for a few minutes in silence, and then I lowered my glasses. The fellow steering gazed straight in front of him. Now daylight had come he seemed changed in a queer indefinable way. He no longer whistled jauntily. He was his usual stolid seaman self.

"We shall be docked by nine-thirty. We've made good time," I said.

"Yes, sir," he said.

Already I could see a black dot far ahead, and a wisp of smoke. The tugs were lying off for us. Carter was in my old place on the fo'c'sle head. The men were at their stations. I, on the captain's bridge, would bring his ship to port. He called me to him, five minutes before the tugs took us in tow, when the first gulls were wheeling overhead.

"Blunt," he said, "I've been thinking. That captain fellow you spoke to in the night, on board that sailing craft. You say he wore a black patch over one eye. Did he by any chance have an empty sleeve pinned to his breast as well?"

I did not answer. We looked at one another in silence. Then a shrill whistle warned me that the pilot's boat was alongside. Somewhere, faint and far, the echo sounded like a boatswain's pipe.

The Lover

It was ten-thirty on a wet morning in January. The telephone boxes were empty on the Piccadilly Circus subway, empty save for one at the right-hand corner by the entrance to Shaftesbury Avenue.

A woman stood there, her lips pressed close to the mouthpiece, the pennies clutched in her hand. She moved impatiently and flung a glance over her shoulder, and rattled the receiver.

"But I've repeated the number three times already. I tell you I want Gerrard 10550—Gerrard 10550." She bit her lip and tapped her foot nervously on the floor. "Of course there is somebody there. Will you please ring them again?"

He turned over in bed and reached for a cigarette. He yawned, stretched himself, and fumbled for his dressing-gown. Then he flung aside the bedclothes and strolled over towards his dressing-table.

He ran the comb through his hair and peered at the dark shadows beneath his eyes. His hand wandered towards the bottle of Bromo Seltzer. When the telephone rang he frowned, and, making no attempt to answer it, wandered into the bathroom. The steaming water foamed from the taps; his dressing-gown slipped to the floor.

He lay back in his bath, a large sponge pressed to his chest, and watched his pale limbs beneath the water, flabby and mushroom-coloured. The smoke from his cigarette curled towards the ceiling. Still the telephone continued to ring on the little table beside the bed.

"Yes, Gerrard 10550. Can you clear the line again? There must be some mistake."

The woman's voice was very weary now, flat, with an added note of supplication. She raised her eyes and read once more the rules for the public telephone service.

*

He wrapped himself in a large warm towel and lit another cigarette. The rain splashed against the window. What an infernal row the telephone was making! He padded with bare feet into the bedroom.

"Hullo, what is it? Speak up; I can't hear a word."

The woman tilted her hat on the back of her head; her bag fell from her hand and crashed on the floor, spilling her change.

"At last! Oh heavens, what a morning! Do you know I've been waiting here nearly half-an-hour? Were you asleep?"

"I suppose I was. What a time to ring, anyway! What d'you want?"

"What do you imagine? Don't you realise I have crept out of the house in this pouring, filthy rain, dressed anyhow, caring for nothing, husband and children waiting at home—only to speak to you. And then because I've wakened you up from sleep you snap at me in this beastly way . . . "

"Listen," he said quickly, "if you want to make a scene, go and make it to somebody else and not to me. I mean to say—life's too short . . . "

"Oh! you don't understand what I am going through because of you! I'm miserable, miserable. I haven't seen you for five days, and you don't apparently care."

"My dear, it's ridiculous to work yourself into such a state. You know perfectly well I'm terribly busy. I've not had a single moment."

"Where were you last night?"

"I worked until late, if you must know, and then went to bed."

"How do I know that you're speaking the truth?" Her voice was hard, suspicious. She could imagine the shrug of his shoulders.

"Oh, hell! If you're in that sort of mood, goodbye."

"No, no! I didn't mean it! Don't go! I am a fool." She clung to the receiver as though she was with him.

"Well, damn it! You make things difficult. What do you think I did?" There was a pause.

The woman fumbled for her handkerchief; she felt her mouth drag at the corner.

"What—what are you doing today?" she began desperately.

"Literally haven't a moment today," answered the voice

briskly. "I'm up to my eyes in work. I've got to finish a story for an American paper."

"Couldn't I—couldn't I come and sit with you?"

"No. I can't work with anyone around; you must know that by now."

"What about this evening, or a second for lunch today? I've kept it absolutely free, thinking we should be together. I'm going off my head these long, empty days—this endless rain, this never seeing you for one single moment."

"I'm afraid it's impossible."

How far the voice sounded, how distant! If only she could be with him now!

"If you only knew how much I love you!" she said.

He moved restlessly and glanced at the clock on the mantel-piece. "Listen. What's the use of all this? I've got to do some work."

"Then we aren't going to see each other at all today? I might just as well go away, go abroad, go right away from you. You don't care if you never see me again; you hate the sight of me; you . . ."

The senseless words poured from her mouth.

He closed his eyes wearily and yawned. "Why go into all that now? You know how I hate scenes—discussions. Why are you complaining? After all, we've had a good time; it's been good fun; we haven't hurt anybody. What's the point of all this tangle of nerves?"

"I'm sorry. I didn't mean to be tiresome, only it's never seeing you, never hearing you. Swear you aren't angry—promise you aren't angry. You see, I've been so unhappy. I'm loathsome, selfish—and you have your work. But if perhaps—loving you as I do—you . . ."

"Well, look, I'll ring some time later in the week. Goodbye."

She jabbed furiously at the receiver. "Wait—wait! What are you doing tomorrow at half-past three?"

But there was no reply.

She straightened her hat and wandered uncertainly away.

He lifted the receiver again and waited until the hotel exchange answered. "I say, if anyone rings again, say I'm working and can't be disturbed."

He stood before the window and watched the rain. What an

effort it was, this continual lying. If one told the truth for one moment there was the devil to pay. Women were a cope—a decided cope. Still, difficult to live without them—one way and another.

He glanced at the letter that had arrived with his breakfast.

" . . . And I'm so anxious for you to meet him, because he really is the most important publisher today. Naturally, a genius like you will find your feet anyway, but it does help to get in with the right people. Anyway, lunch at one as usual at the same place. No one will recognise me there. Isn't convention vile? I would like to shout about us from the house-tops, and we have to sneak to our meetings as though we were ashamed of the most marvellous thing in the world.

"Darling, when I think of last night I . . . "

Good lord! there were three—no, four pages of this. What a woman!

He placed the letter carefully in his note-case. One never knew . . . All the same, she must not shout things from the house-tops. Sort of damn silly thing a woman would do. Still, she did not yet telephone him every hour of the day like the last one. She was very lovely—and very useful.

He wound up the gramophone that she had given him. He supposed he would be able to use her car again today. Impossible to walk a step in this rain. She had suggested giving him a car of his own.

Yes, she really was rather wonderful. He lounged in the chair while the record whispered in his ear: "And that's why Chinks do it—Japs do it."

"Oh, but you look marvellous!" he told her. "Marvellous! Shall we take this little table in the corner?—and then there will be no chance of anyone seeing us. Isn't that a new hat? But, of course, I adore it; I adore everything you wear."

She felt for his hand under the table and sighed.

"You know, sweetheart, when you talk to me like this I feel like chucking up everything and just going away with you. After all, what does scandal matter? We love each other. I don't care about losing my money; we could live in a garret, in a tent."

He forced a laugh. "Aren't you wonderful!"

Surely she would never dream of losing her head to such an

appalling extent! Women had no sense of proportion at all.

"Just think, you and I starving in a garret," she went on dreamily.

"Yes, but it would be the action of a cad," he said quickly. "I should never forgive myself. How could I be so brutal as to drag you away from all your comforts and luxury! It would be criminal." He struck his fist upon the table. Rather dramatic, this. He almost believed it himself. "No," he continued gently, "we must try and content ourselves with things as they are. One day—oh, one day . . . "

He looked into her eyes. He could say this so many times, and it invariably rang true.

"You know," he said, as he glanced down the menu and chose mixed grill at 1s. 9d.—she might expect him to pay— "you know, I don't believe any two lovers have ever understood one another as we do. I can't explain; it's something that comes from the depths of one—a sympathy, a mutual form of self-expression . . . "

"I feel it too," she answered breathlessly. "I'm sure people have said this before, but they've never meant it."

"Never meant it," he agreed gravely.

"Whereas with us, everything is completely natural; neither of us has to pretend," she told him.

"That's what is really so marvellous," he said. "Have some iced water, darling; the wine here is terrible. No, what I was saying is that no two people have ever loved the same way as we have. It's so much more than just sex, you know. Sometimes I feel I could be completely happy if I didn't touch you, if . . . " He saw the cloud come over her face, so he changed his phrase with great presence of mind. "If only one didn't have a bodily existence it would be comparatively simple; you and I would never go through our agonies of separation. As it is I suffer tortures when we are apart."

"I know; that's why we ought to go away," she broke in.

"No, no—you must not. I will not muck up your life." He spoke firmly, and stuck his fork into his mixed grill. "After all, we are happy in our fashion, aren't we? We see each other every day; we love each other; and there is no danger. No one will find out."

"Yes, it's perfect—but somehow—and since just a few days ago

—I want to do so much for you. I want to slave for you; I want to be with you always!"

He had an uneasy pain in the pit of his stomach. Must she still harp on the subject? Was this affair going to be the same as the last one, all over again?

"God! If only I had some money of my own," he said gloomily. He stuck out his jaw and frowned.

"Money! What does money matter?" she said impatiently. "I hate money! I'd like to give it all away, and you and I to go away on some old dirty ship."

He smiled weakly without enthusiasm.

"One day soon we will," she said.

His spirits sank rapidly. "Of course there's no kick in being rich," he remarked carelessly, "but there's no doubt it does mean something in this callous world. One gets tired of striving and fighting, and sometimes one thinks, why write? Why go on? To what end? It's agony, being poor."

"But, darling, you know that you need never want for anything now you have me. All I have is yours, anything you care to ask for."

He wondered if she had forgotten about the car she had promised him.

"I can't go on taking things from you," he muttered. "You don't know how it hurts, how terrible it makes me feel."

"Now you're silly, you forget we are 'us', and not two other people. Loving each other as we do, these things become so simple and so natural. I mean, if our positions were reversed you'd do the same for me. Besides, I adore helping you."

"Do you? If only I wasn't so confoundedly proud."

"Oh! But you're a genius—no one expects you to understand money. You're above the sordid material things of life."

"Um—I suppose I am." He frowned and drummed with his fingers on the table.

Poor lamb, she thought, how artistic he is, how temperamental.

"You will let me help you, won't you?" she pleaded.

He shrugged his shoulders and pushed away his plate. "If you must," he said sullenly.

He decided that the time had come for a change of mood.

"Let's forget money, work, everything but that we are

together," he said smiling. "After all, there is nothing else in the world, is there?"

"Nothing," she agreed.

"If only these people were not here and we were quite alone like yesterday. D'you remember last night?"

"Remember—what do you think?"

Once more she felt for his hand under the table. "Tell me, that woman you told me about, do you ever see her now?"

"Good Lord, no; besides, there was nothing in it, nothing at all. She was never anything more than a friend. She's gone abroad, I believe, with her children." He bent to light a cigarette. Then he closed his eyes and waved aside the smoke. "I want to kiss you for twenty-four hours without stopping."

She revelled in the old, worn words. "Shall we go?" she murmured.

There was a slight awkwardness with the bill. She insisted on paying and he protested. Then, as he looked away, the distasteful moment passed.

To make up for this he hailed a taxi, aggressively rattling the change in his pocket. "But of course I'm going to see you home," he said reproachfully as she held out her hand. The taxi bumped amidst the traffic, and their kisses, though ardent, were unsuccessful.

"If we could be like this always," he lied.

She smiled in ecstasy and fumbled for her powder puff.

He leant back with his feet on the opposite seat and prodded the floor with his stick.

"By the way," he began, "about that car you promised. I've been thinking it over . . . "

The party had been dull, tedious, and after all the man had never turned up. Only his daughter, a young unsophisticated girl, red elbows in evening dress. Not attractive in profile, but too young, much too young. Still, he had made the most of his time. After all, her father was an important man. It never did to let opportunities like this occur merely to pass them by.

He spoke to her early in the evening, and towards the end he was still by her side. "Do you know, I swear I am not flattering you, but the moment I saw you I said to myself, 'There is someone who will understand.' It was something about your eyes, I think."

The girl gazed at him, flushing. "Oh! but nobody has ever talked to me like this before. You see, being my father's daughter they expect me to echo his remarks, and they don't seem to imagine for an instant that I have a mind of my own."

He laughed scornfully. "Absurd! After five minutes with you one realises—so much more than the ordinary thing. I admit I was disappointed not to meet your father this evening," he went on, "but you have made up for it—more than made up for it."

"Of course, you simply must meet him," she exclaimed. "I'm quite sure you would get on famously together."

"You dear thing, that's very sweet and adorable of you. But listen—tell me more about yourself."

She held on to her evening bag with hot, sticky fingers. "Oh! there's nothing, nothing."

"Nonsense. Anyway, I feel we are going to be friends, real friends." He held out his cigarette case and smiled. "You don't smoke? How refreshing. One gets so tired of these women with their eternal cigarettes."

The girl's eyes wandered towards the figure of her hostess, surrounded by a little group of men and women. "She's lovely. Do you know her well?"

"Oh! one comes across her from time to time," he answered carelessly. "But luxury has never appealed to me, I like simple things, books, being alone, or with somebody who understands."

"So do I." They smiled at each other.

"I can talk to you about anything," he said softly, "not only books, but things that matter. It's marvellous to be able to discuss sex with a girl of your age, and not feel self-conscious, not be aware. You're so lovely too, which makes it all the more rare and astounding. You've been told so hundreds of times."

"No—never—"

"But that is absolutely remarkable." He moved closer to her, pressing her knee.

Then his hostess moved from her group towards them. He rose to his feet and made an excuse to the girl.

"For the last hour I've been driven nearly mad," he whispered rapidly. "I haven't seen you for a moment alone. Always surrounded by that infernal crowd. And I've been sitting here, chatting to this little schoolgirl, watching you. Gosh—you look wonderful—wonderful."

"My poor darling—and I imagined you were enjoying yourself."

"As if I ever think of anything but you for a single moment," he said.

She put her finger on her lips. "Hush—someone may hear. Be reasonable and remember tomorrow."

He started, feigning astonishment. "Tomorrow? I don't think I can manage tomorrow."

"But you said at lunch . . . ?"

"Yes, I know, only when I got back I remembered there was an article that must be written."

"Naturally your work comes first. But in the evening?"

"Yes, of course, in the evening."

"Goodnight, my beloved."

"Goodnight."

He wandered down into the hall and saw the girl step into her car. He ran bareheaded down to the pavement. He arranged the rug carefully over her knees.

"I can't tell you what it's done to me—meeting you," he said. "I'm going back to work. I shall think of you."

"How—how wonderful," breathed the girl.

He glanced up at the house behind him, and then bent forward intimately and took her hand. "Listen—are you doing anything tomorrow between five and seven?"

It was midnight when he let himself into his room at the hotel. After all, he had not wasted his time. He flung off his clothes and slipped into his dressing-gown. Then he prepared the room for work. Five cushions on the sofa, and on a stool beside it the gramophone and a case full of records. A box of cigarettes, matches, whisky, and a soda siphon on the floor within reach.

He lay down upon the sofa, settled the cushions behind his head, started a record, and balanced a sheet of foolscap against his knee.

The room filled with smoke and the gramophone played, but the sheet of foolscap remained white and untouched.

Suddenly the telephone rang sharply, screamingly, in his ear.

With a grunt of annoyance he stretched out his hand. A woman's voice came across the wire, whispering, pleading.

"Is that Gerrard 10550? Is that you? Oh! forgive me, but you made me so miserable on the 'phone this morning. I'll try and be patient about not seeing you—but tell me, do you love me as much now as you did in September . . . ?"

The Closing Door

He felt as though he had become part of the room. It was too well known to him. The soft, heavy carpet and these deep leather chairs, even the folds of the curtains discreetly hiding the light of the day—perhaps the room was furnished as a reminder that life was already a dead thing, waving a hand in farewell behind the closed door. The furniture had been chosen with care, calculated to soothe the weary body and ease the jaded mind.

He lay back in one of the deep chairs and gazed steadily at the electric fire. He had only to shut his eyes and surely he would sleep soon, surely he would be carried away to some unconscious place of slumber, where there were no thoughts, no work, no love. The room was silent, too. The taxis hooting outside in Harley Street and the distant traffic rumbling in Marylebone Road; they belonged to another era and another time.

Hanging on the wall above the fireplace was a portrait in oils of a child in a rose-coloured frock with dark curls hanging down her back. Her hat was slung off the back of her head and attached to her neck by a piece of ribbon. Wherever he sat in the room he could not escape her eyes, nor the challenge in them, nor the bright unnatural smile.

He hated the picture and the staring child, yet he knew it was a friend, an old friend, and they were all bound together, he, the child, the deep chairs and the room, they could none of them escape. Automatically he stretched out his hand and found a copy of *Punch* within his reach. There was something of horror in the realisation that *Punch* had always been there, had never been anywhere else. *Punch* was there for eternity. The room knew this too, the room mocked him for his knowledge, but shared his horror with a strange sympathy. "We are here to make things easier for you," whispered the room, "easier for you. Lean back and relax, that's the main thing, to relax."

But the little girl in the picture swung backwards, forwards, backwards, forwards, her cheeks the same colour as her frock, and "Look at me," she shouted, "look at me."

He settled deeper in his chair, his head sunk in his shoulders, his fingers restlessly turning the pages of *Punch,* whose jokes had been stamped upon his mind so long.

Like clockwork, as his eyes fell upon the features of an ex-Prime Minister caricatured as a farmyard animal, the door opened and the butler stood upon the threshold of the room, his voice tone-less yet gentle, as though he knew: "Will you come this way, sir?"

He rose at once, and crossing the room he followed the butler along the carpeted passage to the other room at the end, with the mahogany door.

Now the butler was gone, now the door was closed behind him, now he stood in the high wide room lined with books, and lamps with green shades, a roll-top desk, and a sinister settee like an operating table in one corner of the room. He felt stronger in this room because, although dreading it, loathing it, he was at grips with life, he was no longer waiting in silence.

Besides, someone was here. He came forward from behind his roll-top desk and held out his hands.

"Good morning. What a wonderful day, eh? Spring at last, and I believe we've got it for good. Sit down, my dear boy, sit down. Did you walk here?"

"Yes."

"Then it's more than I did. You may not believe it, but I'm an incredibly lazy man when it comes to physical exercise. In fact, I'm a very bad example to my profession."

He smiled, he shook his head.

Surely if he smiled it meant that there was nothing wrong? Or was he false, concealing behind his mask of assurance the subtle flash of cruelty? It must have been this, because he continued the conversation blandly, smoothly, his hands behind his back, pacing before the bookcase; while the other waited in his chair, swallowing from time to time, his fingers twitching foolishly at his trouser knee, his face upturned.

"I saw that new play they're talking so much about last night," continued the voice. "Didn't think much of it. That fellow is getting old, you know. Time he gave up. Suppose he can't afford to, poor beggar. Has to go on working, like all of us." The other murmured in response, and with his fingers still tapping on his knee he watched the light from the green lamp play upon the ceiling. The room seemed larger than before, and he himself a cramped indefinite thing lost in space, subject to strange torture. Still the voice continued talking.

"Wouldn't mind a holiday myself. Somewhere with a blue sky and the sun. A complete change. That's what everyone needs, a complete change. Pity is that not many people can afford it."

Was it his imagination, or was the voice talking because it was afraid of coming to the point? Afraid of having to tell the truth?

In a second the great figure lost his power, he shrank percept-ibly, he dwindled to a sorry figure with human failings, powerless and absurd. He ceased from pacing before the bookcase, he stood still, his hands behind his back.

"Now you," he said abruptly, "could you afford to take a holiday?"

His victim summoned a smile, his mouth working.

"I don't know," he stammered, "I've never thought about it. Fact is—I've been trying to save lately. Various things crop up—you know how it is. A holiday is such a waste of time unless it's absolutely necessary."

"Yes. Well, it is necessary."

It had come. No more waiting, no more pretence. Hold on, can't you?

"Then—?" It was difficult to frame words into a sentence. It was as though he searched for phrases in a foreign language.

"You see, I want to make things easier for you," said the voice. And it was gentle now, too gentle. Kinder if it had been bitter and harsh. "Miracles very seldom happen, I know that, and so do you. But a different climate, a warm climate, has been known to work wonders. I can't promise anything definite, my dear fellow, I only wish to heaven I could. But there might be a chance."

Powerless, with all his books behind him, all his knowledge, and those bottles in the laboratory! The man in the chair pitied him, felt that something must be said.

"If you could explain—vaguely—" he began.

"You remember I warned you last week," said the voice, "I warned you so that you could prepare yourself, be at least ready. I did not want it to come as a shock. But then I was not sure, I had not completed the final tests. Now there is no doubt, no doubt whatever. Those last X-ray photographs have shown me what I feared."

The man blinked stupidly. He wanted things explained to him as though he were a child. "You called it some long name before," he said. "It's a sort of paralysis, isn't it? That's what you mean, isn't it?"

"Yes, that is the form it takes. Paralysis. Of course, technically, the—"

It did not matter, though, what worked technically. It did not matter what ate its way into his bones, sapped his vitality and his life. He wanted to know what was going to happen to him.

"How long does it take?" he asked.

"It all depends."

The voice was evasive, the figure shrugged its shoulders.

"In your particular case it's rather difficult to say. It might be three months—it might be three years. I can't be definite about that. You will, of course, follow a certain treatment I shall prescribe. As I said before, though, another climate."

Never mind the other climate. Who the hell cared about that?

"I want to know what happens. Does it come suddenly—in a night? Do I wake up and find I can't move? Is that it? Or does it creep slowly, so that one is never quite sure? Gradually an arm getting weak, feeble—and my back more bent— can't you tell me, can't you explain?"

"No, a sudden paralysis attacks some as the result of a stroke, of having lived too hard. You are very young, you don't drink and you live quietly. No, it will not come as a shock."

That was worse, though, surely that was worse. He wondered what was the use of following a treatment if he could not be cured. Perhaps it was the usual method of making things easier to bear. Like the deep chairs in the waiting-room below. Childishly he tried to remember what paralysed people did. Did they lie on their backs? Did they have some sort of employment? Perhaps they had to go to a Home. Surely most paralysed people were beggars, humped in a little chair with a cap outstretched before them. He cleared his throat nervously, watching the doctor's eyes.

"Shall I be—well, sort of absolutely helpless?" he asked awkwardly, sorry for him who had to answer such a question.

The voice did not come for a moment, obviously it was searching for the gentlest phrase.

"Not until the final stages," it said at last. "That would not be for some little time, needless to say. But before that—you will, of course, be considerably handicapped. That is to say, any physical exertion would be out of the question, sport, er—your work—well—my dear boy, I don't have to tell you how extremely painful it is for me to have to break all this to you. Every mortal thing that can be done for you I shall do, you know that. Sympathy is a wretched thing to offer—I—well."

He put his hand on the shoulder of the other, he shook it gently to show what he felt. And the other wished he would take his hand away, he wished that voice would not hold so much pity.

"Oh, it's all right!" he said, with a smile. "It's all right. Don't worry—I mean, I don't mind at all. It's quite all right." He got up from his chair, he pushed it away. "Thanks terribly for all you've done. You've been marvellous to me." He waited for a moment, wondering how to go. "I mustn't keep you," he said, "you must be frightfully busy."

Already the doctor was elbowing him to the door, glad for him to be gone, relieved that he had taken the news so well.

"Will you come along at twelve on Tuesday? Then we can draw up your regime and a definite routine. I don't want to worry you any more today."

"Right. I'll be here on Tuesday. Thanks awfully."

"Tuesday."

The door closed, the voice was silent. The great figure would relax now that he had gone. He would light a cigarette and glance at the clock. After all, it was not he who was going to be paralysed. The butler was standing in the hall, the hat and gloves ready.

"Thank you," said the man who had been sentenced, smiling to show that everything was all right, but avoiding the butler's eyes.

As he crossed the hall he saw through the open door of the waiting-room the picture of the little girl swinging backwards and forwards.

"I told you so," she shouted. "See you Tuesday."

The front door slammed behind him and he stood upon the steps, his hat at the back of his head, the clean cold air fanning his forehead, and he looked up at the sun. It seemed far away, shining brightly and indifferently in a glazed blue sky. And the houses were carved against this sky like frosted buildings on a Swiss post-card, hard and clear. As he walked, people bumped against him laughing, their cheeks glowing, glad that the day was fine. There was something breathless in the air, happy, intoxicating, like a whisper of spring, and because of it everyone must walk quickly, lightly, scarcely brushing the pavement with their feet. Even the horns of the taxis were high-pitched and tuneful, and the rumble of the traffic mellow, absurd. There were two girls sitting on the top of a bus without hats. The sun shone on their hair, the light wind blew it over their faces, and they rocked with laughter. A boy skipped along the pavement bowling a hoop, and a little white terrier ran at his heels yapping excitedly, worrying at his shoes.

It seemed almost that there was a shimmer of green on the trees in Regent's Park, as though at last the tight buds would unfold, relax, opening themselves. On a patch of grass gleamed the first crocus, yellow and fat. Somewhere a bird was singing. Then the man called a taxi, and, climbing into it, he crouched back in the corner, his hat over his eyes.

She kept him waiting as usual. Ten minutes, a quarter of an hour, he did not bother to count. As a rule he would be restless, impatient, bringing out his watch every few minutes, getting up, pacing about. Today, though, it did not matter. For the first time in his life he wished she would not come. He wanted there to be a telephone message saying she could not get off today after all, or even a wire to tell him she had gone away. Because he knew when he saw her he would not be able to be strong. If she were not there, he could forget about everything. He would not think, he would not mind. But when she came and was with him, and they were together—then it was different, then he was weak. He remembered the deep leather chairs in the doctor's waiting-room, and he wanted things to be made easier for him.

It would be easier if he did not have to see her. Perhaps there was a chance that she might say to him today: "I don't love you any more. It's over, our thing. Let's stop seeing each other."

For however much she would hurt him, it did not matter so long as he did not have to hurt her. She would be able to go off, careless, unmindful, nothing mattering any more, finding new people and new places, but she would not be hurt. He could keep his trouble to himself. She would not have to know. Then everything would be all right, then he would not care. Because, anyway, he had got to give up caring about things now.

Only, if she came today the same as she always was, then he was lost.

He did not know how he would tell her. She would not understand. She would look at him with eyes wide and bewildered. "But darling—but darling, it can't make any difference to us, it can't." And she would not see that every word was a fresh torture, thrusting itself deeper, twisting and turning like a knife.

He knew her so well. He knew how she would think for a moment, biting her lip, making a picture of it all to herself, not understanding, young, romantic, absurd.

"I'll look after you—I'll never leave you. We'll go away together." She would pull at his arm, eager and impatient. "It will be all right, won't it?"

She would not be able to grasp the truth of what had happened, of what was going to happen. She would paint it in false colours, because she was ignorant, because she was feminine, because she loved him.

She would shut her eyes and dream a dream of a sunny land, and mountains and a lake, and him lying in a deck-chair with her beside him, giving him grapes. She would lean over him, proud of her strength, loving his helplessness, seeing him as a child. He knew her so well, and that this would be her picture.

For him—he painted no portraits, he saw the truth, naked, sordid and uncoloured. There was nothing beautiful in it. He saw an existence that was a living death—dependent on charity, unable to give protection—or love—or life—and he knew.

He lifted his eyes and he could see that she was coming along the street, half-running, knowing she was late. She waved her hand, even from a distance he saw that she was laughing.

She carried a muff. Small, curly and ridiculous, like a woollen toy. She wore fur at her throat, too, and a fur cap on her head. The tip of her nose was pink from the cold, and her eyes were a robin's eyes, round and inquisitive. She looked like a little bird sniffing at the air. She ran up to him, breathless, squeezing his arm.

"Darling—if you knew," she began, "if you only knew. I've had such a time getting here. Endless shopping, and I had my hair done, and then I had to go to a fitting for a new dress. Have you been waiting *ages*?"

He shook his head, smiling.

"What?" she said, not waiting for his answer. "But the thing is *I'm* late because I would not take a taxi. I just insisted on walking. It's such a lovely, lovely day. It's made me feel—now, I wonder how I can explain it to you? It's made me feel as though life were something so beautiful that I want to hold it close, very close, and shut my eyes and breathe very deep like this. Oh—" She took a long breath, and bit her lip, and looked up to him and laughed. But he did not say anything. He just watched her, smiling stupidly. "Oh, you think I'm mad!" she said, shrugging her shoulders. "Come on, let's walk, I'm ravenous, I want my lunch. But don't you see what I mean about the day? Don't you feel it too? When I woke up this morning the sun was shining straight through the window on to my pillow, and there was a beam of light full of a million flecks of dust, gold dust. There was a smell coming from the trees in the square. Do you know the smell? Of tight buds, and very fresh green leaves, and sunlight on a white pavement?"

He guided her through the stream of traffic because she never looked where she was going. Still he did not say anything.

"I thought to myself that this was a very special day," she went on, "a day when everything seems good, and people are nice, and to be alive is the most *wonderful* thing in the world. Darling, people can't be unhappy on a day like this, can they? Just to see, and to breathe, and to feel, and to smell, that ought to be enough for everyone, don't you think?"

They waited on an island while a stream of traffic passed. High in the sky there was an aeroplane like a golden arrow poised against the sun. They lifted up their faces to look at it, and the far, faint drone came down to them as the hum of a bee in a distant garden. As he watched he thought of the beauty of moving things. That golden arrow of a plane, wending across the sky like a flash of light, the loveliness of ships, the freedom of horses on a stretch of moorland, and riding with the wind in your face. Walking with dogs over a deep ploughed field, or alone in a wet wood, the leaves dark and still, or running on the beach as a child, the sand beneath your feet.

He, too, closed his eyes and breathed deeply, and then he opened them again and smiled and said: "Yes, it's wonderful being alive, wonderful, isn't it?"

The traffic was blocked again and they passed across the street.

"Perhaps we're only feeling like this because it's the beginning of spring," she said, "perhaps it's only for a moment, perhaps it's not going to last. What do you think?"

"I don't know," he said.

"I'm holding it here," she said, "close to my heart, so that it can't escape. It's fluttering, like a bird that wants to fly away. Feel it, feel it."

She pulled his hand to her heart. "Do you hear him beating his wings?" she laughed. "D'you hear? He's so difficult to hold, but we won't let him go, we won't, will we?"

"No," he said.

She tugged at a bunch of violets at her waist.

"I didn't show you these," she told him. "I bought them just before I saw you. They were wet and glistening. I imagined I had picked them in a field with the dew still on the petals. Look, you've got to smell them." She held them up to him, and he buried his face in them deep.

"Doesn't it make you think of summer," she said, "and bathing, and the sea, and woods? Tell me you love them, tell me this beastly horrible winter is over and that spring has really come, never to go again?"

"They're lovely," he said, "lovely," and he went on walking and swinging her hand, and he was thinking, "Anyway we shall have had this, this moment, the street and the sun. They can't take this from us."

The buses rumbled past, red and shining, and open cars, and somebody laughing and somebody without a hat.

"What is it?" she said, smiling up at him. "Everyone is crazy mad today. They none of them care what happens at all. Isn't it glorious, isn't it fun?"

In spite of himself he felt drawn into her mood, into the mood of that moment and that day. Perhaps he had thought too seriously about it, perhaps after all it was not true. Maybe he had seen too darkly, and really it was better to paint pictures as she painted, dream visions as she dreamed, of blue sky and the sun.

Suddenly, as they came to the edge of the pavement, he saw

propped against the wall of a building the crumpled figure of a man, his legs twisted under him, his arms folded horribly, his limp fingers drooping from his white hand. He wore no hat and his glazed eyes, idiot's eyes, watched the passers-by without comprehension, a fixed dull stare.

At his feet his cap lay open, and into this one or two people had dropped a copper. By the side of the cap lay a pile of match-boxes. There was a little slate behind the boxes. On this was written in white chalk:

"I AM COMPLETELY PARALYSED."

His mouth moved and words came from it, inarticulate and strange. Perhaps he was asking people to buy matches. For a moment they both stood before him, blocked in a little crowd, and then she breathed quickly, smothering her nose in the violets, drawing away from him, whose face, without her having noticed, had grown so pale and stern, whose hands strayed mechanically to his pockets in search of sixpence.

"Oh, don't look at that *frightful* man," she said. "Turn away, quick. It will spoil our day if we think about him. Such people ought not be kept alive, it's absolutely criminal."

He peered into her face as they stood on the kerb. The colour had flamed into her cheeks, a dark curl had slipped from beneath her fur cap. Suddenly she looked like the child in the picture.

Then she smiled, she tugged at his arm, brushing her face against his shoulder.

"Darling, it's good to be alive, isn't it? We're going to be happy, you and I, happy—happy."

Indiscretion

I wonder how many people's lives are ruined by a moment's indiscretion? The wrong word at the wrong time—and then finish to all their dreams. They have to go on living with their tongues bitten a second too late. No use calling back the spoken word. What's said is said.

I know of three people who have been made to suffer because of a chance sentence flung into the air. One of them was myself; I lost my job through it. The other fellow lost his illusions. And the woman . . . well, I guess she did not have much left to lose, anyway. Maybe she lost her one chance of security. I have not seen either of them since. The curt, typewritten letter came from him a week later. I packed up then and came away from London, leaving the shreds of my career in the waste-paper basket. In less than three months I read in a weekly rag that he was claiming a divorce. The whole thing was so needless, too. A word from me—a word from her. And all through the sordid little street that runs between Shaftesbury Avenue and Leicester Square.

We stood at the door of the office, he and I. It was icy, it was December. I had a cold in the head, and I did not want to think about Christmas. He came out of his private office and gave me a genial clap on the shoulder.

"You're no advertisement for the time of the year," he said. "Come out and have a bite of lunch."

I thanked him. It is not every day, or every Christmas for that matter, that one's chief broadcasts his invitations. We went to his favourite restaurant in the Strand. I felt better once I had a plateful of beef before me, listening to his easy laugh, watching his familiarity with the waiter. He had the audacity to place a sprig of holly in his button-hole.

"Look here, Chief," I said. "What's the big idea? Are you going to play Santa Claus at a kids' party?"

He laughed loudly, a spot of gravy at the corner of his mouth.

"No," he said, "I am going to be married." I made the usual retort.

"I'm not joking," he went on. "I'm telling you the truth. They all know at the office. I told 'em before I left this morning. Kept it a secret up till now because I didn't want a scene. Aren't you going to congratulate me?"

I watched his smug, self-satisfied expression.

"Hell!" I said. "You don't know what I think about women."

He laughed again, his mood was ridiculous.

"This is different," he told me, "this is the real thing. I've found her at last—the only girl. You know, I'm fond of you, my dear fellow, I'm glad you came along to lunch."

I made some sort of noise of sympathy.

"It's all very sudden, of course," he said, "but I believe in that. I like everything cut and dried. None of your hanging about. We're going to Paris this evening, while this afternoon there will be a short ceremony at a registry office." He pulled out his watch. "In exactly an hour's time," he said, "I shall be a married man."

"Where's your bride?" I asked.

"Packing," he smiled foolishly. "I only decided on this trip yesterday evening. You'll have a tremendous amount of work at the office, I'm afraid, with the Christmas rush."

He leant forward, patronising, confidential. "I have a great deal of faith in you," he said. "I've watched you these few months. You're going to do big things. I don't mind saying . . . " he lowered his voice as though people listened and cared . . . "I don't mind saying that I shall depend on you in the future to work like blazes. You'd like a rise, wouldn't you? Might think of getting married yourself?"

I saw his friendly beam without emotion, and remembered with cynicism a proverb about "a little something makes the whole world kin". I thought of a word that would fit. "That's extremely good of you," I said, "but I shan't marry."

"You're a cynic," he said. "You've no illusions. You see all women in the same pattern. I'm twice your age and look at me—the happiest man alive."

"Perhaps I've been unlucky," I said. "Maybe I've struck the wrong type."

"Ah!" he said. "A bad picker. That's fatal. I flatter myself"—
he opened his mouth to admit a fork-load of food—"that I have
chosen well. You young men are so bitter about life," he went on,
"no romance."

Romance! The word conjured a vision in my mind of a dark
night, with the rain falling, and a small face turned to me, weeping, her hat pulled over her eyes. The last taxi driving away from
the Empire Cinema; men and women in evening dress, hurrying,
bent under umbrellas.

"Romance!" I said. "That's funny." Funnier still the way I
caught hold of one word. It would have been so easy to let it go.

I thought for a moment, turning it over in my head. "The last
time I heard that word," I said, "was from the lips of a girl. I'm
not likely to forget it in a hurry."

He glanced at me inquiringly, surprised at the note in my voice.

"More bitterness?" he suggested. "Why don't you tell me
about it? You're such a silent fellow you never give yourself
away."

"Oh! It's a dull story," I said, "scarcely worth listening to!
Besides, you're going to be married in an hour's time."

"Come on," he laughed, "out with it."

I shrugged my shoulders, yawning slightly, and reached for a
cigarette.

"I ran up against her in Wardour Street," I said. "Queer sort of
place for an adventure, if you come to think of it. Almost too
obvious, perhaps. It's scarcely a beat of mine, anyway. I'm a
retiring sort of chap, as you know, don't go out much. Hate
meeting people, and that kind of thing. Never go to theatres,
never go to parties. Can't afford it, for that matter. My life is
spent between the office and my rooms in Kensington. I read a lot,
hang around museums on Saturdays. Let's admit it, I'm damn
dull! But the point is I scarcely know the West End at all. So
Wardour Street was unfamiliar to me. About six months ago I
came back from the office feeling fed up with the world. You
know how one gets, nervy, irritable, thoroughly dissatisfied with
life in general.

"I hated my rooms suddenly, and I felt that any moment
my landlady would come in and tell me about her sister who
was 'expecting' again. It occurred to me out of the blue, then,

this idea to go to the West End. I took the tube to Leicester Square.

"There's an organ that throbs a sentimental tune, and when you're soaked with this and rubbing knees with your next-door neighbour, they fling a picture on the screen calculated to send you soft inside. That night I was in the right mood. They kept on giving close-ups of the blonde heroine; she seemed to be staring right at me. The usual theme, of course. Lovely innocent girl in love with handsome hero, and the dark blackguard stepping in and trying to ruin her. You're kept on tenterhooks as to whether he ruins her or whether he doesn't. He doesn't, of course, and she finishes with the handsome hero. But even then it leaves you unsatisfied. I sat through the show twice, and stumbled out of my seat at twelve o'clock still living in a land of make-believe.

"When I got outside it was raining. Through a haze I saw people crouching under umbrellas, whisking into taxis. I saw all this as a dream; in my mind I was watching the blonde heroine shut the opening of that tent in the desert. Turning up my collar I began to walk, my head low, hating the rain.

"So I found myself in Wardour Street. I remember glancing up at the name on the corner. A few minutes later somebody bumped into me. It was a girl. Thinly dressed, I noticed, not carrying an umbrella.

" 'I beg your pardon,' I said. She looked up at me, a little white face under a hat pulled low over her brow. Then to my horror she burst into tears. 'I'm most frightfully sorry,' I began. 'Have I hurt you? Is there anything I can do?' She made as if to brush past me, and put her hands to her eyes. 'It's nothing,' she said, choking over her words, 'it was stupid of me.' She looked to the right and left, standing on the edge of the pavement, apparently in some hesitation as to which way she should go. The rain was streaming down, and her little black coat was clinging to her. Half-consciously I remembered the blonde heroine of the picture I had just seen. The tears were still running on her cheeks. I saw her make some attempt to brush them away.

" 'Gosh! How pathetic,' I thought, 'how utterly rotten. And here am I dissatisfied with my life for no reason.' Acting on an impulse I touched her arm. 'Look here,' I said, 'I know it's no business of mine. I've no right to speak to you at all. But—is anything the matter? Can I help you? It's such a filthy night . . . ' She pulled out a wretched little end of handkerchief and began to blow her nose.

" 'I don't know what to do,' she said, 'I don't know what to do.' She was crying again. 'I've never been to London before,' she said, 'I've come up from Shropshire. I was to be married—and there's no address. There's nothing—he's left me. I don't know where to go. There's a man been following me,' she went on timidly, glancing over her shoulder, 'he tried to speak to me twice. He was horrid. I didn't understand . . . '

" 'Good heavens!' I thought, she was scarcely more than a child.

" 'You can't stand here,' I said. 'Don't you know of anywhere? Have you no friends? Isn't there a Home you could go to?' She shook her head, her mouth worked queerly at the corners. 'It's all right,' she said, 'don't bother.' It was no use, I couldn't let her go, not with that frightened gleam in her eyes, in the pouring rain.

" 'Listen,' I said. 'Will you trust me to look after you—just for the moment? Will you come and have something to eat? Then we will try to find a place for you to go.' She looked up at me for a moment, straight in my eyes, and then she nodded her head gravely. 'I think I can trust you,' she said. She said this in such a way—I don't know, it seemed to go straight to my heart. I felt very old and very wise, and she was such a child.

"She put her hand on my arm, still a little scared, a little doubting. I smiled at her. 'That's the way,' I said. We turned back again down Wardour Street. There was a crowd of people in Lyons. She clung tight to my arm, bewildered by them. She chose eggs and bacon and coffee. She ate as though she was starving.

" 'Is this your first meal today?' I asked. She flushed and bit her lips, ashamed.

" 'Yes,' she said. I could have cut my tongue out.

" 'Supposing you tell me,' I said, 'just what it is that has happened.'

"The food had pulled her together, she had lost some of her shyness; she was no longer tearful, hysterical.

" 'I was to be married,' she told me. 'Back in Shropshire he seemed to be so fond of me, so attentive to me and my mother. Why, he was quite a gentleman. We live on a little farm, mother and I, and my sister. It's quiet, you know, away from the big towns. I used to take the produce to Tonsbury on market days. That's where I met him. He was a traveller from a firm in London. He had a little car, too. Nothing poor or shabby about him—constantly with his hand in his pocket. He was always coming to Tonsbury for his firm, and then he would visit me. Then he started courting me—he was ever so handsome. It was all so proper, too. He asked my mother for her consent, and the date and everything was arranged.

" 'Last Sunday he was up at home as usual, laughing and teasing, saying how soon we would have a home of our own. He was to give up travelling, and get a settled job in the firm, and we were to live in London. He insisted on the wedding being in London, too, which was the one upsetting thing, as my mother and sister couldn't leave home.

" 'Yesterday was to have been my wedding day.' I saw she was ready to burst into tears again. I leant across the table and patted her hand.

" 'There, there,' I said stupidly.

" 'We motored up on Tuesday in his little car,' she went on, 'and we came to London yesterday. He had taken rooms at some hotel.' Her words trailed off; I saw she was looking at her plate.

" 'And the blackguard's left you,' I said gently.

" 'He said we were to be married,' she whispered. 'I thought it was all right.' The tears sprang in her eyes. 'He went this morning, early, before I was awake. The people at the hotel were cruel —I found out then that it was a bad place.' She fumbled for her handkerchief, but I gave her mine.

" 'I couldn't go back there, I daren't ask them for a thing,' she told me, 'and I've been looking for him all day, but I know it's no use now. How can I go home? What will they say? What will they think?' She buried her face in her hands. Poor little thing! She couldn't have been more than eighteen. I tried to keep my voice as gentle as possible.

" 'Have you any money?' I said.

" 'I've seven-and-eightpence,' she said. 'He told me I wouldn't need much.'

"I felt that this was the most impossible situation that had ever happened to anyone at any time. And there she sat looking at me, the tears in her eyes, waiting for me to suggest something.

"Suddenly I became very matter of fact. 'You had better make shift at my lodgings for tonight,' I said, 'and in the morning I'll buy you a ticket and pack you off to Shropshire.'

" 'Oh, I couldn't,' she said awkwardly, 'I don't know you.'

" 'Nonsense,' I said firmly. 'You will be perfectly safe with me.'

"We had some slight argument, of course, but finally I persuaded her.

"She was tired, too. I took her home in a taxi—she nearly fell asleep with her head on my shoulder. My landlady had gone to bed; nobody saw us come in. There was a bit of fire left in the grate. The girl crouched in front of it, spreading her hands to the feeble flame. I remember looking down on her and wondering how I should explain her presence to the landlady in the morning.

"It was then that she looked up at me from the fire, and she smiled without fear for the first time. 'If I wasn't so unhappy,' she said, 'this would be like a romance, wouldn't it?'

"Romance! Funny. It was you saying the word romance just now, chief, that brought this story back to me."

I squashed my cigarette in the ash-tray.

"Well, go on," he said. "It's not finished yet, is it?"

"That was the finish of the romance," I said.

"How d'you mean?" he said. "Did she go back to Shropshire?"

I laughed. "That girl never saw Shropshire in her life," I told him. "I woke next morning and she had gone, of course. She had my pocket-book with all my worldly goods."

He stared at me in amazement. "Good Lord." He whistled, blowing out his cheeks. "Then you mean to say she was deceiving you the whole time? There wasn't a word of truth in her story?"

"Not a word!"

"But didn't you put the police on her tracks? Didn't you do something, make some effort?"

I shook my head. "Even if they had found her, I doubt if I could have legitimately retrieved my worldly goods."

"You mean you suspected her story before you left Lyons?" he asked.

"No," I said. "I didn't suspect her once."

"I don't understand," he said. "If she was nothing but a common swindler, why not inform the police?"

I sighed wearily. "You see, chief, the point is I didn't walk the streets all night, nor did I sleep on the sitting-room sofa . . ."

For a few minutes we sat in silence. He looked thoughtful, he stroked his chin. "You were a damn fool, and that's all there is to it," he said. "Ever go back to Wardour Street?"

"No," I answered, "never before and never again. My only visit."

"Extraordinary how you were so easily mistaken," he said. "I can spot that type of girl a mile off. Of course, it's the sort of thing to make you steer clear of women, I agree. But they're not all like that, my dear fellow—not all." He smiled. "Sometimes you find a really genuine case of a young, unsophisticated girl, with no money, let down by some blackguard."

"For instance?" I inquired.

"As a matter of fact, I was thinking of my own girl," he confessed, "the girl who has consented to become my wife this afternoon. When I met her six weeks ago she was quite new to London. Left an orphan quite suddenly, poor kid, without a bean. Very good family, she's shown me letters and photos and things. She was making a wretched living as a typist in Birmingham, and her swine of an employer made love to her. She ran away, scared to death. Thank heaven I came along. Someone would have got hold of her. First time I met her she had twisted her ankle going down that filthy moving stairway on the Piccadilly tube. However, that's not the point." He broke off in the middle of his speech and called for the bill. "If you could see her," he began again. "She's the loveliest thing."

Into his eyes crept that blue suffused haze of the man who has not yet loved, but will have loved by midnight.

"I guess I'm the happiest man alive," he said, "she's far too good for me." The bill was paid, we rose and left the room.

"Tell you what," he said, "come and see us off by the four o'clock train at Victoria. The good old Christmas spirit, eh?"

And because I was idle, because I was bored, because there was no reason to do it at all, I consented.

"I'll be there," I said.

I remember taking the tube to Victoria, and, not finding a seat, swinging from side to side, clinging to a strap.

I remember standing in a queue to buy a platform ticket, and being jostled by a crowd of pushing, feverish people. I remember walking senselessly up and down a platform, peering into the windows of first-class carriages, yelled at by porters. I remember wondering why I had come at all. Then suddenly I saw him, his big, red, cheerful face, smiling at me from the closed window of a Pullman car. He put up his hand and waved, shouting something through the glass I could not hear. He turned and moved down the car, coming to the open door, at the entrance.

"Thought you'd given us the miss," he shouted. "Good boy— turned up after all."

He pulled the girl forward, laughing self-consciously, scarlet with pride and satisfaction.

"Here's the bride," he said. "I want you two to be great friends. Show yourself, my darling."

I stood motionless with my hat in my hand. "A happy Christmas to you," I said. She leant from the window staring at me.

Her husband gazed at us both with a quick, puzzled frown. "I say, have you two met before?" he said.

Then she laughed affectionately, and, putting her arms round his neck, she flung into the air her silly little gesture of bravado, mistress of the situation, but speaking without forethought, reckless, a shade too soon. The guard waved his little green flag.

"But, of course, I know your face," she said. "Didn't we run up against each other once in Wardour Street?"

Angels and Archangels

The Rev. James Hollaway, Vicar of St Swithin's, Upper Chesham Street, was seriously displeased.

For six weeks he had been obliged to leave his parish in the hands of his curate, and now he had returned to find the man had profited by his absence to preach sedition among the masses. In this incredibly short space of time the whole tone of the services had altered, the entire atmosphere of the church had changed. The inhabitants of Mayfair, the titled, the celebrated and the wealthy, who formed the congregation of St Swithin's, had assisted at Mass as usual during the beloved Vicar's absence, and had found in his place a raw young man of no attraction, of no breeding, whose very accent was not above reproach.

And this was not all. Instead of officiating humbly, with an attempt at self-effacement, as one who knows he can never step into the shoes of the absent, who is there merely on sufferance, someone to be passed with averted eyes and a patient sigh, this curate had the supreme audacity to imagine himself a person of importance, authorised to attack and to condemn. He stood in the pulpit, small and plain-featured, an unworthy representative of that Vicar whose voice had thrilled thousands, and whose eyes had drawn the most reserved of women to the portals of confession.

Then, before the members of the congregation had time to lose themselves in the deeper interests of their own thoughts, the unknown curate had looked down upon them with a gleam of contempt, while coldly and calmly he proceeded to tell them what he thought of them.

The venom of the snake has been described as painful, a torture that is impossible to endure, but the words of the little curate were more poisonous than the serpent's tooth, they seared deep into the souls of his listeners. The half-hour during which he preached was the most embarrassing and uncomfortable that has ever been passed under the roof of St Swithin's. If ever sentences screamed for censorship, it was felt that the sermon of the Rev. Patrick Dombey should have been erased entirely with a blue pencil. When he had finished there was not a cheek among the congregation that was not coloured a bright puce, there was not a throat that had not been cleared at least ten times. No man could look his neighbour in the face. There was not a boot that had not tapped nervously upon the floor, nor a glove that had not been torn in two places by the hot twisted hands of its wearer.

The Vicar was to be away six weeks, and this was only the first instalment. The band of the devout and faithful left St Swithin's that Sunday morning like a flock of agitated geese. Needless to say, they did not return the following week, and one and all they wrote a letter of protest to their beloved Vicar.

The Rev. James Hollaway received his mail on the verandah of the lovely house in Devon where he was recovering from his attack of influenza.

At first he did not consider the matter as desperate. He even read some of the letters aloud to his hostess, the fair and faithful Duchess of Attleborough.

"You see, my dear Norah," he began, with a beautiful little gesture of resignation, "I cannot even be away for one week—they clamour for me. What is one to do?"

She bent over his chair and fanned him gently with her handkerchief.

"You are so unselfish, Jim," she told him, "I believe you would be ready to go back at once, and kill yourself, rather than feel you are leaving things in the hands of an incompetent curate. But I forbid you—I insist on keeping you here as my prisoner. You are still so weak, you need looking after."

He shook his head with the movement she adored. "You are spoiling me," he said gently.

"You are a child in matters of health," she went on. "It would be suicide to return. Who is this Patrick Dombey, anyway?"

He shrugged his shoulders contemptuously. "Some Cambridge fellow recommended to me very highly. Been working in Whitechapel, I believe. I suppose he has ridiculous Socialistic ideas. I was obliged to make use of him, I had no one. You remember Smith, my previous curate? He is in a sanatorium, with his wife.

Tubercular, poor fellow, not much hope for him, I'm afraid."

He smiled peacefully as she handed him his morning peach.

"Then you will promise to stay here till you're really well, and leave St Swithin's to look after itself?" she pleaded.

He caught at her hand and pressed it.

" 'O woman, in our hours of ease . . . ' " he quoted softly.

The weeks passed, and disquieting rumours continued to reach the Vicar in Devon. It appeared that the curate, far from being dismayed at the revolt of the faithful flock, had even encouraged their absence, and had filled the church with followers of his own, men and women from the lowest ranks of life. These people came from the worst quarters of the East End, and, ill-fed, ill-clad and dirty, sprawled across the pews so lately occupied by the lovely ladies of society.

The glory of St Swithin's was no more. The famous church in Mayfair, whose incense-laden atmosphere had caused strong hunting peers to weep with emotion, and whose soulful organ and sweet-voiced choir-boys against a background of glittering candles had brought the gayest revue actress to her knees, was now given up to a sordid crowd of slum-dwellers from Whitechapel who did not even know the meaning of genuflexion.

The Vicar, despite his conscience and his clear call to duty, might yet have dismissed the matter temporarily from his mind, confident that on his return all would be well and that, anyway, the rumours were exaggerated, had it not been for a certain column in a prominent newspaper.

"During the absence of the Vicar," it ran, "the most extraordinary scenes have been witnessed at St Swithin's, Upper Chesham Street. The curate-in-charge, the Rev. Patrick Dombey, has, by a series of brilliant sermons, succeeded in attracting enormous crowds, so much so that last Sunday the queue at the church doors reached as far as Chesham Place.

"Many members of the congregation had walked from the worst slum districts in London to attend the service.

"The usual devotees and supporters, who are such warm admirers of the Vicar, did not attend, but their absence was hardly noticeable, for there was barely standing-room in the church; the pews and even the aisles were tightly packed. We predict a great future in store for this outspoken young clergyman, whose enthusiastic listeners are not confined to a single class, but to all sorts and conditions of men."

The eyes of the Vicar of St Swithin's narrowed as he read the article, and he flushed under his skin. He laid aside the newspaper, and drummed with his fingers on his knee. This cocksure young curate had gone a little too far. He was making an unnecessary bid for popularity, and he would have to be stopped at all costs.

The Rev. James Hollaway rose from his chair in search of his hostess, but first he threw his newspaper carelessly into a waste-paper basket.

"Norah," he said, "I've given in to you too long, but now the time has come for me to leave you. The man must return to his harness, the shepherd must return to his flock."

He smiled down at her, running his fingers through his thick grey hair.

"Tell me," he said, "about the train service from here. I feel that tomorrow evening at the latest . . ."

The Vicar leaned back in his chair, his eyes half-closed, his finger-tips pressed together. The curate stood before him on the hearth-rug.

"Before I venture a word of criticism upon your conduct," began the Vicar in smooth tones, "I want to remind you that when I left London six weeks ago I was a sick man. One of the best physicians in London had ordered me complete repose. It was only his insistence that persuaded me finally to accept the Duchess of Attleborough's offer of her house. I went, as you know, leaving all my responsibilities in your hands. You came to me at a moment's notice; there was no option but to accept your services. I need hardly say that I trusted you. What happens because of this trust? I am allowed no peace, no attempt to recover my health and strength. I am worried perpetually by my parishioners to return. And here you see me, barely convalescent as yet, obliged to take on my duties once more because you have proved yourself incompetent and worse."

He paused for breath, and the curate seized his opportunity to speak.

"I'm sorry you've been worried," he said. "I regret very much that anything I have said has disturbed your much-needed rest and quiet. At the same time, I am anxious to know how I have failed you. Incompetent, you say? May I know why?"

The Vicar cleared his throat. "Certainly," he answered. "I have it on good authority that because of your first sermon, and the objectionable tone you took, and the expressions you used, not one member of the congregation returned the following Sunday. They were shocked; more than this—they were horrified. Superfluous to add that I received countless letters of complaint."

"And yet," said the curate quietly, "St Swithin's has been overflowing every Sunday since."

The Vicar looked mildly amused. "My dear fellow, I'm afraid a certain amount of ridiculous publicity has gone to your head. Of course, as a journalistic 'stunt', your effort is to be congratulated. Finding the church empty, you were obliged to fill it as best you could. Merely the old parable of the blind and the halt, 'Go out into the highways and hedges,' and so on. I smiled to myself when I heard the news. 'This boy is absurdly young,' I said to the Duchess. 'He has possibly no idea of the harm he is doing. He fancies himself another Savonarola.' But I have the welfare of my church and my people at heart. I could not rest in Devon whilst St Swithin's was becoming a vaudeville turn and my curate a laughing-stock before the world."

The young priest turned white, and dug his nails into his hand. "I think you have got your facts a little wrong," he said. "I don't know what you mean by a journalistic stunt. I came to St Swithin's straight from one of the poorest parishes in the East End, where I have seen men and women die from hunger and cold, and stunted pale-faced boys and girls drink to prevent themselves from thinking. I tried not to make them hate me. Little by little they began to trust me, they realised I wasn't afraid. They asked me questions about Christ and I told them the truth. When I stood in the pulpit at St Swithin's for the first time, it seemed to me that the church was a good imitation of a faked one at Hollywood. The crowd who made up the congregation were excellent supers. The women were very beautiful and the men well-fed. I remembered the church in the slums that I had left. It was dark and unattractive. Nobody who came there ever washed. They were eminently suited to a religion that has for its God somebody born in a stable. Your congregation at St Swithin's belonged to another world. They were there for an hour's amusement before a heavy meal. I took tremendous pleasure in picturing Christ alive today, and being blackballed by all their clubs . . . "

The Vicar struck his fist on the desk. "This is nothing less than blasphemy," he said.

"Oh, you can call it what you like,' answered the curate. "That's what your parishioners felt when I told them the truth about themselves. As you said just now, they didn't come back. Their morning had been made too uncomfortable for them to face another. The following Sunday I expected to celebrate Mass to an empty church, instead of which, it was filled with men and women from the slums. They had no wish to be flattered or amused. They came because they wanted to be told about God. I see now that I must have made a great mistake; it was foolish of me to speak in that way if I have any ambition to rise in the Church. You were quite right when you called me incompetent. Is there anything more you wish to say to me?"

The Vicar rose to his full majestic height, and pointed with one finger to the door.

"You had better leave the room before I begin to lose my temper," he said softly. "And I want you to understand one thing. Those ideas of yours are dangerous. One day you will regret them. And I am a very powerful man. You can go now. That's all."

The curate turned and went from the room without a word.

When he had gone, the Vicar reached to the cupboard on the wall. He poured himself out a whisky and soda, and lit a cigarette. Then he sat down, his chin in his hand, and began to think.

It was a quarter past eleven in the evening. The Vicar of St Swithin's, Upper Chesham Street, was returning in a taxi from the first night at the Frivolity Theatre. The piece, a light comedy, had been something of a flop. He had made no attempt to go round and see Nancy afterwards. He hated to be tactless.

As the taxi drew into Lower Mallop Street, he remembered that Number Nineteen was the address of his curate, Patrick Dombey. With a half interest he glanced up at the building, and was aware of a light in the front room, partially blurred by a thin curtain. He supposed the fellow read Socialistic tracts late into the night. As the taxi drew past, he glanced once more at the covered window. This time a shadow was reflected on the blind, the shadow of a woman. For a moment the Vicar remained motionless. Then he tapped on the glass to the driver. Three minutes later he was ringing the bell of Number Nineteen, a strange smile of triumph upon his lips.

The door was opened by the curate himself. He seemed a little shaken at the sight of the Vicar.

"Is anything wrong at St Swithin's?" he asked.

The Rev. James Hollaway brushed past him into the passage.

"No," he said. "The fact is, I was returning from the theatre, and it struck me as I passed here that perhaps I had been a little hasty with you this morning. I am not a man to bear malice. Could we have a chat in your room?"

The curate hesitated a moment before replying. "I have somebody there," he said quietly.

"Oh! Pity. Couldn't you send them away?"

"Not very well."

Before he could be prevented, the Vicar had glanced through the crack in the door. He saw a woman standing in the corner of the room. She appeared to have been crying. The tears had blotched her make-up. She was cheaply over-dressed. There could be no doubt as to her profession.

The Vicar raised his eyebrows and closed the door gently. "Rather a late visitor," he murmured. Then, as the curate made no reply, he laid his hand upon his shoulder. "I think you owe me some explanation for this, Dombey," he said.

The young priest looked into his face.

"I have told her she can stay here tonight," he said steadily. "She's frightened; she doesn't know where to go. She is a thief, you see. She isn't much good at it, either. She tried to steal a watch from an old man in Piccadilly. She was nearly caught. She took hold of my arm in a desperate attempt to save herself. She was shaking all over with terror, and it was impossible for me to betray her. I pretended she was with me—I brought her back here. I don't believe she'll ever steal anything again. If I'd given her up they would have sent her to prison; she'd have become a hardened criminal in time. No—I'm not going to send her away."

The Vicar whistled softly to himself. "My dear fellow," he began, "don't bother to tell me all this. After all, I've been young myself once. I know what temptation is. We are human, are we not? But you cannot possibly keep her here any longer. Somebody may have seen her."

The curate flushed all over his face. "You deliberately misunderstand," he said. "You know I've not brought her here for myself. She's like a frightened little cat that has lost its sense. Haven't you any idea of common humanity?"

The Vicar's face hardened, his eyes narrowed. "If you persist in lying, I see myself forced by my conscience and my duty towards God to treat this matter seriously. You have committed a grave offence, Dombey. Have you anything further to say?"

The curate shrugged his shoulders. "You will be able to make out an excellent case against me, won't you? You realise that my conscience won't allow me to betray this girl as a thief. Therefore I stand convicted. Goodbye to ambition and all that. That's what you mean, I suppose? Rather an ugly story—the young curate and the fallen woman. No, I've got nothing more to say."

The Vicar turned, and opened the front door of the lodging-house. "I shall do what I believe to be right," he said slowly. "You are suspended from further duty, Dombey. This is a matter for the Bishop alone."

Ten minutes later he was back in the library of his own house. He lay in his chair, his eyes closed, a faint smile playing upon his lips.

Suddenly the telephone rang at his elbow.

"Hullo," he said. "Yes, Nancy, my dear, speaking . . . Oh! don't be absurd. You were wonderful, quite wonderful . . . I didn't come round because I feared a crowd . . . Yes, the play needs tightening up, of course . . . Depressed, you say? What utter nonsense! . . . Unhappy? . . . My dearest child, is there anything I can do? . . . What, now? Isn't it rather late?" He glanced at his clock. The hands pointed to five minutes to midnight. "Nancy, you naughty little girl, you know you can get anything you want . . . Stop crying at once, dear child . . . Yes, I'll come round right away . . ."

St Swithin's was itself again once more. Gone were the slum crowds who had debased its holy atmosphere for six weeks. Gone were the rough-tongued men and women, the ill-fed, unwashed children. Gone was the plain-featured curate who had brought shame upon the House of God. Once more the waxen lilies breathed a pure air, once more the deep-toned organ throbbed its message to the rafters. The pews were filled with the devout, with the very faithful. The sweet-voiced choir-boys swayed in time to the music. The candles glittered, and the incense floated upon the air.

When the Vicar leaned from his pulpit it seemed as though he waited for applause. The shepherd had returned to the flock. He spread out his arms, he threw back his magnificent head, and spoke to them in the soft tones they loved.

"For there has been a wolf amongst you," he told them: "there has been a wolf amongst the lambs."

Tears came into the eyes of his listeners. They remembered the hard-voiced curate and his bitter sayings, they remembered his evil-smelling followers from the slums.

"My house has been called a house of prayer," cried the Vicar, "but he has made it a den of thieves."

How appropriate were the words he used. How beautiful were the sentiments he expressed. Later, as he chanted before the High Altar, it seemed to the Vicar that his very voice had purified the air. His beloved congregation were with him again. There was a duchess in the front pew, an earl and a couple of actresses immediately behind.

The slum-dwellers had left no trace of their lamentable presence. St Swithin's and her worshippers remained as symbols of eternity.

"Therefore, with Angels and Archangels, and all the glorious company of Heaven, we praise and magnify Thy Holy Name..."

Split Second

Mrs Ellis was methodical and tidy. Unanswered letters, unpaid bills, the litter and rummage of a slovenly writing-desk were things that she abhorred. Today, more than usual, she was in what her late husband used to call her "clearing" moods. She had wakened to this mood; it remained with her throughout breakfast and lasted the whole morning. Besides, it was the first of the month, and as she ripped off the pages of her daily calendar and saw the bright clean 1 staring at her, it seemed to symbolise a new start to her day.

The hours ahead of her must somehow seem untarnished like the date; she must let nothing slide.

First she checked the linen. The smooth white sheets lying in rows upon their shelves, pillow slips beside, and one set still in its pristine newness from the shop, tied with blue ribbon, waiting for a guest who never came.

Next, the store cupboard. The stock of homemade jam pleased her, the labels, and the date in her own handwriting. There were also bottled fruit, and tomatoes, and chutney to her own recipe. She was sparing of these, keeping them in reserve for the holidays when Susan should be home, and even then, when she brought them down and put them proudly on the table, the luxury of the treat was spoilt by a little stab of disappointment; it would mean a gap upon the store cupboard shelf.

When she had closed the store cupboard and hidden the key (she could never be quite certain of Grace, her cook), Mrs Ellis went into the drawing-room and settled herself at her desk. She was determined to be ruthless. The pigeonholes were searched, and those old envelopes that she had kept because they were not torn and could be used again (to tradesmen, not to friends) were thrown away. She would buy fresh buff envelopes of a cheap quality instead.

Here were some receipts of two years back. Unnecessary to

keep them now. Those of a year ago were filed, and tied with tape. A little drawer, stiff to open, she found crammed with old counterfoils from her chequebook. This was wasting space. Instead, she wrote in her clear handwriting, "Letters to Keep". In the future, the drawer would be used for this purpose.

She permitted herself the luxury of filling her blotter with new sheets of paper. The pen tray was dusted. A new pencil sharpened. And, steeling her heart, she threw the stub of the little old one, with worn rubber at the base, into the waste-paper basket.

She straightened the magazines on the side table, pulled the books to the front on the shelf beside the fire—Grace had an infuriating habit of pushing them all to the back—and filled the flower vases with clean water. Then with a bare ten minutes before Grace popped her head round the door and said, "Lunch is in," Mrs Ellis sat down, a little breathless, before the fire, and smiled in satisfaction. Her morning had been very full indeed. Happy, well spent.

She looked about her drawing-room (Grace insisted on calling it the lounge and Mrs Ellis was forever correcting her) and thought how comfortable it was, and bright, and how wise they had been not to move when poor Wilfred suggested it a few months before he died. They had so nearly taken that house in the country, because of his health, and his fad that vegetables should be picked fresh every morning, and then luckily—well, hardly luckily, it was most terribly sad and a fearful shock to her—but before they had signed the lease Wilfred had a heart attack and died. Mrs Ellis was able to stay on in the home she knew and loved, and where she had first come as a bride ten years before.

People were inclined to say the locality was going downhill, that it had become worse than suburban. Nonsense. The blocks of flats that were going up at the top of the road could not be seen from her windows, and the houses, solid like her own, standing in a little circle of front gardens, were quite unspoilt.

Besides, she liked the life. Her mornings, shopping in the town, her basket over her arm. The tradesmen knew her, treated her well. Morning coffee at eleven, at the Cosy Café opposite the bookshop, was a small pleasure she allowed herself on cold mornings—she could not get Grace to make good coffee—and in the summer the Cosy Café sold ice cream. Childishly, she would hurry back with this in a paper bag and eat it for lunch; it saved thinking of a sweet.

She believed in a brisk walk in the afternoons, and the heath was so close to hand it was just as good as the country; and in the evenings she read, or sewed, or wrote to Susan.

Life, if she thought deeply about it, which she did not, because to think deeply made her uncomfortable, was really built round Susan. Susan was nine years old, and her only child.

Because of Wilfred's ill-health and, it must be confessed, his irritability, Susan had been sent to boarding school at an early age. Mrs Ellis had passed many sleepless night before making this decision, but in the end she knew it would be for Susan's good. The child was healthy and high-spirited, and it was impossible to keep her quiet and subdued in one room with Wilfred fractious in another. It meant sending her down to the kitchen with Grace, and that, Mrs Ellis decided, did not do.

Reluctantly, the school was chosen, some thirty miles away. It was easily reached within an hour-and-a-half by Green Line bus, the children seemed happy and well cared for, the principal was grey-haired and sympathetic, and as the prospectus described it, the place was a "home from home".

Mrs Ellis left Susan, on the opening day of her first term, in agony of mind, but constant telephone calls between herself and the headmistress during the first week reassured her that Susan had settled placidly to her new existence.

When her husband died, Mrs Ellis thought Susan would want to return home and go to a day school, but to her surprise and disappointment the suggestion was received with dismay, and even tears.

"But I love my school,' said the child. "We have such fun, and I have lots of friends."

"You would make other friends at a day school," said her mother, "and think, we would be together in the evenings."

"Yes," answered Susan doubtfully, "but what would we do?"

Mrs Ellis was hurt, but she did not permit Susan to see this. "Perhaps you are right," she said. "You are contented and happy where you are. Anyway, we shall always have the holidays."

The holidays were like brightly coloured beads on a frame, and stood out with significance in Mrs Ellis's engagement diary, throwing the weeks between into obscurity.

How leaden was February, in spite of its twenty-eight days; how blue and interminable was March, for all that morning coffee at the Cosy Café, the choosing of library books, the visits with friends to the local cinema, or sometimes, more dashing, a matinée "in town".

Then April came, and danced its flowery way across the calendar. Easter, and daffodils, and Susan with glowing cheeks whipped by a spring wind, hugging her once again; honey for tea, scones baked by Grace ("You've been and grown again"), those afternoon walks across the heath, sunny and gay because of the figure running on ahead. May was quiet, and June pleasant because of wide-flung windows, and the snapdragons in the front garden; June was leisurely. Besides, there was the school play on Parents' Day, and Susan, with bright eyes, surely much the best of the pixies, and although she did not speak her actions were so good.

July dragged until the twenty-fourth, and then the weeks spun themselves into a sequence of glory until the last week in September. Susan at the sea . . . Susan on a farm . . . Susan on Dartmoor . . . Susan just at home, licking an ice cream, leaning out of a window.

"She swims quite well for her age," thus, casually, to a neighbour on the beach. "She insists on going in, even when it's cold."

"I don't mind saying," this to Grace, "that I hated going through that field of bullocks, but Susan didn't mind a scrap. She has a way with animals."

Bare scratched legs in sandals, summer frocks outgrown, a sun-hat, faded, lying on the floor. October did not bear thinking about . . . But, after all, there was always plenty to do in the house. Forget November, and the rain, and the fogs that turned white upon the heath. Draw the curtains, poke the fire, settle to something, the *Weekly Home Companion*, Fashions for Young Folk. Not that pink, but the green with the smocked top and a wide sash would be just the thing for Susan at parties in the Christmas holidays. December . . . Christmas . . .

This was the best, this was the height of home enjoyment. As soon as Mrs Ellis saw the first small trees standing outside the florist's and those orange boxes of dates in the grocer's window, her heart would give a little leap of excitement. Susan would be home in three weeks now. Then the laughter and the chatter. The nods between herself and Grace. The smiles of mystery. The furtiveness of wrappings.

All over in one day like the bursting of a swollen balloon; paper ribbon, cracker novelties, even presents, chosen with care, thrown aside. But no matter. It was worth it. Mrs Ellis, looking down upon a sleeping Susan tucked in with a doll in her arms, turned down the light and crept off to her own bed, sapped, exhausted. The egg cosy, Susan's handiwork at school, hastily stitched, stood on her bedside table. Mrs Ellis never ate boiled eggs, but, as she said to Grace, there is such a gleam in the hen's eye; it's very cleverly done.

The fever, the pace of the New Year. The Circus, the panto-mime. Mrs Ellis watched Susan, never the performers. "You should have seen her laugh when the seal blew the trumpet; I've never known a child with such a gift for enjoyment."

And how she stood out at parties, in the green frock, with her fair hair and blue eyes. Other children were so stumpy. Ill-made little bodies or big shapeless mouths. "She said, 'Thank you for a lovely time,' when we left, which was more than most of them did. And she won at musical chairs."

There were bad moments too, of course. The restless night, the high spot of colour, the sore throat, the temperature of 102. Shaking hands on the telephone. The doctor's reassuring voice. And his footsteps on the stairs, a steady, reliable man. "We had better take a swab, in case." A swab? That meant diphtheria, scarlet fever? A little figure being carried down in blankets, an ambulance, hospital . . . ?

Thank God, it proved to be a relaxed throat. Lots of them about. Too many parties, keep her quiet for a few days. Yes, Doctor, yes. The relief from dread anxiety, and on and on with-out a stop, the reading to Susan from her *Playbook Annual*, story after story, terrible and trite, "and so Nicky Nod *did* lose his treasure after all, which just served him right, didn't it, children?"

"All things pass," thought Mrs Ellis, "Pleasure and pain, and happiness and suffering, and I suppose my friends would say my life is a dull one, rather uneventful, but I am grateful for it, and contented, and although sometimes I feel I did not do my utmost for poor Wilfred—his was a difficult nature, luckily Susan has not inherited it—at least I believe I have succeeded in making a happy home for Susan." She looked about her, that first day of the month, and noticed with affection and appreciation those bits and pieces of furniture, the pictures on the walls, the ornaments on the mantelpiece, all the things she had gathered about her during ten years of marriage, which meant herself, her home.

The sofa and two chairs, part of an original suite, were worn but comfortable. The pouf by the fire, she had covered it herself. The fire irons, not quite so polished as they should be, she must speak to Grace. The rather melancholy portrait of Wilfred in that dark corner behind the bookshelf, at least he looked distinguished. And was, thought Mrs Ellis to herself, hastily. The flower picture showed more to advantage over the mantelpiece; the green foliage harmonised so well with the green coat of the Staffordshire figure who stood with his lady beside the clock.

"I could do with new covers," thought Mrs Ellis, "and curtains too, but they must wait. Susan had grown so enormously the last few months. Her clothes are more important. The child is tall for her age."

Grace looked round the door. "Lunch is in," she said.

"If she would open the door outright," thought Mrs Ellis, "and come right into the room, I have mentioned it a hundred times. It's the sudden thrust of the head that is so disconcerting, and if I have anyone to lunch . . ."

She sat down to guinea-fowl and apple charlotte, and wondered if they were remembering to give Susan extra milk at school this term, and the Minidex tonic; the matron was inclined to be forgetful.

Suddenly, for no reason, she laid her spoon down on the plate, swept with a wave of such intense melancholy as to be almost unbearable. Her heart was heavy. Her throat tightened. She could not continue her lunch.

"Something is wrong with Susan," she thought. "This is a warning that she wants me."

She rang for coffee and went into the drawing-room. She crossed to the window and stood looking at the back of the house opposite. From an open window sagged an ugly red curtain, and a lavatory brush hung from a nail.

"The district *is* losing class," thought Mrs Ellis. "I shall have lodging-houses for neighbours soon."

She drank her coffee, but the feeling of uneasiness, of apprehension, did not leave her. At last she went to the telephone and rang up the school.

The secretary answered. Surprised, and a little impatient, surely. Susan was perfectly all right. She had just eaten a good lunch. No, she had no sign of a cold. No one was ill in the school. Did Mrs Ellis want to speak to Susan? The child was outside with the others, playing, but could be called in if necessary.

"No," said Mrs Ellis, "it was just a foolish notion on my part that Susan might not be well. I am so sorry to have bothered you."

She hung up the receiver, and went to her bedroom to put on her outdoor clothes. A good walk would do her good. She gazed in satisfaction upon the photograph of Susan on the dressing-table. The photographer had caught the expression in her eyes to perfection. Such a lovely light on the hair too.

Mrs Ellis hesitated. Was it really a walk she needed? Or was this vague feeling of distress a sign that she was overtired, that she had better rest? She looked with inclination at the downy quilt upon her bed. Her hot-water bottle, hanging by the washstand, would take only a moment to fill. She could loosen her girdle, throw off her shoes, and lie down for an hour on the bed, warm with the bottle under the downy quilt. No. She decided to be firm with herself. She went to the wardrobe, and got out her camel coat, wound a scarf round her head, pulled on a pair of gauntlet gloves and walked downstairs.

She went into the drawing-room, made up the fire and put the guard in front of it. Grace was apt to be forgetful of the fire. She opened the window at the top so that the room should not strike stuffy when she came back. She folded the daily papers ready to read when she returned, and replaced the marker in her library book.

"I'm going out for a little while. I shan't be long," she called down to the basement to Grace.

"All right, ma'am," came the answer.

Mrs Ellis caught the whiff of cigarette, and frowned. Grace could do as she liked in the basement, but there was something not quite right about a maidservant smoking.

She shut the front door behind her, went down the steps and into the road, and turned left towards the heath. It was a dull, grey day. Mild for the time of year, almost to oppression. Later, there would be fog, perhaps, rolling up from London the way it did, in a great wall, stifling the clean air.

Mrs Ellis made her "short round", as she always called it. Eastward, to the Viaduct ponds, and then back, circling, to the Vale of Health.

It was not an inviting afternoon, and she did not enjoy her walk. She kept wishing she was home again, in bed with a hot-water bottle, or sitting in the drawing-room beside the fire, soon to shut out the muggy, murky sky, and draw the curtains. She walked swiftly past nurses pushing prams, two or three of them in groups chatting together, their charges running ahead. Dogs barked beside the ponds. Solitary men in macintoshes stared into vacancy. An old woman on a seat threw crumbs to chirping sparrows. The sky took on a darker, olive tone. Mrs Ellis quickened her steps. The fairground by the Vale of Health looked sombre, the merry-go-round shrouded in its winter wrappings of canvas, and two lean cats stalked each other in and out of the palings. A milkman, whistling, clanked his tray of bottles and, lifting them to his cart, urged the pony to a trot.

"I must," thought Mrs Ellis inconsequently, "get Susan a bicycle for her birthday. Nine is a good age for a first bicycle."

She saw herself choosing one, asking advice, feeling the handle-bars. The colour red, perhaps. Or a good blue. A little basket on the front and a leather bag, for tools, strapped to the back of the seat. The brakes must be sound but not too gripping, otherwise Susan would topple headfirst over the handle-bars and graze her face.

Hoops were out of fashion, which was a pity. When she had been a child there had been no fun like a good springy hoop, struck smartly with a little stick, bowling its way ahead of you. Quite an art to it, too. Susan would have been good with a hoop.

Mrs Ellis came to the junction of two roads and crossed to the opposite side; the second road was her own, and her house the last one on the corner.

As she did so she saw the laundry van swinging down towards her, much too fast. She saw it swerve, heard the screech of its brakes. She saw the look of surprise on the face of the laundry boy. "I shall speak to the driver next time he calls," she said to herself. "One of these days there will be an accident." She thought of Susan on the bicycle, and shuddered. Perhaps a note to the manager of the laundry would do more good. "If you could possibly give a word of warning to your driver, I should be grateful. He takes his corners much too fast." And she would ask to remain anonymous. Otherwise the man might complain about carrying the heavy basket down the steps each time.

She had arrived at her own gate. She pushed it open, and noticed with annoyance that it was nearly off its hinges. The men calling for the laundry must have wrenched at it in some way and done the damage. The note to the manager would be stronger still. She would write immediately after tea. While it was on her mind.

She took out her key and put it in the Yale lock of the front door. It stuck. She could not turn it. How very irritating. She rang the bell. This would mean bringing Grace up from the basement, which she did not like. Better to call down, perhaps, and explain the situation. She leant over the steps and called down to the kitchen. "Grace, it's only me," she said, "my key has jammed in the door; could you come up and let me in?"

She paused. There was no sound from below. Grace must have gone out. This was sheer deceit. It was an agreed bargain between them that when Mrs Ellis was out Grace must stay in. The house must not be left. But sometimes Mrs Ellis suspected that Grace did not keep to the bargain. Here was proof.

She called once again, rather more sharply this time. "Grace?"

There was a sound of a window opening below, and a man thrust his head out of the kitchen. He was in his shirt sleeves. And he had not shaved.

"What are you bawling your head off about?" he said.

Mrs Ellis was too stunned to answer. So this was what happened when her back was turned. Grace, respectable, well over thirty, had a man in the house. Mrs Ellis swallowed, but kept her temper.

"Perhaps you will have the goodness to ask Grace to come upstairs and let me in," she said.

The sarcasm was wasted, of course. The man blinked at her, bewildered. "Who's Grace?" he said.

This was too much. So Grace had the nerve to pass under another name. Something fanciful, no doubt. Shirley, or Marlene. She was pretty sure now what must have happened. Grace had slipped out to the public house down the road to buy this man beer. The man was left to loll in the kitchen. He might even have been poking his fingers in the larder. Now she knew why there was so little left on the joint two days ago.

"If Grace is out," said Mrs Ellis, and her voice was icy, "kindly let me in yourself. I prefer not to use the back entrance."

That would put him in his place. Mrs Ellis trembled with rage. She was seldom angry; she was a mild, even-tempered woman. But this reception, from a lout in shirt sleeves at her own kitchen window, was rather more than she could bear. It was going to be unpleasant, the interview with Grace. Grace would give notice, in all probability. But some things could not be allowed to slide, and this was one of them.

She heard shuffling footsteps coming along the hall. The man had mounted from the basement. He opened the front door and stood there, staring at her.

"Who is it you want?" he said.

Mrs Ellis heard the furious yapping of a little dog from the drawing-room. Callers . . . This was the end. How perfectly frightful, how really overwhelmingly embarrassing. Someone had called and Grace had let them in, or, worse still, this man in his shirt sleeves had done so. What would people think?

"Who is in the drawing-room, do you know?" she murmured swiftly.

"I think Mr and Mrs Bolton are in, but I'm not sure," he said. "I can hear the dog yapping. Was it them you wanted to see?"

Mrs Ellis did not know a Mr and Mrs Bolton. She turned impatiently towards the drawing-room, first whipping off her coat and putting her gloves in her pocket.

"You had better go down to the basement again," she said to the man, who was still staring at her. "Tell Grace not to bring tea until I ring. These people may not stay."

The man appeared bewildered. "All right," he said, "I'm going down. But if you want Mr and Mrs Bolton again, ring twice."

He shuffled off down the basement stairs. He was drunk, no doubt. He meant to be insulting. If he proved difficult, later in the evening, after dark, it would mean ringing for the police.

Mrs Ellis slipped into the lobby to hang up her coat. No time to go upstairs if callers were in the drawing-room. She fumbled for the switch but the bulb had gone. Another pinprick. Now she could not see herself in the mirror.

She stumbled over something, and bent to see what it was. It was a man's boot. And here was another, and a pair of shoes, and beside them a suitcase and an old rug. If Grace had allowed that man to put his things in her lobby, then Grace would go tonight. Crisis had come. High crisis.

Mrs Ellis opened the drawing-room door, forcing a smile of welcome, not too warm, upon her lips. A little dog rushed towards her, barking furiously.

"Quiet, Judy," said a man, grey-haired, with horn spectacles, sitting before the fire. He was clicking a typewriter.

Something had happened to the room. It was covered with books and papers. Odds and ends of junk littered the floor. A parrot, in a cage, hopped on its perch and screeched a welcome. Mrs Ellis tried to speak, but her voice would not come. Grace had gone raving mad. She had let that man into the house, and this one too, and they had brought the most terrible disorder; they had turned the room upside down; they had deliberately, maliciously, set themselves to destroy her things.

No. Worse. It was part of a great thieving plot. She had heard of such things. Gangs went about breaking into houses. Grace, perhaps, was not at fault. She was lying in the basement, gagged and bound. Mrs Ellis felt her heart beating much too fast. She also felt a little faint.

"I must keep calm," she said to herself, "whatever happens, I must keep calm. If I can get to the telephone, to the police, it is the only hope. This man must not see that I am planning what to do."

The little dog kept sniffing at her heels. "Excuse me," said the intruder, pushing his horn spectacles on to his forehead, "but do you want anything? My wife is upstairs."

The diabolic cunning of the plot. The cool bluff of his sitting there, the typewriter on his knees. They must have brought all this stuff in through the door to the back garden; the French window was ajar. Mrs Ellis glanced swiftly at the mantelpiece. It was as she feared. The Staffordshire figures had been removed, and the flower picture too. There must be a car, a van, waiting down the road . . . Her mind worked quickly. It might be that the man had not guessed her identity. Two could play at bluff. Memories of amateur theatricals flashed through her mind.

Somehow she must detain these people until the police arrived. How fast they had worked. Her desk was gone, the bookshelves too, nor could she see her armchair. But she kept her eyes steadily on the stranger. He must not notice her brief glance round the room.

"Your wife is upstairs?" said Mrs Ellis, her voice strained, yet calm.

"Yes," said the man, "if you've come for an appointment, she always makes them. You'll find her in the studio. Room in the front."

Steadily, softly, Mrs Ellis left the drawing-room, but the wretched little dog had followed her.

One thing was certain. The man had not realised who she was. They believed the householder out of the way for the afternoon, and that she, standing now in the hall, listening, her heart beating, was some caller to be fobbed off with a lie about appointments.

She stood silently by the drawing-room door. The man had resumed typing on his machine. She marvelled at the coolness of it, the drawn-out continuity of the bluff. There had been nothing in the papers very recently about large-scale robberies. This was something new, something outstanding. It was extraordinary that they should pick on her house. But they must know she was a widow, on her own, with one maidservant. The telephone had already been removed from the stand in the hall. There was a loaf of bread on it instead, and something that looked like meat wrapped up in newspaper. So they had brought provisions . . . There was a chance that the telephone in her bedroom had not yet been taken away, nor the wires cut. The man had said his wife was upstairs. It may have been part of his bluff, or it might be that he worked with a woman accomplice. This woman, even now, was probably turning out Mrs Ellis's wardrobe, seizing her fur coat, ramming the single string of cultured pearls into a pocket.

Mrs Ellis thought she could hear footsteps in her bedroom. Her anger overcame her fear. She had not the strength to do battle with the man, but she could face the woman. And if the worst came to the worst, she would run to the window, put her head out, and scream. The people next door would hear. Or someone might be passing in the street.

Stealthily, Mrs Ellis crept upstairs. The little dog led the way with confidence. She paused outside her bedroom door. There was certainly movement from within. The dog waited, his eyes fixed upon her with intelligence.

At that moment the door of Susan's small bedroom opened, and a fat elderly woman looked out, blowzy and red in the face. She had a tabby cat under her arm. As soon as the dog saw the cat it started a furious yapping.

"Now that's torn it," said the woman. "What do you want to bring the dog upstairs for? They always fight when they meet. Do you know if the post's been yet? Oh, sorry. I thought you were Mrs Bolton." She brought an empty milk bottle from under her other arm and put it down on the landing. "I'm blowed if I can manage the stairs today," she said, "somebody else will have to take it down for me. Is it foggy out?"

"No," said Mrs Ellis, shocked into a natural answer, and then, feeling the woman's eyes upon her, hesitated between entering her bedroom door and withdrawing down the stairs. This evil-looking old woman was part of the gang and might call the man from below.

"Got an appointment?" said the other. "She won't see you if you haven't booked an appointment."

A tremor of a smile appeared on Mrs Ellis's lips. "Thank you," she said, "yes, I have an appointment."

She was amazed at her own steadiness, and that she could carry off the situation with such aplomb. An actress on the London stage could not have played her part better.

The elderly woman winked and, drawing nearer, plucked Mrs Ellis by the sleeve. "Is she going to do you straight or fancy?" she whispered. "It's the fancy ones that get the men. You know what I mean!" She nudged Mrs Ellis and winked again. "I see by your ring you're married," she said. "You'd be surprised—even the quietest husbands like their pictures fancy. Take a tip from an old pro. Get her to do you fancy."

She lurched back into Susan's room, the cat under her arm, and shut the door.

"It's possible," thought Mrs Ellis, the faint feeling coming over her once again, "that a group of lunatics have escaped from an asylum, and in their terrible, insane fashion they have broken into my house not to thieve, not to destroy my belongings, but because in some crazed, deluded fashion they believe themselves to be at home."

The publicity would be frightful once it became known. Headlines in the papers. Her photograph taken. So bad for Susan. Susan . . . That horrible, disgusting old woman in Susan's bedroom.

Emboldened, fortified, Mrs Ellis opened her own bedroom door. One glance revealed the worst. The room was bare, stripped. There were several lights at various points, and a camera on a tripod. A divan was pushed against the wall. A young woman, with a crop of thick fuzzy hair, was kneeling on the floor, sorting papers.

"Who is it?" she said. "I don't see anyone without an appointment. You've no right to come in here."

Mrs Ellis, calm, resolute, did not answer. She had made certain that the telephone, though it had been moved like the rest of her things, was still in the room. She went to it and lifted the receiver.

"Leave my telephone alone," cried the shock-haired girl, and she began to struggle to her knees.

"I want the police," said Mrs Ellis firmly to the exchange, "I want them to come at once to 17 Elmhurst Road. I am in great danger. Please report this message to the police at once."

The girl was beside her now, taking the receiver from her. "Who's sent you here?" said the girl, her face sallow, colourless, against the fuzzy hair. "If you think you can come in snooping, you're mistaken. You won't find anything. Nor the police, neither. I have a trade licence for the work I do."

Her voice had risen, and the dog, alarmed, joined her with high-pitched barks. The girl opened the door and called down the stairs. "Harry?" she shouted. "Come here and throw this woman out."

Mrs Ellis remained quite calm. She stood with her back to the wall, her hands folded. The exchange had taken her message. It would not be long now before the police arrived.

She heard the drawing-room door open from below and the man's voice called up, petulant, irritated. "What's the matter?" he shouted. "You know I'm busy. Can't you deal with the woman? She probably wants a special pose."

The girl's eyes narrowed. She looked closely at Mrs Ellis. "What did my husband say to you?" she said.

Ah, thought Mrs Ellis triumphantly, they're getting frightened. It's not such an easy game as they think. "I had no conversation with your husband," she said quietly; "he merely told me I should find you upstairs. In this room. Don't try and bluff with me. It's too late. I can see what you have been doing." She gestured at the room.

The girl stared at her. "You can't put any phony business over on me," she said. "This studio is decent, respectable, everyone knows that. I take camera studies of children. Plenty of clients can testify to that. You've got no proof of anything else. Show me a negative, and then I might believe you?"

Mrs Ellis wondered how long it would be before the police came. She must continue to play for time. Later, she might even feel sorry, perhaps, for this wretched deluded girl who had wrought such havoc in the bedroom, believing herself to be a photographer; but this moment, now, she must be calm, calm.

"Well?" said the girl. "What are you going to say when the police come? What's your story?"

It did not do to antagonise lunatics. Mrs Ellis knew that. They must be humoured. She must humour this girl until the police came. "I shall tell them that I live here," she said gently. "That is all they will need to know. Nothing further."

The girl looked at her, puzzled, and lit a cigarette. "Then it is a pose you want?" she said. "That call was just a bluff? Why don't you come clean and say why you're here?"

The sound of their voices had attracted the attention of the old woman in Susan's room. She tapped on the door, which was already open, and stood on the threshold.

"Anything wrong, dear?" she said slyly to the girl.

"Push on out of it," said the girl impatiently, "this is none of your business. I don't interfere with you, and you don't interfere with me."

"I'm not interfering, dear," said the woman, "I only wanted to know if I could help. Difficult client, eh? Wants something out-size?"

"Oh, shut your mouth," said the girl.

The girl's husband, Bolton or whatever his name was, the

spectacled man from the drawing-room, came upstairs and into the bedroom.

"Just what's going on?" he said.

The girl shrugged her shoulders and glanced at Mrs Ellis. "I don't know," she said, "but I think it's blackmail."

"Has she got any negatives?" said the man swiftly.

"Not that I know of. Never seen her before."

"She might have got them from another client," said the elderly woman, watching.

The three of them stared at Mrs Ellis. She was not afraid. She had the situation well in hand.

"I think we've all become a little overwrought," she said, "and much the best thing to do would be to go downstairs, sit quietly by the fire, and have a little chat, and you can talk to me about your work. Tell me, are you all three photographers?"

As she spoke, half of her mind was wondering where they had managed to hide her things. They must have bundled her bed into Susan's room; the wardrobe was in two parts, of course, and could be taken to pieces very soon; but her clothes . . . her ornaments . . . these must have been concealed in a lorry. Somewhere, there was a lorry filled with all her things. It might be parked down another road, or might have been driven off already by yet another accomplice. The police were good at tracing stolen goods, she knew that, and everything was insured; but such a mess had been made of the house; insurance would never cover that, unless there was some clause, some proviso against damage by lunatics; surely the insurance people would not call that an act of God . . . Her mind ran on and on, taking in the mess, the disorder, these people had created, and how many days and weeks would it take for her and Grace to get everything straight again?

Poor Grace. She had forgotten Grace. Grace must be shut up somewhere in that basement with that dreadful man in shirt sleeves, another of the gang, not a follower at all.

"Well," said Mrs Ellis with the other half of her mind, the half that was acting so famously, "shall we do as I suggest and go downstairs?" She turned and led the way, and to her surprise they followed her, the man and his wife, not the horrible old woman. She remained above, leaning over the banisters.

"Call me if you want me," she said.

Mrs Ellis could not bear to think of her fingering Susan's things in the little bedroom. "Won't you join us?" she said, steeling herself to courtesy. "It's far more cheerful down below."

The old woman smirked. "That's for Mr and Mrs Bolton to say," she said, "I don't push myself."

"If I can get all of them pinned into the drawing-room," thought Mrs Ellis, "and somehow lock the door, and make a tremendous effort at conversation, I might possibly keep their attention until the police arrive. There is, of course, the door into the garden, but then they will have to climb the fence, fall over that potting shed next door. The old woman, at least, would never do it."

"Now," said Mrs Ellis, her heart turning over inside at the havoc of the drawing-room, "shall we sit down and recover ourselves, and you shall tell me all about this photography."

But she had scarcely finished speaking before there was a ring at the front door, and a knock, authoritative, loud. The relief sent her dizzy. She steadied herself against the door. It was the police. The man looked at the girl, a question in his eye.

"Better have 'em in," he said, "she's got no proof." He crossed the hall and opened the front door. "Come in, officer," he said. "There's two of you, I see."

"We had a telephone call," Mrs Ellis heard the constable say, "some trouble going on, I understand."

"I think there must be some mistake," said Bolton. "The fact is, we've had a caller and I think she got hysterical."

Mrs Ellis walked into the hall. She did not recognise the constable, nor the young policeman from the beat. It was unfortunate but it did not really matter. Both were stout, well-built men.

"I am not hysterical," she said firmly, "I am perfectly all right. I put the telephone call through the exchange."

The constable took out a notebook and a pencil. "What's the trouble?" he said. "But give me first your name and address."

Mrs Ellis smiled patiently. She hoped he was not going to be a stupid man. "It's hardly necessary," she said, "but my name is Mrs Wilfred Ellis of this address."

"Lodge here?" asked the constable.

Mrs Ellis frowned. "No," she said, "this is my house, I live here." And then, because she saw a look flash from Bolton to his wife, she knew the time had come to be explicit. "I must speak to you alone, Constable," she said, "the matter is terribly urgent; I don't think you quite understand."

"If you have any charge to bring, Mrs Ellis," said the officer, "you can bring it at the police station at the proper time. We were informed that somebody lodging here at Number 17 was in danger. Are you, or are you not, the person who gave that information to the exchange?"

Mrs Ellis began to lose control.

"Of course I am that person," she said. "I returned home to find that my house had been broken into by thieves, these people here, dangerous thieves, lunatics, I don't know what they are, and my things carried away, the whole of my house turned upside down, the most terrible disorder everywhere." She talked so rapidly, her words fell over themselves.

The man from the basement had now joined them in the hall. He stared at the two policemen, his eyes goggling. "I saw her come to the door," he said. "I thought she was balmy. Wouldn't have let her in if I had known."

The constable, a little nettled, turned to the interrupter. "Who are you?" he said.

"Name of Upshaw," said the man, "William Upshaw. Me and my missus has the basement flat here."

"That man is lying," said Mrs Ellis, "he does not live here; he belongs to this gang of thieves. Nobody lives in the basement except my maid—perhaps I should say cook-general—Grace Jackson, and if you will search the premises you will probably find her gagged and bound somewhere, and by that ruffian." She had now lost all restraint. She could hear her voice, usually low and quiet, rising to a hysterical pitch.

"Balmy," said the man from the basement, "you can see the straw in her hair."

"Quiet, please," said the constable, and turned to the young policeman, who murmured something in his ear. "Yes, yes," he said, "I've got the directory here."

He consulted another book. Mrs Ellis watched him feverishly. Never had she seen such a stupid man. Why had they sent out such a slow-witted fool from the police station?

The constable now turned to the man in the horn spectacles. "Are you Henry Bolton?" he asked.

"Yes, officer," replied the man eagerly, "and this is my wife. We have the ground floor here. She uses an upstairs room for a studio. Camera portraits, you know."

There was a shuffle down the stairs, and the evil old woman came to the foot of the banisters. "My name's Baxter," she said, "Billie Baxter they used to call me in my old stage days. Used to be in the profession, you know. I have the first-floor back here at Number 17. I can witness this woman came as a sort of Paul Pry, and up to no good. I saw her looking through the keyhole of Mrs Bolton's studio."

"Then she doesn't lodge here?" asked the constable. "I didn't think she did; the name isn't in the directory."

"We have never seen her before, officer," said Bolton. "Mr Upshaw let her into the house through some error; she walked into our living-room, and then forced her way into my wife's studio, threatened her, and in hysterical fashion rang for the police."

The constable looked at Mrs Ellis. "Anything to say?" he said.

Mrs Ellis swallowed. If only she could keep calm, if only her heart would not beat so dreadfully fast, and the terrible desire to cry would not rise in her throat.

"Constable," she said, "there has been some terrible mistake. You are new to the district, perhaps, and the young policeman too—I don't seem to recognise him—but if you would kindly get through to your headquarters, they must know all about me; I have lived here for years. My maid Grace has been with me a very long time; I am a widow; my husband, Wilfred Ellis, has been dead two years; I have a little girl of nine at school. I went out for a walk on the heath this afternoon, and during my absence these people have broken into my house, seized or destroyed my belongings—the whole place is upside down; if you would please get through immediately to your headquarters . . . "

"There, there," said the constable, putting his notebook away, "that's all right; we can go into all that quietly down at the station. Now do any of you want to charge Mrs Ellis with trespassing?"

There was silence. Nobody said anything.

"We don't wish to be unkind," said Bolton diffidently. "I think my wife and I are quite willing to let the matter pass."

"I think it should be clearly understood," interposed the shock-haired girl, "that anything this woman says about us at the police station is completely untrue."

"Quite," said the officer. "You will both be called, if needed, but I very much doubt the necessity. Now, Mrs Ellis"—he turned to her, not harshly in any way, but with authority—"we have a car outside, and we can run you down to the station, and you can tell your story there. Have you a coat?"

Mrs Ellis turned blindly to the lobby. She knew the police station well; it was barely five minutes away. It was best to go there direct. See someone in authority, not this fool, this hopeless, useless fool. But in the meantime, these people were getting away with their criminal story. By the time she and an additional police force returned, they would have fled. She groped for her coat in the dark lobby, stumbling again over the boots, the suitcases. "Constable," she said softly, "here, one minute."

He moved towards her. "Yes?" he said.

"They've taken away the electric bulb," she said rapidly in a low whisper. "It was perfectly all right this afternoon, and these boots, and this pile of suitcases, all these have been brought in, and thrown here; the suitcases are probably filled with my ornaments. I must ask you most urgently to leave the policeman in charge here until we return, to see that these people don't escape."

"That's all right, Mrs Ellis," said the officer. "Now, are you ready to come along?"

She saw a look pass between the constable and the young policeman. The young policeman was trying to hide his smile. Mrs Ellis felt certain that the constable was *not* going to remain in the house. And a new suspicion flashed into her mind. Could this officer and his subordinate be genuine members of the police force? Or were they, after all, members of the gang? This would explain their strange faces, their obvious mishandling of the situation. In which case they were now going to take her away to some lair, drug her, kill her possibly.

"I'm not going with you," she said swiftly.

"Now, Mrs Ellis," said the constable, "don't give any trouble. You shall have a cup of tea down at the station, and no one is going to hurt you."

He seized her arm. She tried to shake it off. The young policeman moved closer.

"Help," she shouted, "help . . . help . . . "

There must be someone. Those people from next door, she barely knew them, but no matter, if she raised her voice loud enough...

"Poor thing," said the man in shirt sleeves, "seems sad, don't it? I wonder how she got like it."

Mrs Ellis saw his bulbous eyes fixed on her with pity, and she nearly choked.

"You rogue," she said, "how dare you, how dare you!" But she was being bundled down the steps, through the front garden and into the car, and there was another policeman at the wheel of the car; and she was thrust at the back, the constable keeping a steady hold upon her arm. The car turned downhill, past the stretch of heath; she tried to see out of the windows where they were going, but the bulk of the constable prevented her. After twisting and turning the car stopped, to her great surprise, in front of the police station. Then these men were genuine, after all. They were not members of the gang. Stupified for a moment, but relieved, thankful, Mrs Ellis stumbled from the car. The constable, still holding her arm, led her inside.

The hall was not unfamiliar; she remembered coming once before, years ago, when the ginger cat was lost; there was somebody in charge always, sitting at a sort of desk, everything very official, very brisk. She supposed she would stop here in the hall, but the constable led her on to an inner room, and here was another officer seated at a large desk, a more superior type altogether, thank heaven, and he looked intelligent.

She was determined to get her word in before the constable spoke. "There has been great confusion," she began. "I am Mrs Ellis, of 17 Elmhurst Road, and my house has been broken into, robbery is going on at this moment on a huge scale; I believe the thieves to be very desperate and extraordinarily cunning; they have completely taken in the constable here, and the other policeman..."

To her indignation this superior officer did not look at her. He raised his eyebrows at the constable, and the constable, who had taken off his hat, coughed and approached the desk. A police-woman, appearing from nowhere, stood beside Mrs Ellis and held her arm.

The constable and the superior officer were talking together in low tones. Mrs Ellis could not hear what they were saying. Her legs trembled with emotion. She felt her head swim. Thankfully, she accepted the chair dragged forward by the policewoman, and in a few moments she was given a cup of tea. She did not want it, though. Precious time was being lost.

"I must insist that you hear what I have to say," she said, and the policewoman tightened her grip on Mrs Ellis's arm. The officer behind the desk motioned her forward, and she was assisted to another chair, the policewoman remaining beside her all the while.

"Now," he said, "what is it you want to tell me?"

Mrs Ellis gripped her hands together. She had a premonition that this man, in spite of his superior face, was going to prove as great a fool as the constable.

"My name is Ellis," she said, "Mrs Wilfred Ellis, of 17 Elmhurst Road. I am in the telephone book. I am very well known in the district, and have lived at Elmhurst Road for ten years. I am a widow, and I have one little girl of nine years at present at school. I employ one maidservant, Grace Jackson, who cooks for me and does general work. This afternoon I went for a short walk on the heath, round by the Viaduct and the Vale of Health ponds, and when I returned home I found my house had been broken into; my maid had disappeared; the rooms were already stripped of my belongings and the thieves were in possession of my home, putting up a stupendous act of bluff that deceived even the constable here. I put the call through to the exchange, which frightened the thieves, and I endeavoured to keep them pinned in my drawing-room until help arrived."

Mrs Ellis paused for breath. She saw that the officer was paying attention to her story, and kept his eyes fixed upon her.

"Thank you," he said, "that is very helpful, Mrs Ellis. Now, have you anything you can show me to prove your identity?"

She stared at him. Prove her identity? Well, of course. But not here, not actually on her person. She had come away without her handbag, and her calling cards were in the writing desk, and her passport—she and Wilfred had been to Dieppe once—was, if she remembered rightly, in the left-hand pigeonhole of the small writing desk in her bedroom.

But she suddenly remembered the havoc of the house. Nothing would be found . . .

"It's very unfortunate," she said to the officer, "but I didn't take my handbag with me when I went out for my walk this afternoon. I left it in the chest-of-drawers in the bedroom. My calling-cards are in the desk in the drawing-room, and there is a passport—rather out of date; my husband and I did not travel much—in a pigeonhole in a small desk in my bedroom. But everything has been upset, taken by these thieves. The house is in utter chaos."

The officer made a note on the pad beside him. "You can't produce your identity card or your ration book?" he asked.

"I have explained," said Mrs Ellis, governing her temper. "My calling-cards are in my writing-desk. I don't know what you mean by ration book."

The officer went on writing on his pad. He glanced at the policewoman, who began feeling Mrs Ellis's pockets, touching her in a familiar way. Mrs Ellis tried to think which of her friends could be telephoned to, who could vouch for her, who could come at once by car and make these idiots, these stone-witted fools, see sense. "I must keep calm," she told herself again, "I must keep calm." The Collins were abroad; they would have been the best, but Netta Draycott should be at home; she was usually at home about this time because of the children.

"I have asked you," said Mrs Ellis, "to verify my name and address in the telephone book. If you refuse to do that, ask the postmaster, or the manager of my bank, a branch of which is in the High Street, where I cashed a cheque on Saturday. Finally, would you care to ring up Mrs Draycott, a friend of mine, 21 Charlton Court, the block of flats in Charlton Avenue, who will vouch for me?"

She sat back in the chair, exhausted. No nightmare, she told herself, could ever have the horror, the frustrated hopelessness, of her present plight. Little incident piled on little incident. If she had only remembered to bring her handbag, there was a calling-card case in her handbag. And all the while those thieves, those devils, breaking up her home, getting away with her precious things, her belongings . . .

"Now, Mrs Ellis," said the officer, "we have checked up on your statement, you know, and they won't do. You are not in the telephone book, nor in the local directory."

"I assure you I am," said Mrs Ellis with indignation. "Give me the book and I'll show you."

The constable, still standing, placed the books before her. She ran her finger down the name of Ellis to the position on the left-hand page where she knew it would be. The name Ellis was repeated, but not hers. And none with her address or number. She looked in the directory and saw that beside 17 Elmhurst Road were the names of Bolton, of Upshaw, of Baxter . . . She pushed both books away from her. She stared at the officer.

"There is something wrong with these books," she said, "they are not up to date, they are false, they are not the books I have at home."

The officer did not answer. He closed the books. "Now, Mrs Ellis," he said, "I can see you are tired, and a rest would do you good. We will try to find your friends for you. If you will go along now, we will get in touch with them as soon as possible. I will send a doctor to you, and he may chat with you a little and give you a sedative, and then, after some rest, you will feel better in the morning and we may have news for you."

The policewoman helped Mrs Ellis to her feet. "Come along now," she said.

"But my house?" said Mrs Ellis. "Those thieves, and my maid Grace, Grace may be lying in the basement. Surely you are going to do something about the house? You won't permit them to get away with this monstrous crime? Even now we have wasted a precious half-hour—"

"That's all right, Mrs Ellis," said the officer, "you can leave everything in our hands."

The policewoman led her away, still talking, still protesting, and now she was being taken down a corridor, and the police-woman kept saying: "Now, don't fuss, take it calmly; no one's going to hurt you," and she was in a little room with a bed; heavens . . . it was a cell, a cell where they put the prisoners, and the policewoman was helping her off with her coat, unpinning the scarf that was still tied round her hair, and because Mrs Ellis felt so faint the policewoman made her lie down on the bed, covered her with the coarse grey blanket, placed the little hard pillow under her head.

Mrs Ellis seized the woman's hands. Her face, after all, was not unkind. "I beg of you," she said, "ring up Hampstead 4072, the number of my friend Mrs Draycott, and ask her to come here. The officer won't listen to me. He won't hear my story."

"Yes, yes, that will be all right," said the policewoman.

Now somebody else was coming into the room, the cell. Clean-shaven, alert, he carried a case in his hands. He said good evening to the policewoman, and opened his case. He took out a stethoscope and a thermometer. He smiled at Mrs Ellis. "Feeling a little upset, I hear," he said. "Well, we'll soon put that to rights. Now, will you give me your wrist?"

Mrs Ellis sat up on the hard narrow bed, pulling the blanket close. "Doctor," she said, "there is nothing whatever the matter with me. I admit I have been through a terrible experience, quite enough to unnerve anyone; my house has been broken into; no one here will listen to my story, but I am Mrs Ellis, Mrs Wilfred Ellis, if you can possibly persuade the authorities here . . . "

He was not listening to her. With the assistance of the police-woman he was taking her temperature, under her arm, not in the mouth, treating her like a child; and now he was feeling her pulse, dragging down her eyelids, listening to her chest . . . Mrs Ellis went on talking.

"I realise this is a matter of routine. You are obliged to do this. But I want to warn you that my whole treatment, since I have been brought here, since the police came to my house before that, has been infamous, scandalous. I don't personally know our M.P., but I sincerely believe that when he hears my story he will take the matter up, and someone is going to answer for the consequences. Unfortunately I am a widow, no immediate relatives, my little daughter is away at school; my closest friends, a Mr and Mrs Collins, are abroad, but my bank manager . . . "

He was dabbing her arm with spirit; he was inserting a needle, and with a whimper of pain Mrs Ellis fell back on to the hard pillow. The doctor went on holding her arm, and Mrs Ellis, her head going round and round, felt a strange numb sensation as the injection worked into her bloodstream. Tears ran down her cheeks. She could not fight. She was too weak.

"How is that?" said the doctor. "Better, eh?"

Her throat was parched, her mouth without saliva. It was one of those drugs that paralysed you, made you helpless. But the emotion bubbling within her was eased, was still. The anger, the fear and frustration that had keyed her nerves to a point of con-traction seemed to die away. She had explained things badly. The folly of coming out without her handbag had caused half the trouble. And the terrible, wicked cunning of those thieves. "Be still," she said to her mind, "be still. Rest now."

"Now," said the doctor, letting go her wrist, "supposing you tell me your story again. You say your name is Mrs Ellis?"

Mrs Ellis sighed and closed her eyes. Must she go into it all again? Had they not got the whole thing written down in their notebooks? What was the use, when the inefficiency of the whole establishment was so obvious? Those telephone books, directories, with wrong names, wrong addresses. Small wonder there were burglaries, murders, every sort of crime, with a police force that was obviously rotten to the core. What was the name of the Member? It was on the tip of her tongue. A nice man, sandy-haired, always looked so trustworthy on a poster. Hampstead was a safe seat, of course. He would take up her case ...

"Mrs Ellis," said the doctor, "do you think you can remember now your real address?"

Mrs Ellis opened her eyes. Wearily, patiently, she fixed them upon the doctor. "I live at 17 Elmhurst Road," she said mechanically. "I am a widow, my husband has been dead for two years. I have a little girl of nine at school. I went for a short walk on the heath this afternoon after lunch, and when I returned—"

He interrupted her. "Yes," he said, "we know that. We know what happened after your walk. What we want you to tell us is what happened before."

"I had lunch," said Mrs Ellis. "I remember perfectly well what I ate. Guinea fowl and apple charlotte, followed by coffee. Then I nearly decided to take a nap upstairs on my bed, because I was not feeling very well, but decided the air would do me good."

As soon as she said this, she regretted it. The doctor looked at her keenly. "Ah!" he said. "You weren't feeling very well. Can you tell me what the trouble was?"

Mrs Ellis knew what he was after. He and the rest of the police force at the station wanted to certify her as insane. They would make out that she had suffered from some brainstorm, that her whole story was fabrication.

"There was nothing much the matter," she said quickly. "I was rather tired from sorting things during the morning. I tidied the linen, cleared out my desk in the drawing-room—all that took time."

"Can you describe your house, Mrs Ellis?" he said. "The

furniture, for instance, of your bedroom, your drawing-room?"

"Very easily," she answered, "but you must remember that the thieves who broke into the house this afternoon have done what I begin to fear is irreparable damage. Everything had been seized, hidden away. The rooms were strewn with rubbish, and there was a young woman upstairs in my bedroom pretending to be a photographer."

"Yes," he said, "don't worry about that. Just tell me about your furniture, how the various things were placed, and so on."

He was more sympathetic than she had thought. Mrs Ellis launched into a description of every room in her house. She named the ornaments, the pictures, the position of the chairs and tables.

"And you say your cook is called Grace Jackson?"

"Yes, Doctor, she has been with me several years. She was in the kitchen when I left this afternoon; I remember most distinctly calling down to the basement and saying that I was going for a short walk and would not be long. I am extremely worried about her, Doctor. Those thieves will have got hold of her, perhaps kidnapped her."

"We'll see to that," said the doctor. "Now, Mrs Ellis, you have been very helpful, and you have given such a clear account of your home that I think we shan't be long in tracing it, and your relations. You must stay here tonight, and I hope in the morning we shall have news for you. Now, you say your small daughter is at school? Can you remember the address?"

"Of course," said Mrs Ellis, "and the telephone number too. The school is High Close, Bishops' Lane, Hatchworth, and the telephone number is Hatchworth 202. But I don't understand what you mean about tracing my home."

"There is nothing to worry about," said the doctor. "You are not ill, and you are not lying, I quite realise that. You are suffering from a temporary loss of memory that often happens to all sorts of people, and it quickly passes. We've had many cases before." He smiled. He stood up, his case in his hand.

"But it isn't true," said Mrs Ellis, trying to raise herself from the pillow. "My memory is perfectly all right. I have given you every detail I can think of; I have told you my name, where I live, a description of my home, the address of my daughter at school . . ."

"All right," he said. "Now, don't worry. Just try to relax and have a little sleep. We shall find your friends for you."

He murmured something to the policewoman and left the cell. The policewoman came over to the bed and tucked in the blanket.

"Now, cheer up," she said, "do as the doctor said. Get a little rest. Everything will be all right, you'll see."

Rest ... but how? Relax ... But to what purpose? Even now her house was being looted, sacked, every room stripped. The thieves getting clear away with their booty, leaving no trace behind them. They would take Grace with them; poor Grace could not come down to the police station to give witness to her identity. But the people next door, the Furbers, surely they would be good enough; it would not be too much trouble ... Mrs Ellis supposed she should have called, been more friendly, had them to tea, but after all, people did not expect that unless they lived in the country, it was out of date. If the police officer had not got hold of Netta Draycott then the Furbers must be got in touch with at once ...

Mrs Ellis plucked at the policewoman's sleeve. "The Furbers," she said, "next door, at number 19, they will vouch for me. They are not friends of mine, but they know me well by sight. We have been neighbours for quite six years. The Furbers."

"Yes," said the policewoman, "try to get some sleep."

Oh, Susan, my Susan, if this had happened in the holidays, how much more fearful; what would we have done? Coming back from an afternoon walk to find those devils in the house, and then, who knows, that dreadful photographer woman and her husband taking a fancy to Susan, so pretty, so fair, and wanting to kidnap her ... At least the child was safe, knew nothing of what was happening, and if only the story could be kept out of the newspapers, she need never know. So shameful, so degrading, a night spent in a prison cell through such crass stupidity, such appalling blunders ...

"You've had a good sleep, then," said the policewoman, handing her a cup of tea.

"I don't know what you mean," said Mrs Ellis. "I haven't slept at all."

"Oh, yes, you have." The woman smiled. "They all say that."

Mrs Ellis blinked, sat up on the narrow bed. She had been

speaking to the policewoman only a moment before. Her head ached abominably. She sipped at the tea, tasteless, unrefreshing. She yearned for her bed at home, for Grace coming in noiselessly, drawing the curtains.

"You're to have a wash," said the policewoman, "and I'll give you a comb through, and then you are to see the doctor again."

Mrs Ellis suffered the indignity of washing under supervision, of having her hair combed; then her scarf and coat and gloves were given to her again and she was taken out of the cell, along the corridor, back through the hall to the room where they had questioned her the night before. This time a different officer sat at the desk, but she recognised the police constable, and the doctor too.

The last came towards her with that same bland smile on his face. "How are you feeling today?" he said. "A little more like your true self?"

"On the contrary," said Mrs Ellis, "I am feeling very unwell indeed, and shall continue to do so until I know what has happened at home. Is anyone here prepared to tell me what has happened since last night? Has anything at all been done to safeguard my property?"

The doctor did not answer, but guided her towards the chair at the desk. "Now," he said, "the officer here wants to show you a picture in a newspaper."

Mrs Ellis sat down in the chair. The officer handed her a copy of the *News of the World*—a paper Grace took on Sundays; Mrs Ellis never looked at it—and there was a photograph of a woman with a scarf round her head and chubby cheeks, wearing some sort of light-coloured coat. The photograph had a red circle round it, and underneath was written: "Missing from Home, Ada Lewis, aged 36, widow, of 105 Albert Buildings, Kentish Town." She handed the paper back across the desk. "I'm afraid I can't help you," she said. "I don't know this woman."

"The name Ada Lewis conveys nothing to you?" said the officer. "Nor Albert Buildings?"

"No," said Mrs Ellis, "certainly not."

Suddenly she knew the purpose of the interrogation. The police thought that she was this missing woman, this Ada Lewis from Albert Buildings. Simply because she wore a light-coloured coat and had a scarf round her hair. She rose from the chair.

"This is absolutely preposterous," she said. "I have told you my name and my address, and you persist in disbelieving me. My detention here is an outrage; I demand to see a lawyer, my own lawyer . . . " But wait, she hadn't needed the services of a lawyer since Wilfred died, and the firm had moved or been taken over by somebody else; better not give the name; they would think she was lying once again; it was safer to give the name of the bank manager . . .

"One moment," said the officer, and she was interrupted once again, because somebody else came into the room, a seedy, common-looking man in a checked shabby suit, holding his trilby hat in his hand. "Can you identify this woman as your sister, Ada Lewis?" asked the officer.

A flush of fury swept Mrs Ellis as the man stepped forward and peered into her face. "No, sir," he said, "this isn't Ada. Ada isn't so stout, and this woman's teeth seem to be her own. Ada wore dentures. Never seen this woman before."

"Thank you," said the officer, "that's all. You can go. We will let you know if we find your sister."

The seedy-looking man left the room. Mrs Ellis turned in triumph to the officer behind the desk. "Now," she said, "perhaps you will believe me?"

The officer considered her for a moment, and then, glancing at the doctor, looked down at some notes on his desk. "Much as I would like to believe you," he said, "for it would save us all a great deal of trouble if I could, unfortunately I can't. Your facts have been proved wrong in every particular. So far."

"What do you mean?" said Mrs Ellis.

"First, your address. You do not live at 17 Elmhurst Road because the house is occupied by various tenants who have lived there for some time and who are known to us. Number 17 is an apartment house and the floors are let separately. You are not one of the tenants."

Mrs Ellis gripped the sides of her chair. The obstinate, proud, and completely unmoved face of the officer stared back at her. "You are mistaken," she said quietly. "Number 17 is not a lodging-house. It is a private house. My own."

The officer glanced down again at his notes. "There are no people called Furber living at number 19," he went on. "Number 19 is also a lodging-house. You are not in the directory under the name of Ellis, nor in the telephone book. There is no Ellis on the register of the branch of the bank you mentioned to us last night. Nor can we trace anyone of the name of Grace Jackson in the district."

Mrs Ellis looked up at the doctor, at the police constable, at the policewoman, who was still standing by her side. "Is there some conspiracy?" she said. "Why are you all against me? I don't understand what I have done . . . " Her voice faltered. She must not break down. She must be firm with them, be brave, for Susan's sake. "You rang up my friend at Charlton Court?" she asked. "Mrs Draycott, that big block of flats?"

"Mrs Draycott is not living at Charlton Court, Mrs Ellis," said the police officer, "for the simple reason that Charlton Court no longer exists. It was destroyed by a fire bomb."

Mrs Ellis stared at him in horror. A fire bomb? But how perfectly terrible! When? How? In the night? Disaster upon disaster . . . Who could have done it, anarchists, strikers, unemployed, gangs of people, possibly those who had broken into her house? Poor Netta and her husband and children; Mrs Ellis felt her head reeling . . .

"Forgive me," she said, summoning her strength, her dignity, "I had no idea there had been such a fearful outrage. No doubt part of the same plot, those people in my house . . . "

Then she stopped, because she realised they were lying to her; everything was lies; they were not policemen; they had seized the building; they were spies; the government was to be overthrown; but then why bother with her, with a simple harmless individual like herself; why were they not getting on with the civil war, bringing machine guns into the street, marching to Buckingham Palace; why sit here, pretending to her?

A policeman came into the room and clicked his heels and stood before the desk. "Checked up on all the nursing homes," he said, "and the mental homes, sir, in the district, and within a radius of five miles. Nobody missing."

"Thank you," said the officer. Ignoring Mrs Ellis, he looked across at the doctor. "We can't keep her here," he said. "You'll have to persuade them to take her at Moreton Hill. The matron *must* find a room. Say it's a temporary measure. Case of amnesia."

"I'll do what I can," said the doctor.

Moreton Hill. Mrs Ellis knew at once what they meant by

Moreton Hill. It was a well-known mental home somewhere near Highgate, very badly run, she always heard, a dreadful place.

"Moreton Hill?" she said. "You can't possibly take me there. It has a shocking reputation. The nurses are always leaving. I refuse to go to Moreton Hill. I demand to see a lawyer—no, my doctor, Dr Godber; he lives in Parkwell Gardens."

The officer stared at her thoughtfully. "She must be a local woman," he said; "she gets the names right every time. But Godber went to Portsmouth, didn't he? I remember Godber."

"If he's at Portsmouth," said Mrs Ellis, "he would only have gone for a few days. He's most conscientious. But his secretary knows me. I took Susan there last holidays."

Nobody listened to her, though, and the officer was consulting his notes again. "By the way," he said, "you gave me the name of that school correctly. Wrong telephone number, but right school. Co-educational. We got through to them last night."

"I'm afraid then," said Mrs Ellis, "that you got the wrong school. High Close is most certainly not co-educational, and I should never have sent Susan there if it had been."

"High Close," repeated the officer, reading from his notes, "is a co-educational school, run by a Mr Foster and his wife."

"It is run by a Miss Slater," said Mrs Ellis, "a Miss Hilda Slater."

"You mean it *was* run by a Miss Slater," said the officer. "A Miss Slater had the school and then retired, and it was taken over by Mr and Mrs Foster. They have no pupil there of the name of Susan Ellis."

Mrs Ellis sat very still in her chair. She looked at each face in turn. None was harsh. None was unfriendly. And the police-woman smiled encouragement. They all watched her steadily. At last she said: "You are not deliberately trying to mislead me? You do realise that I am anxious, most desperately anxious, to know what has happened? If all that you are saying is some kind of a game, some kind of torture, would you tell me so that I know, so that I can understand?"

The doctor took her hand, and the officer leant forward in his chair. "We are trying to help you," he said. "We are doing everything we can to find your friends."

Mrs Ellis held tight to the doctor's hand. It had suddenly become a refuge. "I don't understand," she said, "what has happened. If I am suffering from loss of memory, why do I remember everything so clearly? My address, my name, people, the school . . . Where is Susan; where is my little girl?" She looked round her in blind panic. She tried to rise from the chair. "If Susan is not at High Close, where is she?"

Someone was patting her on the shoulder. Someone was giving her a glass of water.

"If Miss Slater had retired to give place to a Mr and Mrs Foster, I should have heard, they would have told me," she kept repeating. "I telephoned the school only yesterday. Susan was quite well, and playing in the grounds."

"Are you suggesting that Miss Slater answered you yourself?" enquired the officer.

"No, the secretary answered. I telephoned because I had . . . what seemed to me a premonition that Susan might not be well. The secretary assured me that the child had eaten a good lunch and was playing. I am not making this up. It happened yesterday. I tell you, the secretary would have told me if Miss Slater was making changes in the school."

Mrs Ellis searched the doubtful faces fixed upon her. And momentarily her attention was caught by the large 2 on the calendar standing on the desk.

"I *know* it was yesterday," she said, "because today is the second of the month, isn't it? And I distinctly remember tearing off the page in my calendar, and because it was the first of the month I decided to tidy my desk, sort out my papers, during the morning."

The police officer relaxed and smiled. "You are certainly very convincing," he said, "and we can all tell from your appearance, the fact that you have no money on you, that your shoes are polished, and other little signs, that you do definitely belong somewhere in this district; you have not wandered from any great distance. But you do not come from 17 Elmhurst Road, Mrs Ellis, this is quite certain. For some reason, which we hope to discover, that address has become fixed in your mind, and other addresses too. I promise you everything will be done to clear your mind and to get you well again; and you need have no fear about going back to Moreton Hill; I know it well, and they will look after you there."

Mrs Ellis saw herself shut up behind those grey forbidding

walls, grimly situated, frowning down upon the further ponds the far side of the heath. She had skirted those walls many times, pitying the inmates within. The man who came with the groceries had a wife who became insane. Mrs Ellis remembered Grace coming to her one morning full of the story, "and he says they've taken her to Moreton Hill." Once inside, she would never get out. These men at the police station would not bother with her any more. And now there was this new, hideous misunderstanding about Susan, and the talk of a Mr and Mrs Foster taking over the school.

Mrs Ellis leant forward, clasping her hands together. "I do assure you," she said, "that I don't want to make trouble. I have always been a very quiet, peaceable sort of person, not easily excited, never quarrelsome, and if I have really lost my memory I will do what the doctor tells me, take any drugs or medicines that will help. But I am worried, desperately worried, about my little girl and what you have told me about the school and Miss Slater's having retired. Would you do just one thing for me? Telephone the school and ask them where you can get in touch with Miss Slater. It is just possible that she has taken the house down the road and removed there with some of the children, Susan amongst them; and whoever answered the telephone was new to the work and gave you vague information."

She spoke clearly, without any sort of hysteria or emotion; they must see that she was in deadly earnest, and this request of hers was not wild fancy.

The police officer glanced at the doctor, then he seemed to make up his mind. "Very well," he said, "we will do that. We will try to contact this Miss Slater, but it may take time. Meanwhile, I think it is best if you wait in another room while we put through the enquiry."

Mrs Ellis stood up, this time without the help of the policewoman. She was determined to show that she was well, mentally and bodily, and quite capable of managing her affairs without the assistance of anybody, if it could be permitted. She wished she had a hat instead of the scarf, which she knew instinctively was unbecoming, and her hands were lost without her handbag. At least she had gloves. But gloves were not enough. She nodded briskly to the police officer and the doctor—at all costs she must show civility—and followed the policewoman to a waiting room.

This time she was spared the indignity of a cell. Another cup of tea was brought to her.

"It's all they think about," she said to herself, "cups of tea, instead of getting on with their job."

Suddenly she remembered poor Netta Draycott and the terrible tragedy of the fire bomb. Possibly she and her family had escaped and were now with friends, but there was no immediate means of finding out. "Is it all in the morning papers about the disaster?" she asked the policewoman.

"What disaster?" said the woman.

"The fire at Charlton Court the officer spoke to me about."

The policewoman stared at her with a puzzled expression. "I don't remember him saying anything about a fire," she said.

"Oh, yes, he did," said Mrs Ellis. "He told me that Charlton Court had been destroyed by fire, by some bomb. I was aghast to hear it because I have friends living there. It must surely be in all the morning papers."

The woman's face cleared. "Oh, that," she said. "I think the officer was referring to some fire bomb during the war."

"No, no," said Mrs Ellis impatiently. "Charlton Court was built a long time after the war. I remember the block being built when my husband and I first came to Hampstead. No, this accident apparently happened last night, the most dreadful thing."

The policewoman shrugged her shoulders. "I think you're mistaken," she said; "there's been no talk of any accident or disaster here."

An ignorant, silly sort of girl, thought Mrs Ellis. It was a wonder she had passed her test into the force. She thought they only employed very intelligent women. She sipped her tea in silence. No use carrying on any sort of conversation with her. It seemed a long while before the door opened, but when it did it was to reveal the doctor, who stood on the threshold with a smile on his face.

"Well," he said, "I think we're a little nearer home. We were able to contact Miss Slater."

Mrs Ellis rose to her feet, her eyes shining. "Oh, Doctor, thank heaven . . . Have you news of my daughter?"

"Steady a moment now. You mustn't get excited or we shall

have all last night's trouble over again, and that would never do. I take it, when you refer to your daughter, you mean someone who is called, or was called, Susan Ellis?"

"Yes, yes, of course," said Mrs Ellis swiftly. "Is she all right, is she with Miss Slater?"

"No, she is not with Miss Slater, but she is perfectly well. I have spoken to her on the telephone myself, and I have her present address here in my notebook." The doctor patted his breast pocket and smiled again.

"Not with Miss Slater?" Mrs Ellis stared in bewilderment. "Then the school *has* been handed over; you spoke to these people called Foster. Is it next door? Have they moved far? What has happened?"

The doctor took her hand and led her to the seat once more. "Now," he said, "I want you to think quite calmly and quite clearly and not be agitated in any way, and your trouble will be cleared up, your mind will be free again. You remember last night you gave us the name of your maid, Grace Jackson?"

"Yes, Doctor."

"Now take your time. Tell us a little about Grace Jackson."

"Have you found her? Is she at home? Is she all right?"

"Never mind for the moment. Describe Grace Jackson."

Mrs Ellis was horribly afraid poor Grace had been found murdered, and they were going to ask her to identify the body. "She is a big girl," she said, "at least not really a girl, about my own age, but you know how one is inclined to talk of a servant as a girl; she has a large bust, rather thick ankles, brownish hair, grey eyes, and she would be wearing, let me see, I think she may not have changed into her cap and apron when those thieves arrived; she was still probably in her overalls. She is inclined to change rather late in the afternoon; I have often spoken about it; it looks so bad to open the front door in overalls, slovenly, like a boarding-house. Grace has good teeth and a pleasant expression, though of course if anything has happened to her she would hardly—" Mrs Ellis broke off. Murdered, battered. Grace would not be smiling.

The doctor did not seem to notice this. He was looking closely at Mrs Ellis. "You know," he said, "you have given a very accurate description of yourself."

"Myself?" said Mrs Ellis.

"Yes. Figure, colouring, and so on. We think, you know, it is just possible that your amnesia has taken the form of mistaken identity and that you are really Grace Jackson, believing yourself to be a Mrs Ellis, and now we are doing our best to trace the relatives of Grace Jackson."

This was too much. Mrs Ellis swallowed. Outraged pride rose in her. "Doctor," she said rapidly, "you have gone a little too far. I bear no sort of resemblance to my maid, Grace Jackson, and if and when you ever find trace of the unfortunate girl, she would be the first to agree with me. Grace has been in my employment seven years; she came originally from Scotland; her parents were Scottish, I believe—in fact, I know it, because she used to go for her holiday to Aberdeen. Grace is a good, hard-working, and I like to think honest girl; we have had our little ups and downs, but nothing serious; she is inclined to be obstinate; I am obstinate myself—who is not?—but . . . "

If only the doctor would not look at her in that smiling, patronising way. "You see," he said, "you do know a very great deal about Grace Jackson."

Mrs Ellis could have hit him. He was so self-assured, so confident. "I must keep my temper," she told herself. "I must, I must . . . " Aloud she said: "Doctor, I know about Grace Jackson because, as I have told you, she has been in my employment for seven years. If she is found ill or in any way hurt, I shall hold the police force here responsible, because, in spite of my entreaties, I do not believe they kept a watch on my house last night. Now perhaps you will be good enough to tell me where I can find my child. She, at least, will recognise me."

Mrs Ellis considered she had been very restrained, very calm. In spite of terrible provocation she had not lost control of herself.

"You insist that your age is thirty-five?" said the doctor, switching the subject. "And that Grace Jackson was approximately the same?"

"I was thirty-five in August last," said Mrs Ellis. "I believe Grace to be a year younger, I am not sure."

"You certainly don't look more," said the doctor smiling.

Surely, at such a moment, he was not going to attempt to appease her by gallantry?

"But," he continued, "following upon the telephone conversation I have just had, Grace Jackson would be, today, at least fifty-five or fifty-six."

"There are probably," said Mrs Ellis icily, "several persons of the name of Grace Jackson employed as domestic servants. If you propose tracing every one of them, it will take you and the police force a considerable time. I am sorry to insist, but I must know the whereabouts of my daughter Susan before anything else."

He was relenting; she could see it in his eye. "As a matter of fact," he said, "it happens, very conveniently, that Miss Slater was able to put us in touch with her; we have spoken to her on the telephone, and she is only a short distance away, in St John's Wood. She is not sure, but she thinks she would remember Grace Jackson if she saw her."

For a moment Mrs Ellis was speechless. What in the world was Susan doing in St John's Wood? And how monstrous to drag the child to the telephone and question her about Grace. Of course she would be bewildered and say she "thought" she would remember Grace, though goodness only knows it was only two months since Grace was waving her good-bye from the doorstep when she left for school.

Then she suddenly remembered the Zoo. Perhaps, if these changes at school were all being decided upon in a great hurry, one of the junior mistresses had taken a party of children up to London to the Zoo, to be out of the way. The Zoo or Madame Tussaud's.

"Do you know where she spoke from?" asked Mrs Ellis sharply. "I mean, somebody was in charge, somebody was looking after her?"

"She spoke from 2a Halifax Avenue," said the doctor, "and I don't think you will find she needs any looking after. She sounded very capable, and I heard her turn from the telephone and call to a little boy named Keith to keep quiet and not make so much noise, because she couldn't hear herself speak."

A tremor of a smile appeared on Mrs Ellis's lips. How clever of Susan to have shown herself so quick and lively. It was just like her, though. She was so advanced for her age. Such a little companion. But Keith . . . It sounded very much as though the school *had* suddenly become co-educational; this was a mixed party being taken to the Zoo or Madame Tussaud's. They were all having lunch, perhaps, at Halifax Avenue, relations of Miss Slater's, or these Fosters, but really the whole thing was most inexcusable, that changes should come about like this, and the children be taken backwards and forwards from High Close to London without any attempt to notify the parents. Mrs Ellis would write very strongly to Miss Slater about it, and if the school had changed hands and was to be co-educational, she would remove Susan at the end of the term.

"Doctor," she said, "I am ready to go to Halifax Avenue at once, if the authorities here will only permit me to do so."

"Very well," said the doctor. "I am afraid I can't accompany you, but we have arranged for that, and Sister Henderson, who knows all about the matter, will go with you."

He nodded to the policewoman, who opened the door of the waiting room and admitted a severe middle-aged woman in nurse's uniform. Mrs Ellis said nothing, but her mouth tightened. She was very sure that Sister Henderson had been summoned from Moreton Hill.

"Now, Sister," said the doctor cheerfully, "this is the lady, and you know where to take her and what to do; and I think you will only be a few minutes at Halifax Avenue, and then we hope things will be straightened out."

"Yes, Doctor," said the nurse. She looked across at Mrs Ellis with a quick professional eye.

"If only I had a hat," thought Mrs Ellis, "if only I had not come out with nothing but this wretched scarf, and I can feel bits and pieces of hair straggling at the back of my neck. No powder compact on me, no comb, nothing. Of course I must look terrible to them, ungroomed, common . . ."

She straightened her shoulders, resisted an impulse to put her hands in her pockets. She walked stiffly towards the open door. The doctor, the Sister, and the policewoman conducted her down the steps of the police station to a waiting car. A uniformed chauffeur was to drive, she was thankful to see, and she climbed into the car, followed by the Sister.

The awful thought flashed through her mind that there might be some charge for the night's lodging in the cell and for the cups of tea; also, should she have tipped the policewoman? But anyway, she had no money. It was impossible. She nodded brightly to the policewoman as a sort of sop, to show she had no ill feeling. She felt rather different towards the doctor. She bowed rather formally, coldly. The car drove away.

Mrs Ellis wondered if she was expected to make conversation with the Sister, who sat stalwart and forbidding at her side. Better not, perhaps. Anything she said might be taken as evidence of mental disturbance. She stared straight in front of her, her gloved hands primly folded on her lap. The traffic jams were very bad, worse than she had ever known. There must be a motor exhibition on. So many American cars on the road. A rally, perhaps . . .

She did not think much of Halifax Avenue when they came to it. Houses very shabby, and quite a number with windows broken. The car drew up at a small house that had 2a written on the pillar outside. Curious place to take a party of children for lunch. A good Lyons café would have been so much better.

The Sister got out of the car and waited to help Mrs Ellis. "We shan't be long," she said to the chauffeur.

"That's what you think," said Mrs Ellis to herself, "but I shall certainly stay with Susan as long as I please."

They walked through the piece of front garden to the front door. The Sister rang the bell. Mrs Ellis saw a face looking at them from the front window and then quickly dart behind a curtain. Good heavens . . . It was Dorothy, Wilfred's younger sister, who was a schoolteacher in Birmingham; of course it was, it must be . . . Everything became clearer; the Fosters must know Dorothy; people to do with education always knew each other, but how awkward, what a bore. Mrs Ellis had never cared for Dorothy, had stopped writing to her in fact; Dorothy had been so unpleasant when poor Wilfred died, and had insisted that the writing bureau was hers, and rather a nice piece of jewellery that Mrs Ellis had always understood Wilfred's mother had given to her, Mrs Ellis; and in fact the whole afternoon after the funeral had been spent in such unpleasant argument and discussion that Mrs Ellis had been only too glad to send Dorothy away with the jewellery, and the bureau, and a very nice rug to which she had no right at all. Dorothy was the last person Mrs Ellis wanted to see, and especially in these very trying circumstances, with this Sister at her side, and herself looking so untidy, without a hat or a bag.

There was no time to compose herself because the door opened. No . . . no, it was not Dorothy after all, but . . . how strange, so very like her. That same thin nose and rather peeved expression. A little taller, perhaps, and the hair was lighter. The resemblance, though, was really quite extraordinary.

"Are you Mrs Drew?" asked the Sister.

"Yes," answered the young woman, and then because a child was calling from an inner room she called back over her shoulder impatiently, "Oh, be quiet, Keith, do, for heaven's sake."

A little boy of about five appeared along the hall dragging a toy on wheels. "Dear little fellow," thought Mrs Ellis, "what a tiresome nagging mother. But where are all the children; where is Susan?"

"This is the person I have brought along for you to identify," said the Sister.

"You had better come inside," said Mrs Drew rather grudgingly. "I'm afraid everything's in a fearful mess. I've got no help, and you know how it is."

Mrs Ellis, whose temper was beginning to rise again, stepped neatly over a broken toy on the door mat and, followed by the Sister, went into what she supposed was this Mrs Drew's living-room. It was certainly a mess. Remains of breakfast not cleared away—or was it lunch?—and toys everywhere, and some material for cutting out spread on a table by the window.

Mrs Drew laughed apologetically. "What with Keith's toys and my material—I'm a dressmaker in my spare time—and trying to get a decent meal for my husband when he comes home in the evening, life isn't a bed of roses," she said. Her voice was *so* like Dorothy's. Mrs Ellis could hardly take her eyes off her. The same note of complaint.

"We don't want to take up your time,' said the Sister civilly, "if you will just say whether this person is Grace Jackson or not."

The young woman, Mrs Drew, stared at Mrs Ellis thoughtfully. "No," she said at length, "I'm sure she is not. I haven't seen Grace for years, not since I married; I used to look her up in Hampstead occasionally before then; but she had quite a different appearance from this person. She was stouter, darker, older too."

"Thank you," said the Sister, "then you are sure you have never seen this lady before?"

"No, never," said Mrs Drew.

"Very well then," said the Sister, "we needn't detain you any longer."

She turned, as though to go, but Mrs Ellis was not to be fobbed off with the nonsense that had just passed.

"Excuse me," she said to Mrs Drew, "there has been a most unfortunate misunderstanding all round, but I understand you spoke to the doctor at the police station at Hampstead this morning, or someone did from his house, and that you have a party of school children here from High Close, my child amongst them. Can you tell me if she is still here; is anyone from the school in charge?"

The Sister was about to intervene, but Mrs Drew did not notice this, because the little boy had come into the room, dragging his toy. "Keith, I *told* you to stay outside," she nagged.

Mrs Ellis smiled at the boy. She loved all children. "What a pretty boy," she said, and she held out her hand to him. He took it, holding it tight.

"He doesn't usually take to strangers," said Mrs Drew, "he's very shy. It makes me wild at times when he won't speak and hangs his head."

"I was shy myself as a child, I understand it," said Mrs Ellis.

Keith looked up at her with confidence and trust. Her heart warmed to him. But she was forgetting Susan . . . "We were talking about the party from High Close," she said.

"Yes," said Mrs Drew, "but that police officer was rather an idiot, I'm afraid, and got everything wrong. My name was Susan Ellis before I married, and I used to go to school at High Close, and that's where the mistake came in. There are no children from the school here."

"What a remarkable coincidence," said Mrs Ellis, smiling, "because my name is Ellis, and my daughter is called Susan, and an even stranger coincidence is that you are so like a sister of my late husband's."

"Oh?" said Mrs Drew. "Well, the name is common enough, isn't it? The butcher is Ellis, down the road."

Mrs Ellis flushed. Not a very tactful remark. And she felt suddenly nervous, too, because the Sister was advancing and was leaning forward as though to take her by the arm and walk to the front door. Mrs Ellis was determined not to leave the house. Or, at any rate, not to leave it with the Sister.

"I've always found High Close such a homey sort of school," she said rapidly, "but I am rather distressed about the changes they are making there, and I am afraid it is going to be on rather a different tone in the future."

"I don't think they've changed it much," said Mrs Drew. "Most small children are horrible little beasts, anyway, and it does them good not to see too much of their parents and to be thoroughly well mixed up with every sort of type."

"I'm afraid I don't agree with you on that," said Mrs Ellis. So peculiar. The tone, the expression might have been Dorothy's.

"Of course," said Mrs Drew, "I can't help being grateful to old Slaty. She's a funny old stick, but a heart of gold, and she did her best for me, I'll say that, and kept me in the holidays after my mother was killed in a street accident."

"How good of her," said Mrs Ellis, "and what a dreadful thing for you."

Mrs Drew laughed. "I was pretty tough, I think," she said. "I don't remember much about it. But I do remember my mother was a very kind person, and pretty too. I think Keith takes after her."

The little boy had not relinquished Mrs Ellis's hand.

"It's time we were getting along," said the Sister. "Come now, Mrs Drew has told us all we need to know."

"I don't want to go," said Mrs Ellis calmly, "and you have no right to make me go."

The Sister exchanged a glance with Mrs Drew. "I'm sorry," she said in a low tone, "I shall have to get the chauffeur. I wanted them to send another nurse with me, but they said it wouldn't be necessary."

"That's all right," said Mrs Drew. "So many people are bats these days, one extra doesn't make much difference. But perhaps I had better remove Keith to the kitchen, or she may kidnap him."

Keith, protesting, was carried from the room.

Once again the Sister looked at Mrs Ellis. "Come along now," she said, "be reasonable."

"No," said Mrs Ellis, and with a quickness that surprised herself she reached out to the table where Mrs Drew had been cutting out material, and seized the pair of scissors. "If you come near me, I shall stab you," she said.

The Sister turned and went quickly out of the room and down the steps, calling for the chauffeur. The next few moments passed quickly, but for all this Mrs Ellis had time to realise that her tactics were brilliant, rivalling the heroes of detective fiction. She crossed the room, opened the long French windows that gave on to a back yard. The window of the bedroom was open; she could hear the chauffeur calling.

"Tradesmen's entrance is ajar," he shouted. "She must have gone this way."

"Let them go on with their confusion," thought Mrs Ellis, leaning against the bed. "Let them. Good luck to them in their running about. This will take down some of the Sister's weight. Not much running about for her at Moreton Hill. Cups of tea at all hours, and sweet biscuits, while the patients are given bread and water."

The movement went on for some time. Somebody used the telephone. There was more talk. And then, when Mrs Ellis was nearly dozing off against the bed valance, she heard the car drive away. Everything was silent. Mrs Ellis listened. The only sound was the little boy playing in the hall below. She crept to the door and listened once again. The wheeled toy was being dragged backwards and forwards, up and down the hall. And there was a new sound coming from the living-room. The sound of a sewing-machine going at great speed. Mrs Drew was at work.

The Sister and the chauffeur had gone. An hour, two hours must have passed since they had left. Mrs Ellis glanced at the clock on the mantelpiece. It was two o'clock. What an untidy, scattered sort of room, everything all over the place. Shoes in the middle of the floor, a coat flung down on a chair, and Keith's cot had not been made up; the blankets were rumpled anyhow.

"Badly brought up," thought Mrs Ellis, "and such rough, casual manners. But poor girl, if she had no mother ... "

She took a last glance round the room, and she saw with a shrug of her shoulder that even Mrs Drew's calendar had a printing error. It said 1952 instead of 1932. How careless ...

She tiptoed to the head of the stairs. The door of the living-room was shut. The sound of the sewing-machine came at breathless speed. "They must be hard up," thought Mrs Ellis, "if she has to do dressmaking. I wonder what her husband does for a living." Softly she crept downstairs. She made no sound. And if she had, the sound of the sewing-machine would have covered it. As she passed the living-room door it opened. The boy stood there, staring at her. He said nothing. He smiled. Mrs Ellis smiled back at him. She could not help herself. She had a feeling that he would not give her away.

"Shut the door, Keith, *do*," nagged his mother from within. The door slammed. The sound of the sewing-machine became more distant, muffled. Mrs Ellis let herself out of the house and slipped away . . . She turned northward, like an animal scenting direction, because northward was her home.

She was soon swallowed up in traffic, the buses swinging past her in the Finchley Road. Her feet began to ache and she was tired, but she could not take a bus or summon a taxi because she had no money. No one looked at her; no one bothered with her; they were all intent upon their business, either going from home or returning, and it seemed to Mrs Ellis, as she toiled up the hill towards Hampstead, that for the first time in her life she was friendless and alone. She wanted her house, her home, the consolation of her own surroundings; she wanted to take up her normal, everyday life that had been interrupted in so brutal a fashion. There was so much to straighten out, so much to do, and Mrs Ellis did not know where to begin or whom to ask for help.

"I want everything to be as it was before that walk yesterday," thought Mrs Ellis, her back aching, her feet throbbing. "I want my home. I want my little girl."

And here was the heath once again. This was where she had stood before crossing the road. She even remembered what she had been thinking about. She had been planning to buy a red bicycle for Susan. Something light—but strong, a good make.

The memory of the bicycle made her forget her troubles, her fatigue. As soon as all this muddle and confusion were over, she would buy a red bicycle for Susan.

Why, though, for the second time, that screech of brakes when she crossed the road, and the vacant face of the laundry boy looking down at her?

Daphne du Maurier
The House on the Strand £1.50

Dick Young was lent a house in Cornwall by his friend Professor Lane. During his stay he agreed to be a guinea-pig for the Professor's new research drug – a drug which transports him from the house at Kilmarth back to the fourteenth century. There, in the manor of Tywardreath, he witnesses intrigue, adultery and murder . . .

I'll Never Be Young Again £1.50

Hesta was so much in Richard's blood that ne lost all liberty of thought and action. His former life faded into insignificance as he found happiness in Montparnasse, shedding his youthful illusions in an obsessive love. But could Hesta replace Richard's need to write, or his ambition to reach out from under the shadow of a famous father and find his own success . . . ?

'Daphne du Maurier's descriptions of riding in Norwegian mountains, of life before the mast and in foreign capitals ring as true as her transcription of a young man's thoughts and talk'. PUNCH

Jamaica Inn £1.50

The cold walls of Jamaica Inn smelt of guilt and deceit. Its dark secrets made the very name a byword for terror among honest Cornish folk.

Young Mary Yellan found her uncle was the apparent leader of strange men who plied a strange trade. Was there more to learn? She remembered the fear in her aunt's eyes . . .

'An exciting brew . . . for a late evening's reading' SATURDAY REVIEW

Daphne du Maurier
My Cousin Rachel £1.50

Ambrose married Rachel, Countess Sangaletti, in Italy and never
returned home. His letters to his cousin Philip hinted that he was
being poisoned, and when Philip arrived in Italy, Ambrose was
dead

Rachel comes to England, and soon Philip too is torn between
love and suspicion. Is she the angel she seems? Or is she a
scheming murderess?

'The tension is admirably built up and maintained. The ending is
dramatic, surprising and masterly'   QUEEN

Frenchman's Creek £1.50

While the gentry of Cornwall strive to capture the daring
Frenchman who plunders their shores, the beautiful Lady Dona
finds excitement, danger and a passion she never knew before as
she dares to love a pirate – a devil-may-care adventurer who risks
his life for a kiss . . .

'A heroine who is bound to make thousands of friends, in spite of
her somewhat questionable behaviour'   SUNDAY TIMES

Rebecca £1.50

One of the most appealing heroines in all of fiction... brilliantly
conceived, masterfully executed, Daphne du Maurier's
unforgettable tale of love, mystery and suspense is a story-telling
triumph that will be read and re-read. *Rebecca* is known to
millions through its outstandingly successful stage, screen and
television versions: and the characters in this timeless romance
are hauntingly real.

Daphne du Maurier
Mary Anne £1.50

In the glittering, corrupt world of Regency London, Mary Anne Clarke had beauty, brains and wit – but no money. Spurred on by the demands of a drunken husband, a wastrel brother and four children, she chose an exacting profession aimed for the top – and soon became the mistress of the Duke of York.

For her family she needed a fortune – and she got it the wrong way. The scandal rocked the country from palace to Parliament and Mary Anne Clarke became the most famous woman in England.

The Loving Spirit £1.50

A powerful exuberant romance of Cornwall, through three generations of passion and drama, of sailing ships and the glory of wind and sea.

Janet Coombe was born with the loving spirit, and passed it on to her son Joseph. When it reappears in her great-granddaughter Jennifer, the barrier of the years breaks down as they are carried beyond all prudence in their need to love and be loved.

'Miss du Maurier creates on the grand scale . . . a rich vein of humour and satire, observation, sympathy, courage, a sense of the romantic are here'   OBSERVER

Rule Britannia £1.50

US marines land in Cornwall and Mad – a world-famous ex-actress – defies them; rallying her family, friends and neighbours to protect their heritage. Unforgettable characters from the pen of a favourite storyteller . . .

Leonard St Clair
Obsessions £1.50

The seventeenth of July was to be a glittering day for European and American high Society: the wedding of Orsino di Ascoli, multi-millionaire at the head of a titanic business empire, and Erin Deering, star of the cinema screen.

From the shadows, others are watching; among them Lisa di Ascoli, the seductive heiress with the heart of ice. The shadows are filled with hate and vengeance. The shadows reach back over four decades to the hour when priceless gems were torn from the breast of a dead Tsarina as Bolshevik bullets cut down the Imperial Romanovs in Ekaterinburg on the seventeenth of July...

Susan Howatch
The Sins of the Fathers £2.50

From Wall Street to the quiet of an English country churchyard, Susan Howatch's magnificent narrative traces the fortunes of the Van Zale dynasty through two decades of wealth, ambition and struggle, until the sins of the fathers are finally visited upon the next generation.

Selected Bestsellers

☐ **Gone with the Wind**	Margaret Mitchell	£2.95p
☐ **Robert Morley's Book of Worries**	Robert Morley	£1.50p
☐ **The Totem**	David Morrell	£1.25p
☐ **The Alternative Holiday Catalogue**	edited by Harriet Peacock	£1.95p
☐ **The Pan Book of Card Games**	Hubert Phillips	£1.50p
☐ **The New Small Garden**	C. E. Lucas Phillips	£2.50p
☐ **Food for All the Family**	Magnus Pyke	£1.50p
☐ **Everything Your Doctor Would Tell You If He Had the Time**	Claire Rayner	£4.95p
☐ **Rage of Angels**	Sidney Sheldon	£1.75p
☐ **A Town Like Alice**	Nevil Shute	£1.50p
☐ **Just Off for the Weekend**	John Slater	£2.50p
☐ **A Falcon Flies**	Wilbur Smith	£1.95p
☐ **The Deep Well at Noon**	Jessica Stirling	£1.75p
☐ **The Eighth Dwarf**	Ross Thomas	£1.25p
☐ **The Music Makers**	E. V. Thompson	£1.50p
☐ **The Third Wave**	Alvin Toffler	£1.95p
☐ **Auberon Waugh's Yearbook**	Auberon Waugh	£1.95p
☐ **The Flier's Handbook**		£4.95p

All these books are available at your local bookshop or newsagent, or can be ordered direct from the publisher. Indicate the number of copies required and fill in the form below

3

Name———————————————————————————
(block letters please)

Address———————————————————————————

Send to Pan Books (CS Department), Cavaye Place, London SW10 9PG
Please enclose remittance to the value of the cover price plus:
25p for the first book plus 10p per copy for each additional book ordered to a maximum charge of £1.05 to cover postage and packing Applicable only in the UK
While every effort is made to keep prices low, it is sometimes necessary to increase prices at short notice. Pan Books reserve the right to show on covers and charge new retail prices which may differ from those advertised in the text or elsewhere